# Melt With You

## ALSO BY JENNIFER DUGAN

*Hot Dog Girl*

*Verona Comics*

*Some Girls Do*

# Melt With You

## JENNIFER DUGAN

putnam

G. P. Putnam's Sons

**G. P. PUTNAM'S SONS**

An imprint of Penguin Random House LLC, New York

First published in the United States of America by G. P. Putnam's Sons,
an imprint of Penguin Random House LLC, 2022

G. P. Putnam's Sons is a registered trademark of Penguin Random House LLC.

Visit us online at penguinrandomhouse.com
Library of Congress Cataloging-in-Publication Data
Names: Dugan, Jennifer, author.
Title: Melt with you / Jennifer Dugan.
Description: New York: G. P. Putnam's Sons, [2022] | Summary: "Two teen girls,
former best friends and one-time lovers, go on a summer road trip
in an ice cream truck"—Provided by publisher.
Identifiers: LCCN 2021049152 (print) | LCCN 2021049153 (ebook) |
ISBN 9780593112564 (hardcover) | ISBN 9780593112571 (epub)
Subjects: CYAC: Dating (Social customs)—Fiction. | Bisexuality—Fiction. | Automobile travel—
Fiction. | Ice cream trucks—Fiction. | Family-owned business enterprises—Fiction. | LCGFT: Novels.
Classification: LCC PZ7.1.D8343 Me 2022 (print) | LCC PZ7.1.D8343 (ebook) | DDC [Fic]—dc23
LC record available at https://lccn.loc.gov/2021049152
LC ebook record available at https://lccn.loc.gov/2021049153

Manufactured in Canada

ISBN 9780593112564
1  3  5  7  9  10  8  6  4  2
FRI

Design by Suki Boynton
Text set in Albertina MT Std

*To everyone who had to get it wrong*
*before they could get it right*

# Melt With You

# ONE

*W*e're getting low on the cookie dough, Mom," I **say**, scooping out my thirty-seventh ice cream cone of the afternoon and passing it to her.

"I'm sorry, the *what?*" Mom gives me a look as she passes the cone to the next person in line. She adjusts the pin-striped hat on her head, careful not to unleash her wavy brown hair—complete with a lone patch of gray she calls her skunk stripe—and crosses her arms, waiting.

I roll my eyes. Right, she's going to make me say it. She always makes me say it. I clutch my hand to my heart and tap my eyelashes together dramatically. "I'm sorry, Mother. I meant we're getting low on I'll Never Let Dough."

"Much better." She laughs. "I'll text Carmen to run some over. She's at the lab anyway."

Carmen is my mom's best friend. They met in seventh grade and have been joined at the hip ever since. About five years ago, when they both found themselves to be divorced single moms trying to work around school hours, they decided to take a risk on a rickety old ice cream truck.

Only instead of the usual melty Spider-Man pops and ice cream sandwiches, they took Carmen's experience as a "taste-maker" at a gourmet candy shop and my mom's experience in marketing and combined it with *both* of their obsessions with romance movies. The result: Love at First Bite, a small-batch ice cream service that operates solely out of this truck and a rented "lab space" at a local commercial kitchen.

Which means instead of cookies and cream, it's I Like Your Boots, and instead of plain vanilla, it's Just Whelmed Waffle Cone. But what they're most famous for is Beauty and the Feast, an "aggressively chocolaty ice cream swirled with French vanilla and a dash of citrus, topped with a blue-and-yellow homemade macaron and an assortment of red rose-petal sprinkles."

"I think this one's for you, Fallon," Mom says, gesturing toward the window. I lean over the freezers, grinning when I see my best friend, Jami, on the other side.

"Hey! I thought you had a lesson today," I say, wiping my hands on a rag. The ice cream might be off them, but the sticky-sweet cream scent will cling to my skin for days. There are worse things, I guess.

"Yeah, I cut out a bit early," Jami says, biting her lip. Her long blond hair is pulled into a low ponytail, and she's still in her riding clothes: tight tan pants and high black boots with sturdy heels. The *Lion King* tank top she scored from Target last week sort of ruins the classy motif she's got going from the waist down, though.

"You can do that?" I raise my eyebrows. Jami takes her riding lessons very seriously, so this is wildly unlike her.

"Kinda." She winces. "I told Stefan I had really bad cramps, and he got so uncomfortable he practically threw me out of the barn."

"Sounds about right." I laugh. Some people are so weird about periods. Like it's this deep, dark, gross thing and not a regular occurrence for, like, a lot of the population.

"Can you take a break?"

I glance at my mom, who nods. The line has died down enough now that she should be able to handle it.

"So, Chloe's home," Jami says when I step out the back of the truck.

I sigh, pulling off my hat and shaking out my hair—wavy brown like my mom's but with more frizz than shine—and hop up onto one of the empty picnic tables behind the truck. The ground around it is littered with cigarette butts from all the random food service workers who park their trucks here sometimes. I guess this is our version of a break room, not that I spend much time back here. There's no cover from the sun, and being whiter than white, I tend to burn in five seconds flat. Jami follows me, sliding onto the bench and eyeing me nervously.

It's not that this was unexpected. Chloe just finished her

freshman year out in California. I knew she had to come home eventually. You can't stay at college forever, I guess.

This is where I probably should mention that Chloe happens to be Carmen's daughter—yes, the same Carmen who co-owns Love at First Bite with my mom.

And also that Chloe used to be my best friend.

And then more.

And then nothing.

Oh, and did I mention Chloe *also* works here?

I toss my hat onto the table beside me. "Maybe I can leave early. I'll hide out at your place until I can convince my mom it would be a massive mistake to schedule us together. I just can't deal with any surprise Chloe visits today."

"I still don't get why you can't just work somewhere else."

I love Jami, but she's constantly teasing me and our other best friend, Prisha, about the "undying loyalty" we seem to have to our respective family businesses: me, the ice cream truck; Prisha, her dad's grocery store. She doesn't get that these are our families' livelihoods. Not only are we expected to help, but they actually, truly *need* us to. Jami's mom's an accountant at a big commercial firm; it's not the same.

I shake my head. "You know they can't afford to hire someone else."

"Responsible to the end." Jami sighs.

"It's not just that," I say, because we've been over this. "Besides, I worked it out last night. If we each cut our hours a little, we can stagger our schedules so that we never have to be here at the same time. It seems like the best solution all around."

"We leave in a month!" Jami says, widening her big eyes cartoonishly. "Are you sure you should be cutting hours right now?"

The trip. Right. The other thing I forgot to mention. Jami and I have been planning a trip to Montreal for almost a year now. It's supposed to be our last hurrah before we get ripped apart by college. Jami is going to RISD for architecture, with a minor in performance, and I'm heading to UT Austin, my dad's alma mater, to study business. My friends tease that I should go to school for film, since I'm obsessed with movies—horror in particular—but I don't know. It doesn't seem like a good idea to load up on student loans for something my Dad calls "frivolous" when he's all too happy to help out with tuition now that I'm following in his footsteps.

We picked Montreal primarily because of Jami's obsession with cathedrals, but it's really for the both of us. She can study the building design, and I'll get the chance to scope out the filming location of one of my favorite indie horror movies of all time, *Too Dead to Die*, directed by my hero, the absolutely incredible Adya Mulroney. Because if I *were* going to do something "frivolous," it would be directing smart, funny, feminist horror exactly like hers.

There's just one problem: Jami fronted my broke ass's whole share of the money. The ice cream business really slows down during winter in upstate New York—shocking,

I know—so I barely got any hours for the past nine months. Still had to always be on call, though, so it's not like I could add in another job. Oh, and did I mention Jami funded our trip with the money that was supposed to go toward her textbooks this fall? Yeah.

Normally, I'd be the human embodiment of the wince emoji over that, but it currently feels like a much smaller problem compared to a summer spent working with my ex. If I have to stand next to Chloe and mix up The Malt in Our Stars, a strawberry milkshake drizzled in dark chocolate fudge and sprinkled with smashed-up heart candies—Chloe's favorite flavor, by the way, perhaps an omen I definitely should *not* have ignored—I'll absolutely scream.

"I'll figure it out. Don't worry," I say, and I mean it.

"Cool." She nods. "I'm not trying to, like, be all up in your face about it, but I leave in a few days, and I'd like to be sure our trip is even happening before I go."

"It'll happen," I say firmly, because I *need* this trip to look forward to.

"The refund deadline is—"

"I'll get the money, I promise," I say, because I will, no matter what it takes. "I wish you weren't leaving, though."

Now that school's over, Jami's getting ready to head out to Stars in the Woods, an immersive three-week theater experience that only the best of the best get invited to. Jami has been the lead in literally every school play since the third grade. She's been going to the camp for years, and now, finally, she's been brought on as a senior counselor and assistant director—an actual paying job. Those three weeks alone will be more than enough to cover her half of the trip.

"Three weeks," she says. "And I promise I'll facetime you from the forest every day."

"Or just take me with you. I wouldn't have to see the Wicked Witch of the West all summer, I'd have enough money to pay for our trip, and we wouldn't have to be apart. Win-win-win." I grin, wishing it could really be that easy.

She narrows her eyes. "You hiding some performing arts experience I don't know about?"

"Oh, totally," I say, and then we both laugh because the one time she convinced me to actually try out for a play, I puked during my audition. I am not the girl who gets in front of people and sings and dances. I'm the girl who sits in the back of the auditorium during rehearsals, doing her math homework while quietly bemoaning the lackluster choices the director is making.

"Right," she says. "Looks like you're staying put, then. Besides, even the cook jobs are wait-listed at this point. You snooze, you lose."

I sigh. "I can't believe I have to slog through the start of summer with Chloe here and you gone."

"Maybe it won't be that bad," Jami says. "It's been almost a year. Maybe you two could—"

"Could what?" Now she's starting to sound like my mother, who's desperate for Chloe and me to make up, even though she doesn't really know what happened between us in the first place. No thank you.

"Okay, I'm not going there with you today. Just admit that at some point you *do* need to get over what happened."

"Do I?"

Jami huffs out a breath and drops her head back. "Seriously, Fallon, you are the most stubborn girl I've ever met in my entire life."

I gently boop her on the nose. "And you love me for it."

"Only very, very occasionally," she says, shoving me.

I clutch my heart dramatically and then grab her hand, tugging us both up to standing.

"Come on, let's go see if my mom will let me leave early."

# TWO

ow was Jami's?" Mom heads toward the kitchen, tossing her Love at First Bite apron over the arm of the couch I'm on, which sends the scent of heavy cream and sugar wafting my way. Seriously? I did not just take an hour-long hot shower to escape that smell for this.

I pause what I'm watching—another bad horror movie I've seen a dozen times before—nudging the apron off the couch and looking at my mom. "It was fun. Thanks for letting me cut out of work early. Pri came over too, and we all went swimming."

"Oh, nice," she says, barely listening. "You want to split this?" Mom holds up a perfectly shrink-wrapped pizza. It's from a local pizza place, but they started selling them to grocery stores about a year ago. It inspired my mom to try to get distribution lined up for her ice cream, which is actually and thrillingly already in progress. If all goes well, they'll be closing on a deal soon that could put Love at First Bite on the map.

"Definitely," I say, hopping up as she preheats the oven.

"So, what happened today? You never ask to leave early."

"It's summer break!" I say. "I'm legally obligated to go swimming with my friends at least a few times, aren't I?"

"Hmm," Mom says, unwrapping the pizza and shoving it into the oven. "Are you sure this doesn't have anything to do with Chloe coming home?"

And there it is. I knew it was coming. I don't know why I even bothered trying to lie.

"Oh, is she home already?" I try to sound nonchalant, but my mom just stares at me, so I add a halfhearted "Cool."

"Yeah," she says, pulling down some plates. "It'll be nice to have you both back at the truck."

"About that," I say, and she freezes. "I kind of don't want to be scheduled with her, if we can avoid it."

"I don't see how we'll be able to avoid it."

I grab my notebook off the coffee table and carry it over to her. "I was kind of working on that last night, actually. I think it will work if you cut both of our hours just a little."

Mom crosses her arms. "What about saving for the trip?"

And, oh, I was definitely prepared for this question. "I wouldn't have enough before we left, but I *would* by the end of the summer. Jami says as long as she has the money before orientation, she's cool with it."

Mom frowns, probably wishing I hadn't thought this out

so well. But I did. I'm good at this. I always have a plan, and a backup plan, and a way to execute both. I can daydream five hundred scenarios for how something could play out before most people have thought of one.

Unfortunately, lately my only backup plan is "run away and hide." It's not that it's the only option; it's just that when it comes to anything to do with Chloe—and by default, working with her at Love at First Bite—all logic and planning goes right out the window.

My mom crinkles her forehead and tosses the oven mitts on the counter. "Really, Fallon?"

I shrug again, not sure what else to say. My mom knows about Chloe and me. Well . . . sort of. She knows we used to be best friends, and she knows we had a falling-out. She doesn't—and won't—know anything beyond that.

I know my mom just wishes we would get our shit together and go back to being best friends so that she and Carmen can go back to reliving their youth vicariously through us. But I should tell you now, it's not going to happen. And not in a famous-last-words kind of way. It's seriously *not* going to happen.

Because Chloe Shapiro is the worst thing that ever happened to me.

My mom sighs. "If you would just tell me what went on between you two, I could help you figure this out. It's been nearly a year! You don't just throw away friendships like this, and you've never been one to hold a grudge. What is going on?"

"It's not a grudge."

And that's not a lie. A grudge doesn't begin to cover what this is. This is anger and betrayal unfurling until just the thought of her makes me itchy and sad, like my skin is too tight, and everything hurts from the inside out. It's heartbreak in the purest form, in the ugliest form.

But how do you explain that to your mom when she just thinks you're supposed to be best friends forever? She wouldn't get it. Mom considers Carmen her sister, and they always thought Chloe and I would follow in those footsteps. I can tell you, we decidedly did not. When the two of us went from stolen smiles and secret nuzzles to full-on lips on necks and hands wandering down, down, down . . .

"Fallon?" my mom says, and I snap my eyes to her, my cheeks redder than the pizza sauce bubbling in the oven behind us.

"I just can't, Mom. Okay? Please just drop it." I turn to leave. I'm not hungry anymore.

"We need you," my mom says before I even get to the hall. "Full-time. As many hours as you can give us. We can't afford to bring on another person right now, and even if we did, I couldn't train them in time. Carmen leaves *tomorrow*."

I freeze. Damn, I forgot all about Carmen leaving when I was making my grand plan to avoid Chloe.

Remember that distribution deal I mentioned? The one they're close to closing? Well, Carmen's flying down to Dallas tomorrow to attend a big meeting with the potential investors.

Normally, Mom would be there too, but we have two major food truck festivals coming up that we have to drive to. Oh, and did I mention that those two festivals collectively make up the majority of our business income *for the year*? Yeah. Usually, Mom and Carmen handle those on their own, but I managed to convince her to make them a pre-college, mother-daughter road trip, just me and her instead. And if we can handle *those* on our own, there's no reason she should be giving me such a hard time about scheduling right now!

"Look, Carmen is only gone a couple days. And you'll still have either me or Chloe there all the time," I try, even though it hurts just to say her name. "Why does it have to be both of us? You agreed it could just be me and you for the festivals. So why can't it just be you and one of us for a regular shift?"

"You know Chloe's not—"

"Reliable," I say, because yeah, actually, I do know that.

"I was going to say 'serious.' She's not as serious as you are with her work ethic. That's all. And that's not even . . . I mean, she's nineteen. What do you expect?"

"I'm barely eighteen," I remind her.

"Yes, but you're *you*," she says, her eyes meeting mine. "You turned thirty right after your sixth birthday and never looked back."

I don't point out that my so-called maturity was born out of my need to hold things together while my parents' marriage circled the drain. I don't begrudge them that or anything; I get how life works. I love my dad, and our every-other-weekend schedule growing up wasn't that bad. The whole two-Christmases-a-year thing didn't exactly suck either. But still, I was the one stuck doing the laundry and learning how to microwave eggs because I wasn't allowed to touch the stove and they were too busy falling apart to notice when I was hungry.

Mom leans against the counter. "What if I make it worth it to you?"

"I'm listening," I say, even though we both already know that if she truly needs me, I'm gonna show up for her. The same way she always does for me.

"If you stop giving me a hard time about the schedule, I'll let you keep *all* the cash tips from Food for a Cause."

"Wait, seriously?" I ask, my eyes going wide, because that's always a lot of money.

Food for a Cause, the first of our two major festivals this summer, is an annual extravaganza held by a bunch of rich people in Memphis. They bring specialty food trucks in from all over the country and pay them handsomely while way overcharging their guests. I guess the proceeds go to some food pantry in town, although it does sorta feel mostly like an excuse for a bunch of wealthy weirdos to pat themselves on the back for doing the bare minimum. Like, couldn't they just *give* the money to the food pantry in the first place without the big show?

Anyway, my mom's college roommate is the event planner, and for the past three years she's brought in Love at First Bite as one of their special guest vendors. That contract alone accounts for over a third of the business's annual income, and on top of that, those donors, they tip very, *very* well.

"The tips alone will let me pay back Jami."

"If it's anything like last year, it'll do a lot more than that."

"No, I can't take that from you," I say, because no matter how bad I want it, with the alimony stopping, she's going to need it. I know Mom hates when I worry about that stuff, but I've heard her and Dad fighting about it. Dad agreed to pay it until I graduated, and well, I did. Things were tight before; I can't imagine what they'll be like now.

"I already talked to Carmen. Consider it our graduation present to you. We let Chloe have it last year. It's a tradition now."

"Chloe never told me that!"

"She didn't want you to get jealous!"

"Wait a minute. If it's my graduation gift, then why are there strings attached?"

Mom laughs. "That's the deal. Take it or leave it."

"Okay, fine. No one's getting their hours cut, but can you put one of us opening and the other closing? I don't really care who gets what. I just can't do full shifts with her every day. Will you at least *try* to limit the overlap?"

"Fallon—"

"Please?"

"Fine." She sighs. "I'm just sad about it. I always thought you two would be by each other's sides forever, like Carmen and me."

"That rarely happens, though," I say. "The odds of being best friends with someone your whole life is, like, practically zero. I have a bigger chance of getting struck by lightning."

Mom tilts her head. "You never know; it could strike again."

"Rarely in the same place twice."

# THREE

*E*ven if lightning doesn't strike twice, it doesn't mean its effects don't linger, like singed trees trying to burn everything down.

I scrape out a scoop of It's Not You, It's Tea—Earl Grey ice cream—and drop it into a plastic bowl with a sickening squelch. Then I slather it with chocolate and drop on not two but three teaspoons of rainbow sprinkles.

I'd know this order anywhere.

I invented it, after all, two years ago to cheer Chloe up when she found out her celebrity crush got married. It's an off-menu order, and she's pretty much the only one who knows about it.

It figures it would take her barely a day to show up here.

I hold the order out to my mom, but she ignores me and heads over to take the order from the next person in line. Fine, then. I steel myself for coming face-to-face with Chloe for the first time in months, trying not to wonder too hard if this particular order is supposed to be a blatant message to me or just a nod to the past.

You should probably know that I've done a most excellent job of avoiding her up until this point.

I made myself scarce when she came home for spring break, and since it wasn't Love at First Bite's busy season, only one of us needed to work over winter recess. I let her have the hours and begged off, citing an extended visit with my dad across town. I'm sure no one was fooled.

I shove a spoon into the gooey goodness and drop it onto the counter.

"Order up," I yell, looking deliberately over Chloe's head even though she's standing directly in front of me, unimpressed.

"Uh, right here, Fal," she says, raising her hand.

"Okay," I say snottily. Because standing this close to her makes me feel like I'm going to melt or explode, and I'm not particularly in the mood to do either.

"A 'hi' would be nice," Chloe says quietly, pressing her words into all of my wounds.

"A lot of things would be nice," I snap, and shove some napkins at her. Our fingers brush when she takes them, and I jerk my hand back.

Chloe sighs. "What does that *even* mean?"

"It means—"

"Fallon, can you scoop this one for me?" Mom asks, cutting me off before I can say anything else.

I take the order slip from her—two The Malt in Our Stars and a double scoop of Just Whelmed Waffle Cone—while Mom walks to the window, chatting up Chloe about college. Maybe I run the blender extra long and loud to drown out the sound of their voices, but I still can't miss the way Chloe gushes about how much she loves her new school and her new friends.

And probably all her new hookups too. Not that she'd admit that in front of me.

I pour the first shake into a cup, nearly spilling it all over myself when Mom makes some comment about Chloe having fun, but not *too much* fun. I snap the lid on and loudly clang the metal container back into the machine.

My mom turns and gives me a little wink, and for a second, panic slices through me. Does my mom know that Chloe and I hooked up?

Yeah, no. *She can't,* I think as I stab the buttons to start the machine. As impossible as it sounds with not one *but two* very nosey mothers in our midst, we managed to keep that part to ourselves. Or at least I did. I can't speak for the traitor on the other side of the counter—the one who is currently laughing with my mom while blatantly trying to catch my eye.

Okay, rewind.

You probably want a few details. Fine. If you think there must have been a party, a couple drinks, and a tent involved, you're not too far off. I mean, actually, you've nailed it. Which is almost a little creepy. So, yay?

But if you're thinking that also means we got wasted and handsy and one thing led to another, that's where you're wrong. Well, half wrong at least, on my end anyway. Who knows what Chloe thinks happened. We didn't talk after (mostly her choice), and now I don't plan to ever talk to her again (my choice).

Here's what I do know:

Chloe Shapiro has been my best friend since I was old enough to have one. *Had* been, I mean.

Chloe Shapiro is *hot*. A fact that has been lost on absolutely no one, including me, since we were about fourteen or so.

Chloe Shapiro *flirted with me* last summer. A lot. And not in the usual we're-best-friends-so-we're-snuggly way. No, sometime during the summer after her senior year and my junior year, she went from head on my shoulder to lips on my neck.

Chloe Shapiro knew that I liked her back, because I also went from head on *her* shoulder to lips on *her* neck every single chance I got.

Chloe Shapiro then led me on and ripped my heart out.

And we lived miserably ever after.

I know, I know, I know. Right now you're probably thinking that whole best-predictor-of-future-behavior-is-past-behavior thing. And normally I would agree. Her signature catchphrase is "it's not that deep," which she applies to everything from breaking a nail to not getting into her first-choice university. Not to mention the literal pile of exes she's left in her wake. She was never the safest bet. And I'm usually careful, and not just in a finishing-schoolwork-on-time and showing-up-early-for-appointments kind of way. I'm careful with my heart and my body. I don't get ridiculous, one-sided crushes. I don't randomly hook up. I think before I leap. In fact, Chloe was the first . . . Never mind, doesn't matter.

But even though Chloe lives her life like a cannonball on fire, I thought I knew her. She loves hard, hates hard, and gets bored quickly. Twice as quickly as anyone I've ever met in my life. But never with *me*. If I had known that a timeline existed where Chloe could treat me just like any other person in her orbit, our hookup would never have happened.

Period.

I finish up the shakes and slam them down on the counter, which makes Chloe and my mom both jump.

"Order up!" I yell again, clutching a waffle cone stuffed full of vanilla ice cream in my hand, even though this customer is *also* waiting right in front of me.

I go back to my station for cleanup, rubbing the stainless steel down as hard as I can until Mom comes over and puts her hand on my shoulder.

"I think she wants to talk to you," she says, leaning close and speaking quietly. "I told her about the schedule changes."

I glance over to see Chloe lingering awkwardly by the counter. Good. A twisted part of me kind of likes that she's the one walking on eggshells for once.

"No thanks," I say, scrubbing a little harder.

"Fallon," my mom says, her tone stern, "can't you just be polite?"

*No, I can't,* I want to shout, but I also don't want to make my mom mad. Nothing good comes from annoying someone who is both your parent and your boss. I sigh and drop my rag.

"Fine." I groan, smoothing my uniform before walking up to the counter.

Chloe is still trying to look nonchalant, fiddling with her ice cream and her napkins. There's a blue rainbow sprinkle stuck on her bottom lip—a lip that I have kissed and, at one point, desperately wanted to kiss again—but I say nothing. Let her walk around like that all day for all I care.

"My mom told me to be polite, so this is me being polite," I say, crossing my arms.

"I'm glad you said that, because otherwise I wouldn't have been able to tell." Chloe takes another bite of her ice cream, flicking her bright blue eyes to mine. She licks her lips this time, dislodging the sprinkle before bringing her fingers to her mouth with a smirk. I can't tell if she's embarrassed or amused, and I can't tell if I care.

"I got back yesterday," she says, running her hand through her painfully straight blond hair. And okay, we're really doing this. We're really pretending everything is fine.

"Yeah, I heard," I say, and when she quirks an eyebrow, I hastily add, "Jami saw you."

"Oh." Chloe smiles. "How is she? I missed you two over

winter break. Your mom said you were staying with your dad or something."

"Yep. Family bonding."

"And you couldn't have answered any of my texts? I mean, you were across town, not in another galaxy. We could have met up."

"Sorry, my phone was on the fritz," I lie, but she just stares at me. "I was busy."

"Which one?"

"Hmm?"

"Was your phone on the fritz or were you busy?"

"Both?" I say, the word coming out like a question, and this is not how I thought this would go.

"What's the deal with the opposite shifts? And now I'm not going to the food truck festivals either? Your mom said it was some mother-daughter bonding—"

"I have no idea. She makes the schedule," I lie again.

Real talk: I have imagined this moment nearly every day since last September. (Unlike most of August, which I spent crying or fantasizing about Chloe running back to me. Unfortunately, the reality was a lone text from her at the end of the month that just said **hey**, which I roundly ignored.) At any rate, that's left me ten months to prepare for this. Ten months of choreographing our first encounter post-hookup in my head. I had plans. Plans!

For one, it wasn't going to take place in an ice cream truck, which honestly, this part I maybe should have foreseen.

But regardless, I definitely wasn't going to be in my Love at First Bite uniform. You know, the one with the pink heart biting the little purple heart logo on the apron and the dorky little striped hat that doubles as a hairnet.

And Chloe was definitely not going to be perfectly tanned from her time in California, nor would she be wearing tiny cuffed shorts that one hundred percent would have violated our high school's fingertip rule. She looks like a model, and I look like a *Stranger Things* reject.

So how did I picture all this going?

Okay, close your eyes and imagine: The scene would open on me at one of the summer bonfires. I would be standing in the woods, gazing into the night sky, backlit by the orangey-yellow glow of the fire, of course. I'd hear her name carried on whispers from the other kids, and I'd turn my head slowly.

We would make intense eye contact, our faces looking serious in the flickering firelight. All eyes would be on Chloe and me, the audience giving us their rapt attention. The tension would grow heavier and heavier until we were almost smothered by the question of whether I was going to kiss her or slap her.

And then she would say—

"You're such a weirdo."

Wait. What? That's not—

"You're doing that thing again." Real-life Chloe laughs, shredding the napkin in front of her. "I guarantee it."

"What thing?" I pout, crossing my arms.

"That thing where you think so hard, you scrunch up your nose, and we all pretend not to notice that you're, like, directing a movie in your head or something. You are literally the only person I know who writes fanfic of their own life *as they experience it.*"

"I don't . . . That's not—"

"What am I supposed to be doing right now, like, in your perfect version of me?"

I hate that she knows me so well.

But this time when I scrunch up my nose, it's not because I'm thinking hard. "Sorry, some of us have to think things through. We can't all just follow our whims and not worry about the people we hurt."

One side of Chloe's mouth quirks up. "What's that supposed to mean?" She sounds genuinely and infuriatingly confused.

"Heya, can I get two scoops of History, Huh-ney Comb?" a scruffy man in his forties asks as he walks up to us. "And, um, add on some extra rainbow sprinkles, please."

"You order over there," Chloe and I say, rudely and in perfect unison.

His eyes widen and he backs away, heading over toward my mom, who apologizes profusely.

In any other circumstance, I would get yelled at for that, but she's the one who made me talk to Chloe. I could be happily in the back scrubbing down the shake machine. Speaking of which . . .

"Look, I should probably get back to work," I say.

And Chloe, she looks absolutely baffled by this.

Important note: Chloe Shapiro is usually not good at hiding her emotions around me. Like, at all. Which is why my stomach is twisting in really uncomfortable ways. Faking confusion to get out of a fight would never cross her mind. So, what the hell?

"Fallon?" she says, and suddenly I'm the one getting spun around like a milkshake, just from looking into her big doe eyes.

I hate this.

I was supposed to be the cool, calm one.

She was supposed to come home and tell me how much she missed me and how sorry she was. And then I was supposed to say, *Good, your loss,* and then walk away, leaving her in the bonfire. Well, not *in* the bonfire but, like, *beside* the bonfire. I'm not a monster.

"I have to work," I say again.

"Yeah, no, go," Chloe says. Her mouth sets in that displeased line it makes sometimes—the one where it looks like she just ate a bad jelly bean—but then she shakes it off and smiles. "See you around, I guess?"

I don't miss the way her voice sounds like she wants to say something else.

Or the way she swallows hard, her eyes narrowed.

And then, before I can even scrape my pride off the floor, she walks away.

Stealing my epic movie ending for herself.

# FOUR

*J*ami is waiting for me on my front porch after work the next day. She could have gone in. The door is never locked, and she knows this—I even reminded her of that fact when she texted **here!** ten minutes ago and I was still on my way home. But instead she's curled up on one of our porch chairs. Her skirt, white cotton dotted with pink dinosaurs riding red rockets, rustles in the breeze as she scrolls away on her phone. She doesn't even look up as I approach, her eyes scanning the screen in front of her.

"Good news?" I ask, pulling off my apron as I drop onto the seat beside her.

"No, just stuff about the camp. There are so many rules and regulations I have to remember now that I'm a senior counselor. And, like, I get it—we need to keep them alive or whatever. But honestly, I'd rather focus on the production and not on, like, their 'emotional needs.'" She makes air quotes around the last two words, and I stifle a laugh.

"You'll make a great mom someday," I tease, and Jami rolls her eyes.

"Not if I can help it."

She stands up and brushes off her skirt, and I follow her lead, heading inside and into the kitchen. I grab two cans of Coke out of the fridge and pass one to her.

"Can we just not talk about you leaving for a little while?" I ask.

And okay, so maybe I have a little separation anxiety surrounding her leaving. But can you blame me after what happened with Chloe? I constantly remind myself that this is different. This is only for three weeks, and we'll facetime every single day. But I can't help but think, *What if it's not different?*

"Yeah, I'm dying for an update anyway, so spill. How was work?" Jami asks, running a long, delicate finger around the top of the can. "Chloe didn't show her face again, did she?"

"No," I say gratefully. "It was kind of weird. My mom said she's registered for summer classes now or something. I guess she's not that worried about getting hours at the truck after all. She's, like, tutoring on the side too? I actually might be getting *more* hours now and not really have to see her."

"Win-win. But wait, Chloe Shapiro is taking extra classes and *tutoring*?" Jami asks, following me to my bedroom and making herself right at home on one of my oversize beanbag chairs. "Since when is she Little Miss 'I Love School'?"

I shrug because I don't know. It must be part of some new-and-improved college Chloe. She was never a major slouch in high school or anything; we're both pretty solid A or B students—although a lot of that was because I meticulously planned both her homework and mine in my daily planner. But she was never the above-and-beyond tutor type.

I wish that my stomach didn't flip-flop at the idea of her in her glasses helping other kids learn, like a young, hot . . . yeah. Even though my brain is one hundred percent over Chloe Shapiro, my libido probably never will be.

*Screw this.* I'd rather talk about Jami's impending departure than give Chloe another millimeter of brain space.

"Okay, we have exactly forty-eight hours before you're on the plane to Delaware," I say. "How are we going to spend it?"

"Welllll . . ." she says, drawing out the word and then looking away. "That's one little thing I kind of came here to talk about."

"What?"

"A bunch of my friends from theater club are throwing a last-minute bonfire for me tomorrow night. It was supposed to be a surprise, but I figured it out." She winces when I scowl. "I know, I know. But you have to come, please!"

Bonfires. I used to love them. Key words: *used to.* They're a much-celebrated rite of passage for the kids at my school. Birthday? Bonfire. Graduation? Bonfire. Going away? Definitely a bonfire. I used to daydream about when it would be *my* turn to be the guest of honor at one. And now? I haven't been to one since the Chloe incident, which definitely hasn't helped my social standing any.

You're probably still really wondering what happened.

Fine.

Last summer, a huge group of us had gotten together in the woods off Route 146. You know, back down the side roads where the logging trucks go in? It was—and still is—the best party spot in town. Close enough that it's not a total pain to get to, but deep enough in the woods that no one ever bothers you.

It had rained a lot that day, so I was actually glad it was my dad's weekend and I could use his old Wrangler. Mom's Civic could never handle the mud on the unpaved roads.

Chloe had ridden up earlier with some of the other seniors to help set up. It was her going-away party. Well, in a sense. I mean, sure, other kids were leaving too, but they didn't really matter, not like her. Chloe was always the center of it all, at least for me.

The tents were already up when I got there, and I really didn't give them any thought. There was no way Dad was letting me sleep over. He's super strict about curfews and about always knowing where I am on "his time." I had to practically beg him to let me go at all. So I was just planning to make an appearance, hang out for a little bit, and then head back to his place. The next day was Chloe's last morning home before heading off to college, and I wanted to be up early so I didn't miss a second of it. We were going to meet for breakfast. I was going to drive her to the airport.

I had plans. Good, friendly, flirty plans.

Except logic does not exist in the face of Chloe Shapiro's eyes catching the firelight.

The night was a bit of a blur. I followed her around like a lost puppy while she flitted from group to group, saying her goodbyes and joking about how she couldn't wait to escape this place. Chloe was laughing, and I was trying not to cry. My friend Syed was there, and he kept finding me, talking about all the fun we'd have senior year and how it was awesome that we'd have so many classes together. But a year without Chloe? Nothing about that felt awesome.

"You can't logic yourself out of heartbreak," Chloe had said to me once, when I was in tenth grade and had just broken up with Justin Valdez. He was annoyed and kept showing up at my locker. I didn't get why he couldn't see that we didn't make any sense together. We had literally nothing in common besides the fact that we were attracted to each other and equally matched when it came to kissing.

"You can't build a relationship on kissing, not even a tenth-grade one," I had snapped back.

Chloe had just scrunched her face and asked, "Why not?" Like it was a fine and normal thing to just use someone for their looks or date them because they were fun, or because you liked the way their lips felt on yours.

I thought she didn't know what she was talking about, but now I—

"Please, please, please, please, please," Jami begs, snapping me out of my memories. "Don't make me spend my last night home without you."

I sigh, not missing the implication that she's going to go with or without me. But of course I'm going to go. The new me might hate parties, but I'm not a total jerk. I'm not going to ruin her going-away bash, and I'm *definitely* not going to miss the chance to hang out with her before she's sentenced to three weeks in the forest.

"Fiiiiine," I groan, and she wraps her arms around me in a tight hug.

"You are the best, best friend!" Her phone buzzes then, interrupting the mushy moment. "Hey, it's Tayshia," she says, reading the text. "She wants to know if we want to meet her at the coffee shop in an hour. A few people are getting together, I guess."

"Who's going?" I ask. I love hanging out with Tayshia, but she's super close with Chloe too, and I don't want to risk seeing her again. Not yet.

"She didn't say," Jami says, but then she sees my face. "I'll ask."

Her fingers fly over the keypad, and then we both stand there awkwardly, waiting for the three dots to turn into a reply.

"Um, her and John, obviously, and then, uh, JoJo, Dennis, Jay, and . . ." She trails off, but I already know. That's pretty much all of Chloe's old gang. They stayed local for college, so we've been hanging out a lot with them this year.

"And Chloe," I finish for her. "I'll sit this one out, but you should totally go."

"I'm not leaving you here alone."

I roll my eyes. "I'm literally just going to take a shower and chill out tonight."

"You know you have to see her again sometime, right?"

"I did see her, remember? Yesterday when she came to the truck?"

"Yeah, and then you were weird all night."

She's right, but she doesn't have to say it.

"Hey." I pout. "I don't make fun of you when you hide from Tucker."

"That's different."

"How?"

"Because Tucker and I dated for seven months! And you and Chloe—"

I swallow hard and look away. Right. Fair.

Except not fair.

Because I didn't just lose the person I had a crush on after our disastrous hookup. I also lost my best friend. (And my virginity, which I definitely am *not* telling you about right now.) And all of that seems way, way harsher than losing some random boy you've barely known half a year.

"Sorry," she says quietly.

"It's fine," I lie.

# FIVE

"We have a problem," Mom says, dropping onto the couch next to me later that night.

I glance away from my movie, the third horrible horror movie of the night. My mom got me a subscription to Shudder, the Netflix of cheesy horror movies, and I don't intend to let it go to waste. They're the only place you can watch Adya Mulroney's full body of work, and I practically had to beg to get my mom to sign up for another streaming service. She agreed, under the condition that she could take the $5.99 a month straight out of my Love at First Bite paycheck.

"Let me guess: You need me to work a double tomorrow?" I ask, tossing another handful of popcorn into my mouth.

"No, not that," Mom says, picking some lint off her fleece pajama pants. She's freshly scrubbed and out of the shower, the scent of her apricot body wash replacing the sweet scent of ice cream.

I pause the movie just as the monster starts to reanimate for what I'm assuming will be the final jump scare and angle my body toward Mom. And oh, she actually looks upset right now. Like full-on, pinched-mouth, glassy-eyed, trying-not-to-cry upset.

"What's going on?"

Mom opens her mouth, shuts it, and then opens it again. "Carmen's meeting today with the investors didn't go as well as it could have."

"Oh, shit." The words slip out, and the fact that Mom doesn't bother to chastise me for "language" has me even more worried.

Mom bites the side of her nail, her eyebrows pinching together. "They had some production concerns, and even with our ramped-up business plan, they're hesitant to invest. Especially without meeting the whole team in person. Apparently, they didn't get enough of a 'vibe' from me during the Zoom, and they're threatening to walk." She raises her hands and drops them, tears escaping the corners of her eyes before she can catch them.

I hate these investors, whoever they are.

I don't think I've stressed enough how *very goddamn important* this meeting is to us. This expansion would mean no more stressing over seasonal income. Ever. It would mean celebrating instead of crying when the alimony checks stop next month. It would mean Love at First Bite ice cream on the shelf of every high-end specialty grocery store across the country *and* in various funky restaurants up and down the East Coast. It would be a complete and utter game changer. The biggest of big breaks. Life changing.

"Carmen practically *is* the whole team," I argue. "Do these people not get what a family business is?" I imagine a row of hipster thirtysomethings, "investors" and "influencers," rich off their parents' money, peering over their thick plastic glasses at Carmen, spewing crap about "vibes" and the importance of solid handshakes. Yes, yes, I definitely hate them.

"I think they're just nervous. It's understandable in this economy, honestly," she adds, rubbing her temples, and I think she's giving them too much credit. "They want to schedule a meeting with both of us there as soon as possible."

"Luckily, we'll be there in like a week for the food truck festival, so—"

"Sooner than that," she says, and I scrunch up my forehead. I don't see how we can drive to Food for a Cause, work that, and then get to Dallas—our second and final major festival of the year—any sooner than we've already planned to. We're already heading there the morning after FFAC without even taking a day off for a break from driving. There's just no way.

And then it hits me. "You're canceling on FFAC?"

Mom frowns. "I can't. We don't have the cash flow to pay back the deposit they gave us on the contract. They're understanding, but they're not *that* understanding—not to mention the damage it would do to our reputation if we don't show up."

Shit, I hadn't considered that. I don't see how Mom could keep Love at First Bite afloat another year without Dad's money helping to cover expenses as it is. Ruining their reputation by canceling an event at the last minute is definitely off the table.

"What can we do, then?"

"Carmen and I talked, and we think you're old enough now and experienced enough to handle FFAC for us. You've already done a bunch of other festivals as our assistant. We think you could handle taking the lead."

"Mom—"

"I can fly out before the next investor meeting knowing Love at First Bite is in good hands, and then we'll all meet in Dallas for the food truck festival there afterward." She looks panicked, a desperation tinging her hopefulness, which makes the skin on the back of my neck prickle. "If there was any other way, Fallon, I wouldn't be asking. And Clare and Delilah will both be there to help."

Clare and Delilah are my mom's college roommate and her daughter. Clare runs FFAC; it's how we first got the invite. Clare might have thought it was a mistake for my mom to give up her day job after the divorce, but she was determined to be supportive anyway. We see them once or twice a year, making Delilah a sort of de facto cousin, since both my parents were only children.

Still, my stomach sinks at the thought of all those people crowding in line, shouting out their orders. I know how overwhelming it gets at even the small festivals I've worked. I can't imagine how intense it must get at FFAC. Not to mention the whole I-hate-driving-the-truck thing. I'm terrified enough when I have to drive it across town; there's no way I can make it all the way to Memphis. But if she honestly needs me to, what choice do I have?

"If you really think I can handle this alone." I try to force a smile.

"No, I can't let you do this alone," my mom says slowly.

Relief washes over me for a split second before it hits me who she might mean. "Not Chloe, right?"

Mom looks away, and I don't even need to hear her answer before my head is in my hands. This is a nightmare. It has to be. I must have fallen asleep after Jami left, and this is my subconscious working through stuff in the most horrifying way possible. I pinch my arm, hard, but all that gets me is a tiny red welt and a confused look from my very real, very awake mother.

I take it back. The idea of driving alone seems quite nice now. Relaxing, even. Did I say terrifying? I meant exhilarating. But to be fair, even breaking down on the side of a highway in an ice cream truck and potentially being murdered in a ditch sounds better than being stuck in close quarters with Chloe.

"Is there anyone else you can think of?" Mom asks sadly. "I hate asking this of you. But if we miss this event or we blow this expansion deal, there's not going to be a Love at First Bite. We're barely in the black in a good year as it is, and this *hasn't* been a good year."

I know what you're thinking right now. You're thinking, *Why is Fallon being such a dramatic little witch about this? Her mom needs her. Truly, sincerely needs her. Surely, she can scrape her heart off the floor, pin her ego to the wall, and get the job done. Suck it up already, Fallon.*

And you know what? You're one hundred percent right. But knowing that doesn't change anything. It doesn't change the way my stomach churns and my eyes tear up and my skin feels hot and cold and prickly all at once from the thought of being that close to her for so long. It doesn't change how I feel about her—how I *felt* about her. I can't do this. I can't.

"Anyone else. *Please.*"

"What if you also bring Jami? Or Prisha?" Mom asks. "Maybe if there's a third person there, one you trust, so you and Chloe wouldn't be alone . . . I know they've never worked the truck, but—"

"Prisha has to work at her parents' store, and Jami's got camp. You know this."

"Shit," Mom says, which sets my teeth on edge. She never swears, and until tonight, she never let me get away with it around her either.

"I can't do this, Mom."

She drags her fingers over her forehead, like she's massaging away a pending headache. "Fallon, I need you to be reasonable."

And, oh, how I wish I could! How I wish I could just turn this off and everything could go back to the before, to when things were . . . Well, they weren't great, but they were *fine*. I jump up and start pacing.

"What happened between you two? I don't understand!"

I want to say, "Gee, I don't know, Mom. I guess it's hard to stay friends with someone who doesn't seem to think it's a big deal that their body was all over your body!" But that is *not* a conversation I'm having with my mother, especially not when her best friend's daughter makes up the other body in this equation.

I settle on "Just stuff."

We're both quiet then, the air charged. And I don't know whether I should walk away or sit back down. I stare at the TV screen, at the monster frozen in time, and ugh, me too, monster. Me too. A sniffle draws my gaze back to my mom, and crap, she's actually crying again.

I made my mother cry.

I rub my hands over my face with a whispered "damn" and then drop back down to the couch. I take a deep breath, knowing what has to be done.

"I'll figure it out. I'll make it work somehow," I finally say.

My mom looks at me with red eyes. "You will?"

I wrap my arms around myself, dropping my chin to my chest. "If this is seriously the only way to get this done—if you truly have no other alternative in the universe—then yeah, I'm in."

# SIX

*I* swing the mini golf club a little too hard, sending my bright green ball careening straight off the edge of the windmill fan and plunking into a pond dyed an unnatural shade of blue. Behind me, Jami and Prisha tsk.

"You need to finesse it. Like this." Jami taps her ball just right. It skims over the green, deftly traveling between the blades of the windmill before banking left on a little hill and coming to a stop at the very edge of the hole.

Prisha nudges Jami's ball with her hot-pink Converse, and it clanks into the hole with a little thud. "Hole in one!"

I scoff, elbow-deep in the water as I fish out my ball. Prisha sticks her tongue out with a good-natured laugh before heading to the next hole.

Prisha is the final piece of our friendship trio. She moved here from Michigan a couple years ago and seamlessly joined the group. Well, back then it was a quartet, but she sided with me in the friendship divorce.

She sets down her ball with a grin. The bright summer sun breaks from a cloud, making her light brown skin look almost copper as she does a little twirl before taking some practice swings beside the tee. I laugh, forgetting for a moment what a mess my life has become overnight.

But no, I'm not thinking about that. Today is just about the three of us. Prisha has to work tonight and can't make it to the bonfire. Not that her parents would let her go—they are very anti-party, even though Prisha doesn't drink. Thus, a day of mini golf, just the girls.

"You coming? Or are you going to hide in the water all day?" Prisha calls after taking her shot. She taps her fingers across her thigh as she waits, and I try not to notice. In an alternate timeline, one that wasn't marred by Hurricane Chloe, Prisha and I could have been a thing. Maybe even more than a thing. But then she met Kai, and Chloe and I . . .

My fingers finally grasp my ball, and I yank it out of the water. "Coming," I say, a bit of sludge dripping down my arm. I roll the ball around on my shorts in a feeble attempt to dry it off.

A family—two moms and three little kids—is still finishing up the hole ahead of us, so I take my place on the bench between Prisha and Jami to wait. The wood pricks against my legs and digs into the soft skin of my neck as I lean back. But it's a small price to pay; the heat has zapped me of all my energy today.

"You ready for tomorrow?" Prisha asks, bumping Jami with her shoulder.

"I think so," she says, before launching into an excited rant about how they're going to do *Into the Woods* this summer. My joke about *Into the Woods* being literally done *in the woods* only earns me a polite half-laugh, so I'm happy to drop my head back and stare up at the clouds, zoning out to the sound of their chatter.

Prisha taps me on the forehead. "Hey, you good?"

"Oh yeah, yeah," I say. I try to play it off like I've still been listening, but their amused faces tell me I'm busted. "Sorry, I was—"

"Daydreaming," Jami says. "We know."

Ahead of us, one of the kids cries over the clown eating his ball, which means we're almost up. It's the last hole, a giant clown face painted on a wooden board that eats the golf balls. That way the course doesn't have to worry about trusting people to actually walk up and return the balls. Think Skee-Ball but creepier. Instead of nice, normal little rings, it's got a faded, scratched-up mouth that looks more bloody than painted. The nose is bright orange, and the eyes are two black holes leading into the abyss—or probably some ball-return mechanism, if I'm being honest. But still.

"I'm kind of jealous," Prisha says. "Jami is going to be out becoming a Broadway star, and you're going to be out seeing the country with your mom, while I'm stuck here bagging groceries at my dad's store."

"The woods of Delaware are hardly Broadway." Jami laughs.

"And it's, like, a tiny little corner of the country I'll see, at most," I say, leaving out the fact that my mom isn't actually going to be there. I don't want them to worry.

Prisha glares at the clown as soon as the family in front of us leaves. "I'm going to take this sucker down," she says, which I interpret to mean that she intends to get her ball through the eyes, which earns you a free ice cream cone from the snack bar.

It is, admittedly, hard for me to get excited about ice cream given how much of a role it plays in my life.

"Good luck," Jami says as Prisha walks closer to the final hole. I shudder, trying not to think about how weird it is to try to knock a ball through a clown's eye.

Jami comes to stand next to me as Prisha sets her bright blue ball on the little green rubber mat in front of the clown. She crouches down with one eye shut, pointing her putter in the direction of the clown's face as if it really matters, as if the green isn't all topsy-turvy hills anyway. Jami and I both burst out laughing when Prisha licks her finger and holds it in the air before lining up for her shot.

Behind us, the next group of mini golfers—a bunch of older boys probably just home from college—makes noises of impatience from our recently abandoned bench. And god, why is everybody in such a rush to have things end? *Savor the time, people,* I want to tell them, because after this horribly creepy hole, we're all going to be shoved back into the real world. The world where I am stuck in the truck for a week with no one to keep me company but Chloe.

"Are you all packed up for *your* trip?" Jami asks with a smirk.

I shrug, an involuntary frown tugging at my lips.

"Wait, what's that look for?" Prisha puts down her putter, which makes the boys behind us groan. She flips them off as she studies my face. "What's going on?"

And okay, there actually isn't a way to answer this without lying. And I absolutely am not about to start our summer off with lying to my two best friends on my conscience.

"So, about my trip." I wince. "My mom isn't exactly going anymore."

"What?!" Jami asks.

"Can you guys please just go!" one of the boys calls.

Prisha glares at him until he sits back down. She does, however, turn back around and line up her shot all over again. "Is the trip off, then?"

"No, IhavetogowithChloe," I mumble, squeezing my golf ball hard in my hand.

Prisha chooses that exact moment to finally swing for real, and she overshoots from surprise. Her ball rolls up hard to the clown's hair, rolls back down, and gets caught in the ball return. No ice cream for her.

"I could not have heard you right," Jami practically shouts. "Because I swore for a second that you just said you were road tripping to FFAC *with Chloe*."

Prisha looks at me in shock. "Wait, what is happening? Is this the Upside Down? Did we just flip into nightmare mode or something?"

"Look, if you're not going to go, can you let us?" the same boy asks.

"Shut up!" the three of us shout in unison.

"Since when was this the plan?" Jami asks, and I don't miss the nervous look on her face.

I drop my shoulders back, trying and failing to look confident. "Since last night, and it's a long story. Just take your shot, and I'll tell you all about it after."

"You don't want a turn?" Prisha asks, twirling her putter in her hand.

I rub my fingers over my bright green golf ball and shake my head before shoving it in my pocket. Something tells me I'm going to need this little talisman to get me through the rest of this summer, imbued as it is with the memory of fun and friends. It won't be the same as having them there, but at least it will be something—a tangible reminder of a good day and better friends while I'm trapped in a tin can with Hurricane Chloe.

♥

A LITTLE WHILE later, we walk toward the batting cages.

"Maybe this could be good," Jami says.

"Yeah," I say, "I'm sure that's what a mouse thinks right before the trap snaps his neck too."

Jami rolls her eyes as we climb into the bleachers that give us a view of where Prisha's boyfriend, Kai, is practicing. Kai was the captain of our high school varsity baseball team. He's also playing baseball in college, and I'm pretty sure Prisha said he even got a scholarship for it. Kai wasn't super on my radar—sports aren't really my thing—so I haven't kept up. But he and Prisha are pretty serious now, so I'm trying to make an effort.

You know how they say there's always one person who loves the other person a *little* bit more in every relationship? Well, there is one glaring exception to that: Prisha and Kai.

Kai is tall and kind, and while I'm not super into boys, even I can admit that he's cute, with his dark curly hair and easy grin. Kai and Prisha look good together in a way that reminds me I am definitely bi.

He gives us a nod before tensing into position, his muscles taut and sinewy, and he swings at the next ball. There's a crack as his bat connects and sends the ball flying across the batting cage. He checks the speed and then turns toward us with a smile. The ball machine whirs off, and he wipes the sweat off his face with a towel stashed in his gym bag.

"Hey, ladies. How'd it go?" Kai trots over and gives Prisha a kiss on the cheek. She swats him away, teasing that he's "so gross," but we all know she doesn't mean it.

"I didn't win the ice cream. Again." She pouts.

Kai shakes his head. "You know that's rigged, right? I don't think anyone has ever won it."

"Still," she says, and he leans forward and kisses the pout right off her lips.

"Y'all want a ride home?" he asks, like he doesn't know we were counting on it and that Prisha's mom dropped us off here specifically because he was here too.

"That'd be great," Jami says, playing that game where we pretend like just because Kai's the only one with his own car, we don't expect him to drive us around all the time, even though we sort of do.

Once we're all piled into his Subaru, Kai turns up the music and puts down the windows. Thank god, because Jami and I are currently stuffed in the back with what seems to be the entire contents of his baseball bag. While I appreciate the blue pine-tree air freshener he has hanging from his rearview mirror, it does little to combat the fetid stink emanating from the pile of sneakers and workout clothes in his back seat.

"Seriously, Fal, I think going on this road trip with Chloe could be good," Prisha says, turning toward us from the front. I don't miss the way she flicks her eyes to Jami, both of them gauging my reaction.

"Ooooh," Kai says, "isn't that the girl you hooked up with last summer? The one you—"

Prisha punches him in the arm, sparing us from whatever he was going to say next.

And okay, I think I'm going to lose it.

"Ow," he says, rubbing his arm with a fake scowl. "I'm telling Coach!"

Prisha crosses her arms. "Don't be a pig, then! I'm sure Coach would agree with me."

"I wasn't being a pig. I simply asked, respectfully, if that was the girl she hooked up with. And it is, right, Fal?"

"I mean, it was a little more complicated than that," I say. "But yeah."

"Oh shit, sorry," Kai says, and he looks properly admonished. "I thought it was, like, a one-time thing, which would be bad enough, but road tripping with your ex? Yikes."

"Well, it *was* just the one time," I say, not knowing why I need to clarify this point so badly. It's like I don't want to give Chloe any more of me than she deserves. "I mean, technically, but—"

Kai furrows his brows in the mirror. "Wait, then—"

Prisha frowns. "Kai, shh. And Fallon, you don't have to explain yourself to this meathead—*who I love*," she croons when he scowls. "But my point, before my handsome, loving, doesn't-always-think-before-he-talks boyfriend derailed us, is that maybe something positive will come out of this. It's been a year. If it's possible to get closure so you're not walking around like an open wound anymore, this could be how it happens."

She says it so nonchalantly, like I have a broken bone that just needs *time*. She doesn't get it. I don't hate Chloe Shapiro because she blew me off and broke my heart. I hate Chloe Shapiro because her actions made me waste time feeling like shit and had me crying over her instead of doing something actually productive. I hate Chloe Shapiro because her inconsistency and flightiness let me down. I hate Chloe Shapiro because she doesn't seem to hate me at all or even acknowledge that *clearly* we're enemies now.

"Pri does have a point," Jami says, flicking her finger against my arm.

"Yeah, maybe," I mumble, knowing that is absolutely not going to be the case.

# SEVEN

*J*ami insists on driving to the going-away party, even though my mom let me borrow her car. I argue that letting me drive, thus making me the designated driver, means that she could let loose and not have to worry about anything, but she isn't having it. At all.

It doesn't dawn on me until we get there that this was her way of making sure I didn't chicken out or leave the party early. And now I'm effectively stuck here, at her mercy. Resigned, I find a stump near the bonfire and throw my hoodie over it before sitting down.

Jami flits around, occasionally checking in with me, but I'm content to just let her do her thing. The bonfire burns down to more of an aggressively hot campfire, leaving my face feeling scalding hot while my back freezes in the cool night air. There are worse things, I guess, than being fifty percent cold at a party celebrating your best friend leaving, in the spot where you lost not only your virginity but also your *other* best friend, forever.

And I know. *I know.* You're once again wondering, *Why is Fallon being soooooo dramatic all the time? All she does is mope.* Which, fair. I haven't been my best lately.

But there are extenuating circumstances tonight. Returning to the scene of the crime, for one. And then, watching Jami and all our friends—seeing her hugging them and laughing—it just further highlights how everything is changing. We're all going our separate ways this fall, even if we're trying to ignore it.

I think I'm just really goddamn sick of going-away parties.

"Is this seat taken?" someone asks, and I turn my head to see Julie Perez standing there with her boyfriend, Chris. She's pointing to the empty stump next to me with her foot. No, it is decidedly not taken, but judging by how Julie and Chris seem to be making it their mission to make out on every available surface at the party tonight, I'm not exactly in a rush to sit next to them either.

"Uh, no," I say, standing up and brushing off my jeans. "I was going to go get a snack anyway, so have at it. You can have both."

Julie looks at me like she can't decide whether to be relieved or offended but seems to settle on the former with a smile. "Cool, thanks, but we just need one." I walk away as she takes her place on Chris's lap.

The music blares all around us, courtesy of the sound system in Brett Harris's car. I swear even the tree leaves are vibrating from it as I lace through the outskirts of the crowd. I stop and take another sip of my drink, room-temperature beer that makes my head feel a little fuzzy, and I toe my sneaker into the soft dirt of the forest floor.

I wander to the edge of the party, craving a break from the chaos, and somehow find myself in the back, where everyone staying over put up their tents earlier. It's just like last year, and I stare at the spot where everything happened and didn't happen. Where I thought a relationship had started, but really a friendship ended.

It's bullshit, all of it, honestly. It wasn't anything epic or special. It was just two hands meeting, nervous and clumsy, fingers wandering and warm in the most private of places, gasps and teeth and the taste of stale beer on her lips. It was—

"Hey," Chloe says, her voice cutting through the haze.

I spin around fast, blushing, hoping she can't read my mind. I almost reach out to touch her face, my fingers twitching from the memory of her skin, my brain fuzzy enough to miss her—but not quite fuzzy enough to forget how she hurt me. I shove my hand into my pocket and open my mouth, but the only thing that comes out is a mortifying "um."

The music switches to a faster beat, the bass thrumming through my chest, and I press my lips into a hard line at the sight of her smile. I will not smile back. She cannot have that from me.

"I hope it's okay I'm here," she says, her eyes searching mine.

"Why?" I manage to mumble when I finally tear my eyes from hers. I wish I didn't care. I wish it didn't feel good to soak up the sight of her, skin blazing gold in the firelight, biting her lip the way she always does when she thinks she's in trouble and is sure being cute will get her out of it.

"Why do I hope it's okay?" she asks softly.

"Why are you here?" I ask, my voice a bit too loud. A few people turn and stare at us. Fine. Let them.

"Oh." Her lips twitch, her smile falling away. "It sounded like fun? I didn't know this was for Jami until I was already in the car. I came with Tyler and Joe."

"Of course you did," I scoff, turning away. Tyler and Joe have been in love with her since ninth grade. She pretends not to notice, but I'm zero percent surprised she would use them for rides while she's home.

Chloe touches my arm, but I pull it away.

"Are you okay?" she asks. Her voice sounds more worried than mad, but no, she doesn't get to be worried. The only thing I want her to be is gone.

"Do you even really care?" I shout, and she looks legit stunned.

Jami comes up then, wrapping her arm around my shoulders. "She's perfect," she says a little too cheerfully before leading me away. Chloe starts to follow us but then seems to think better of it, disappearing into the crowd while Jami takes me to her car.

Okay. You're right. I *am* a piece of shit for causing drama at Jami's party. I couldn't help it, though.

"I didn't know she'd be here. I swear." And even though Jami has been Team "You Should Talk to Her" all along, I know she means it. She would never sabotage me like this. "Do you want to leave?" Jami asks, but I know she doesn't want to, and I don't want to ruin this night any more than I already have.

"No," I say, but she doesn't believe me. "No, seriously." I shake my head. "It's fine. I'm fine. Go enjoy your party. I swear to god."

Jami crinkles up her forehead, and I can guess what she's thinking. She's probably torn because she wants my words to be true so badly but knows that they aren't. There's no way, and we both know it. But the thing is, even though I definitely am not okay right now, for her I will be. Loyalty over everything, right? Leaving would be a Chloe thing to do.

She smiles, squeezing my hands. "Thanks."

"Now get out of here." I laugh, swatting at her and shooing her away. "Go!"

And she does.

And I hang back in her car, where it's a little bit cold, a little bit dark, and no one else ever comes to say hello.

# EIGHT

"Mmpf?" I mumble into the pillow as someone gently shakes me awake, the smell of coffee wafting in my direction. It takes me a second to realize where I am: on an air mattress in the middle of Jami's floor.

I roll onto my back and am met with an eager-looking Jami, who's already showered and dressed and more put together than anyone has a right to be this early in the morning.

"We have to leave in a half hour," she says, thrusting a coffee cup into my hand. "But if you're not up to it, I can Uber to the airport. My mom said it was fine when she heard how loud you were snoring this morning."

"I do not snore!" Scandalized, I scooch up to a seated position, making the little air mattress dip and wheeze.

"You do after three beers. It was bad."

"Lies!" I take a gulp of the way-too-hot coffee and cough hard. I don't really love coffee the way some people do, but I love that Jami recognized I would probably need a little something to help me get moving today.

I rub the sleep out of my eyes with my empty hand, thinking through the events of the night, like how I sat on the hood of Jami's car watching people party and the way Chloe stayed close, close, close to the fire, like she was giving me as much space as possible.

The fact that I am supposedly leaving on a trip with her tomorrow—one where space will be impossible—isn't lost on me.

"We have to goooooo," Jami sings, channeling her best musical-theater nerd.

"I can't believe how chipper you are today, considering you had, by my count, at least double the booze I did."

"Um, no. That was ginger ale in my cup. Designated driver, remember?" she says, standing back up. "Besides, it's summer-camp day." She twirls around in her skirt, a swooshy sky-blue thing with little black cats printed on it. I smile even though I'm not really feeling it. Happy Jami is contagious.

Jami tosses my clothes to me, not-so-subtly hinting that I need to get out of the pajama pants and hoodie she loaned me last night, and pulls the plug to deflate the air mattress. Within seconds, my butt hits her hardwood floor.

"Do you need to run home first?" she asks, but I shake my head.

"I'll shower later. I just need some toothpaste and a hair tie," I say, heading for the bathroom.

When I get back, she's sitting on her bed writing some-thing on a torn-out piece of notebook paper. Her bright red carry-on and well-worn JanSport backpack are waiting beside her.

"Ready?" I ask.

"Can't wait. But the more important question is, are *you* ready?"

"Well, I do hate airport traffic, but—"

She laughs. "Not that. The trip with Chloe."

"I'll figure it out," I say, hedging, and I grab my purse off her desk. "Besides, at least now we don't have to worry about my paying you back for the trip."

"Honestly? I'd rather cancel than force you into this." Jami frowns.

"I'm not being forced into anything," I lie. I mean, *I am*, but not by her, and it doesn't do anybody any good to say that anyway. "But seriously, we have to go, or we'll be late."

"Here," Jami says, shoving the piece of paper into my hand with a pained smile. "I'd say don't open it until after you leave tomorrow, but I know you, and I know you're going to peek no matter what. Might as well open it now while I'm watching."

I roll my eyes, but she's right. The paper crinkles in my hand as I unfold it and read.

Breathe. You got this.

I fold the note back up and slip it into my bag, my eyes tearing up. I feel like I just got punched in the face with emotion. I know I've been taking this year for granted, every second. And now that she's leaving—even if it's just a trial run for the real thing—I'm so mad at myself.

I wrap her in a hug so tight, the air whooshes out of me. "Thank you. You're the best."

"I know." She laughs and picks up her suitcase.

♥

SOME PART OF me, some way-back, tiny, hidden part of my brain, knew that I would probably hear from Chloe today.

I just didn't think it would be when I was first getting home, still dressed in yesterday's clothes, my eyes puffy from crying after dropping Jami off at the airport.

Her car is parked on the edge of my driveway, two of the tires scraping up our lawn. She's leaning against the car door, waiting for me as I park on the street instead of trying to maneuver my mom's car around her.

I tap my fingers on the steering wheel, not sure whether I want to get out or drive away.

Either option would be better than sitting here paralyzed by all the memories of us in the car together. The thrill of driving alone with her after she passed her driver's test without even practicing. Or the time we were hauling gallons of ice cream for our moms, and she managed to pull her car over just in time to be the tenth caller in a radio contest and win us both sold-out concert tickets. Or when we took it to prom last year, super platonically, because she "forgot to ask anyone else." And the laughing, so much laughing, that ensued as we shoved all my fluffy bright pink tulle into the passenger seat until I looked like a ball of cotton candy with an updo.

Chloe tilts her head and takes a step toward me, and no, no, I don't think I want to have this conversation surrounded by all these memories, thank you very much. I click off the car's ignition and climb out, bracing myself like she's an overeager Labrador gunning to knock me over and not a human being who's here to . . . I don't even know. Is "emotionally devastate me" too strong of a phrase? I can't decide.

"Hi, Fal," she says as I walk up. "At least, I think that's how you greet someone in situations like this."

"Situations like this?"

She scrunches up her face. "Meaning after you've had a weird, public semi-argument with your best friend and aren't totally sure why."

I notice how she says "best friend," present tense, without even the courtesy of adding the word "former" in front of it. I step back, leaning against the old oak tree that grows in front of the duplex we rent.

Chloe must notice the confusion on my face, because she takes another step forward before I hold up my hand to stop her. "What are you doing here?"

She shrugs. "I don't know. Texting and calling you didn't seem to work this year, so I thought I might as well just start showing up everywhere until you acknowledge I exist."

"Okay, stalker," I say without a hint of humor, because that feels like crossing a line I really don't want crossed. Especially not while I'm standing here with pine needles still stuck in my hair from last night.

"You wish."

"I really don't. I'd rather you just left me alone." I push past her, heading to my front door, my heart pounding out of my chest.

"Gonna be pretty hard to avoid me after tonight," she says. "Considering we're going to be occupying the same tiny truck for the foreseeable future."

"Don't remind me," I groan, fishing out my keys.

"Don't you think you at least owe me an explanation?"

I turn around, crossing my arms. "You can't be serious."

"Deadly," she says, walking toward me. She stops a few inches away, pulling a stray pine needle out of my hair. "If you hate me so much, why are you going on this trip with me?"

"Stop." I swat her hand away. "I'm going to help my mom. It has nothing to do with you. AT. ALL. You know as well as I do our moms can't afford for this truck to go under."

"I do. But what I don't know is why we can't be friends anymore."

"Oh, I don't know, Chloe. Maybe it has something to do with what happened last summer."

"Come on, Fal. It's not that deep. It doesn't have to be," she says, and that knocks the wind right out of me.

There are a lot of things on this earth that fall within the parameters of her favorite catchphrase. And apparently, now I'm one of them.

"You should leave," I struggle to get out, walking to my door.

Her nostrils flare, just a little, in annoyance. "What's your problem, Fallon? Really? Like, cards on the table. What the hell?"

"Can you just go?!"

"That is *not* fair."

"Oh, you're one to talk about *fair*."

"What does that even mean?"

And oh. Oh. I am at my breaking point now.

"You left!" I shout. "You just got on a plane like it didn't even matter! You—"

"Oh my god. Is this some weird jealousy thing? Like I went off to college without you and made new friends. Is that what this is? Was I just supposed to sit here and rot in this town while you finished high school?"

I hate how much that stings. How ridiculous she thinks I am for liking her, for feeling jealous when she posted Instagram pics of her hanging all over kids at college just days after our hookup, for thinking we had something real, for missing her when she left.

"I'm not talking about college," I say, because how can she not get this? How can she not understand that when I say "You left," I don't just mean physically?

She stumbles a little. "Wait, what?"

"Just go away, Chloe."

"Not until you talk to me! Make it make sense! You said it was fine that day. And now you're pissed?"

And oh. That.

Yeah, I guess I forgot to tell you about that. About how the next morning we had plans to meet up at our favorite diner and have breakfast before I drove her to the airport. I was so ridiculously excited. It's embarrassing now. I was *actually* going to tell her that . . . Doesn't matter. She didn't show. She texted fifteen minutes after I got there and said she was running late and her mom would just take her to the airport. I wrote back **K**, not sure what else to say, and then drove home, numb.

It was the last time I bothered to respond.

"Fuck you," I say, rushing to unlock my door just so I can have the satisfaction of slamming it behind me, because who does she think she is?

And this is not happening. This trip, being with her? It's off. It's over. I'm calling it now. Mom can find someone else to figure this out, or Chloe can go by her goddamn self. I flip the lock on the door, fully prepared to break the news to my mom and then run to my room, where no one can hurt me, except then I hear Mom talking. She's on the phone, upset.

I creep down the hallway and peek into her room, careful to stay just out of her sight. She's standing in front of the mirror, frantically holding up different outfits still on hangers, her suitcase lying mostly empty on the bed. Her phone, the speaker clicked on, rests right beside it.

Carmen's worried voice hits my ears. "We're so screwed. We are so screwed."

"It's going to be okay," my mom says in the same tone she uses to soothe me when I'm upset. "I'll be there tomorrow. We'll talk to them first thing, and we'll figure it out. We have the production in place; we have the means to do it. You laid the groundwork at the first meeting, and now we just need to seal the deal."

All it takes is one look at her exhausted face, and I know, without even hearing Chloe's car backing out of the driveway and racing down the street, that there is no way I'm going to bail on her. I do not flake on the people I love. I will not.

I'm not like Chloe.

# NINE

*I*n my head, it will go like this: Mom will drive me out to the truck. I will be stoic, despite my general unease, like a soldier going off to war. Because this is a war, at least to me. Chloe showing up at my house felt like a challenge—a gauntlet thrown or whatever.

But I digress.

Back up.

Start over.

It will go like this: We will pull up outside the truck, which my mom readied for the trip the night before. The early-morning sun will splash pink on the clouds. I will be put together, with the perfect winged eyeliner, cute leggings, and my favorite shirt—you know the one, the comfortable heather-gray tee with an illustration of a little kitten and bold black letters that spell out **REAL MEN CUDDLE CATS**. I bought it for my dad for Father's Day one year, and it sat unused in the back of his closet until I reclaimed it. A quick cinched side knot, some ballet flats, and a perfect bun, and we have the ideal cozy-chic summer traveling outfit.

In my head, Chloe will be a disaster, arriving late and disheveled, tampons and pajamas spilling out of her backpack, because she was never good at planning ahead or making sure things went well. She doesn't even own a suitcase as far as I know, which is weird for someone who literally goes to college on the other side of the country. I picture her cramming her belongings into various backpacks and garbage bags, and I smile. She deserves wrinkled clothes.

In my head, I am perfect, and she is the creature lurking in my periphery.

But . . .

The reality is that last night I fell asleep facetiming with Prisha and Jami after Jami got to her hotel. I was trying to shake out my pre-trip jitters. Jami's being bused out to the cabins with all the other campers today, and since she isn't sure how the Wi-Fi will be out there, we wanted to get in as much face time as humanly possible.

Which means I didn't actually pack until five in the morning. And now it's five thirty, and I have to be dropped off at the truck by six fifteen, and I'm still in sweats with my hair a veritable rat's nest. I debate taking a shower, decide not to, and then change my mind again. We're camping the whole way to Memphis, so who knows when my next hot shower will come—probably not until we're in the hotel before FFAC, days from now. By the time I'm done and dressed, my mom is yelling at me that we needed to leave ten minutes ago.

Which is why I show up in a parking lot with dripping-wet hair, no makeup, and wearing a pair of holey sweats and a tank top that rides up. It's hot already, even at six fifteen in the morning. The kind of hot that you know is going to turn into a full-on scorcher in another hour or two. The kind of hot that burns off all the clouds so there's nothing left to see.

I was sort of right in my vision: My mom *did* spend part of last night restocking the truck for us and getting everything ready. Other than the spare vats of ice cream she's hauling toward the truck right now, we're stocked up and ready to go.

You might be wondering how the ice cream in the truck will stay cool for days despite it being five million degrees outside. See also: "Why we're broke right now." Mom and Carmen spent a ton of money on a new freezer unit this spring. When the truck is running, the freezer feeds off the energy made by the engine. When we turn the truck off, it switches over to a generator that lasts a guaranteed thirteen hours.

Before this, Mom and Carmen used to have to overnight-ship ice cream to a freezer storage facility in Memphis before every FFAC event. Not only was it an absolute nightmare logistically and way, way, way too expensive, but there was also always some runoff that melted and refroze on the top of every container. Mom would end up shipping twice the amount of ice cream she thought she would need just so she could skim off what she called the "melty grossness."

It was actually just as delicious as any other ice cream, if not as aesthetically pleasing. But no matter how good it tasted, my mom has standards she won't ever let slip. Maybe that's where I get it from. She says, "It's not just about taste but consistency," and ha, I guess maybe that applies to my Chloe situation too. It's never been about the taste; it's the consistency that's lacking. I wanted the same firm, reasonable, there-for-you ice cream my mom insists on, not Chloe's runny, malleable mess, always going this way or that, refusing to hold itself together.

It used to be adorable. But now it's annoying.

I reach into the trunk and pull out my carry-on—my simple black one nestled beside my mom's bright purple one with ribbons tied to the handle. She's leaving for the airport straight from here. I'm blissfully grateful that Chloe seems to be running late as usual. I want nothing more than a minute alone to decompress and prepare for the trip ahead.

"Hi!" a voice says as soon as I open the double back doors of the truck. I jump back at the sight of Chloe, awake, dressed, and sitting cross-legged in the middle of the floor with her laptop open. "I figured I would get in a little work while I waited for you two."

She says it like it's the most normal thing in the world. Like she was waiting for us awhile, even though it is literally the exact time we said we'd be here. My skin prickles. This is not how it was supposed to go.

Chloe stands up and takes my bag out of my hand. She carries it over and places it down beside her stuff on the little shelf with netting my mom installed to hold personal items safely while driving.

"Thanks," I say reluctantly, because my mom is stepping in behind me and I don't want to be rude and stress her out or, worse, trigger another lecture about having an open mind and how friendship with other women is the most important thing a girl can have in this world.

"There's a cup of coffee for you up front in the cupholder," Chloe says, a nervous smile ghosting across her lips. "I honestly wasn't sure you'd even come."

I lick my lips and shrug because, honestly, I still wish I hadn't, but there's no use saying it out loud when we both already know it.

"Oh! Chloe!" my mom says, looking a little *too* happy to see her. "You beat us here! I'm impressed."

"Yeah," she says, slipping her laptop into its case and tucking it into some other netting on the wall. "I wanted to get a little schoolwork in before we left, and I had to call my mom to figure out how to set the truck up as a hotspot or whatever so I can keep up with my online classes. But don't worry, I took the day of the event off. My professors already know. Besides, it's mostly just readings and posting in the class discussion board anyway."

Who is this ultra-responsible person, and what have they done with my flighty former best friend? Maybe college did change her, or maybe she's just gotten even better at acting like whatever people want her to be.

"Carm is already up?" Mom asks.

Chloe sighs. "I'm not entirely sure that she's gone to sleep yet. I'm so glad you're going out there early. She's beating herself up pretty bad over the meeting. You know how she gets."

My eyes flick back and forth as they talk, wondering when it switched from them having a sort of parent-child relationship to something more like peers. It's unsettling. Is this what happens when you leave for school? When I come back for Thanksgiving break, will my mom be more like a roommate I really love? Or is this just another annoying Chloe thing?

I lean back against the freezer and watch them, looking for any signs that something is amiss. I catch the way Chloe's eyes crinkle when my mom says something funny—the way my mom's forehead pinches when she's being serious and walking us through the generator setup, pointing to all the switches that keep it going, which I've already memorized. I absorb the ten thousand conversations their bodies are having while their mouths are talking.

I turn and make sure the netting is secure, bumping my hip on the edge of the bright silver freezer and trying really hard not to remember the way Chloe's body talked to mine once upon a time. The sound of her sigh, the way her nose scrunches up just a little when she . . .

"Shit," I whisper to myself, struggling with one last strap holding everything down. This is going to be a long week.

"Want some help with that?" Chloe asks, the skin of her bare arm warm against mine when she shoves in beside me and cinches the netting, snapping it into place with ease. Her biceps flex just slightly from the effort. *That's new,* I think, my eyes catching on the tan line on her shoulder when the strap of her tank slips down.

I can't tell if she caught me staring or if she's just pleased with herself for doing something I couldn't, but her familiar easy smirk is back, just like it used to be. It shouldn't send butterflies cascading through my stomach, but it does. She licks her lips, her eyes narrowing just slightly when they meet mine, like she can read my mind. I look away, the butterflies swirling into a tornado that makes my stomach ache.

"Okay, so you two know the deal with this truck," my mom says. "But I want to take you through it one more time again anyway." She crosses her arms with a serious look, like we both weren't practically raised inside of it. Like I haven't been in it every day for forever, and Chloe too until she left for college. "Main freezers, backup freezers, pump, generator, power cords"—she points all around us—"gourmet menus for the event, regular menus in case you run out of the specialty flavors early. Tip jar's under here. Bowls, spoons, napkins, cones—"

"We know, Mom," I say, checking my phone. There are three texts from Prisha already. "You're going to be cutting it really close if you don't leave soon. You know they always have, like, one person working the airport security line on weekdays."

Hazard of a tiny airport. I swear the whole area was

thrilled when they were finally able to slap the word "international" on the front, all of us politely looking away from the fact that the only thing that makes it international is one weekly flight to Canada, which is a mere three-hour drive anyway, even in the worst of traffic.

"Okay, okay—you're right," she says, kissing my forehead. "Do you have everything you need out of the car? Remember you're camping tonight and tomorrow, and then you'll have a hotel for the night before and after FFAC, and then it's on to the Dallas festival, where Carmen and I will be anxiously awaiting your arrival."

"And then I fly back," I say, even though it's a sore spot between me and Mom. She had it in her head that the four of us would drive back together, best-friends style. But we both know that wouldn't work. One, it's illegal; there aren't enough seats in the truck. And two, I would rather die than sit huddled in the back with Chloe for a few extra days. Which reminds me—

"Oh, I almost forgot!" I dart out of the truck and over to Mom's car, opening the back door and sliding out two long bags. "The tents!"

Mom scrunches her forehead. "I still don't see why you need to bring the other—"

"Hush," I say, giving her a peck on the cheek. "Text me when you land, okay?"

"Yes, and drive carefully, both of you. We're really trusting you here. Call Carmen if you need anything while I'm in the air. Anything at all. This is a big deal and—"

"We know," Chloe says, leaning against one of the backup freezers storing huge containers full of extra ice cream. "You can count on us."

I look at Chloe and raise my eyebrows. She's really laying this whole "responsible adult" thing on thick. I can't wait to see how much of it is an act. I'm pretty sure almost all of it is, knowing her.

My mom wraps me in one last big hug. We exchange I love yous and promises to travel safe and text often. She waves at me excitedly from the car, beeping before driving off, and I watch her drive away a little too long, knowing that when I turn around, I'll have to face the reality of what's waiting for me.

"Did you really bring two tents?" Chloe asks, hopping down out of the back of the truck and waving to my mom herself.

"Yep," I say. "One for each of us." I'm challenging her, waiting to see if she says anything more.

"Come on," she says instead, twirling the keys around her pointer finger. "I'm driving."

# TEN

*C*hloe insists that, because she's driving, she doesn't have to follow my carefully planned route—which results in her shoving my phone beneath my seat so hard she's already on the road before I dig it out. Other than this not-so-brief argument, we drive in silence for the first half hour. Neither of us dares to talk, or at least, I don't. What would I even say? *Screw you for ruining my perfectly designed plans once again.* No thank you. I think I'll keep pouting instead.

I eventually take a reluctant sip of my coffee—half regular, half hazelnut—from one of the convenience stores that are local to our area. It's my favorite combo, and I can tell she got the sugar and cream configuration just right. I don't know if I should mention it or ignore it.

I thought it hurt when the only person who actually knew how to make my coffee stopped making it, but somehow this hurts even more. Like she knew—or knows, apparently—and just removed herself from the equation anyway.

But she keeps sneaking glances at me, practically vibrating every time I take a sip, and the pressure to say, well, *anything* becomes overwhelming.

"Thanks," I finally say, and her face splits into a Cheshire Cat grin.

"I wasn't sure if you still took it like that. I was worried Jami had brought you over to the dark side in my absence." I raise an eyebrow, and she theatrically whispers, "I saw they built a Starbucks at the old bank over the winter break. Drive-through and everything."

I shake my head. "Give me cheap gas station coffee, or give me death," I say, and she whoops so sincerely that I laugh.

But when she adds, "That's my girl," the laughter dies in my throat.

Because I'm not, and she made sure of it. I shift in my seat and go back to staring out the window.

"Something I said?" She sneaks another side-glance at me, and the air in the truck suddenly feels heavy and charged, like a storm cloud about to burst.

"You mean besides ignoring the route I spent three hours planning?"

"Come on." She rolls her eyes. "Relax."

I hum in disagreement and tap my nails against the door handle. They're longer than I normally wear them, and the colors alternate in sparkly blue, purple, and pink. I bet she doesn't even notice it or the ten million other things that separate current me from the me of last year.

"What now? Getting ready to jump out?"

"Huh?" I turn my head toward her, but she's staring at the road, her gaze unwavering.

"I asked if you're getting ready to jump out. You keep tapping the handle. If you want me to pull over or slow down enough for a decent chance at a tuck and roll, just say the word."

I narrow my eyes. In any other circumstance, I'd be sure she's joking, but a little part of me—the same little part of me that really *does* want to abandon ship—can't help but think she's serious. Chloe was always the queen of delivering sarcasm so dryly, so sincerely, that you couldn't always tell if she was messing with you or not. I'm not used to being on the receiving end of it, though.

"I wouldn't need you to slow down for a tuck and roll," I say, and her perfectly groomed eyebrows appear over the top edge of her Ray-Ban sunglasses.

"Okay, then," she says, and I hate this heavy awkwardness between us.

She clears her throat and reaches for her coffee. But just as she slides it out of the cupholder, the lid gives way, and the cup splashes back down. Drops of coffee fly everywhere—the dashboard, the shifter, my tank top, and my sweats.

Chloe tears open the center console and grabs some napkins that my mom always keeps stashed there. She swerves a little, frantically patting at my shirt while she tries to drive.

"I'm sorry. I'm so sorry." Her hand skims over my chest, and I practically yelp, shoving it away. She reaches over once more, dabbing at my collarbone before I can snatch the napkin out of her hand.

"Watch the road! I got it."

"Sorry, sorry, sorry," she keeps saying, and I honest to god think she's apologizing for the coffee and not for feeling me up. She probably doesn't even consider that. Doesn't even care. Doesn't even remember that the last time her hands were there, they lingered.

You're probably wondering, *Is Fallon so stuck on this because it's her only frame of reference?*

The answer: *Probably! Yes!*

I don't mean to be some cliché clingy girl who can't get over the person she gave her virginity to. But yeah, Chloe is the first person I ever did anything like that with. The first person I ever even wanted to do that with at all.

People always make such a big deal out of "being someone's first." Like Kai is always saying he would never be someone's first time. Like it's this big taboo thing. Prisha even laughs it off, like, "I know, right?" But he *was* her first. And she was *his*. So, like, you do the math on that one. Is it all just for show?

Regardless, I was definitely not Chloe's first. If someone's hands are on her chest—even for something as innocent as a coffee spill—she has a reasonably sized pool of memories to draw from.

Tia Gordon had that honor in the spring of their junior year. Chloe crawled through my window that night and told me it was "awesome" and that she "couldn't wait to do it again." This was long before I started thinking maybe we could be more, but even back then, the thought of her with someone else annoyed me. I thought it was just because she'd experienced something completely new without me, but now I think it was maybe something else. Jealousy or something uglier.

We pretty much never talked about it again.

Tia cried, like *cried* cried, full-on sobbing in the girls' bathroom when Chloe stopped calling her back. She even face-timed *me* once, wanting to know why Chloe had dropped her so suddenly. "How would I know?" I asked. And she said, "Because you're her favorite." At the time, I preened at that, but now, thinking back, it makes me feel like I was always just another one of her devoted fans like the rest of the queer girls in high school.

I should have paid more attention. I can calculate the odds of just about anything; I can imagine a thousand different scenarios at the drop of a hat. But why couldn't I see that Chloe would eventually drop me the way she dropped Tia, when the evidence was right in front of my face?

When I made my decision to sleep with her, I didn't

properly account for all of her unpredictability and indecisiveness. Like how when she couldn't decide who to take to the tenth-grade dance, she just brought two dates, and they weren't even mad when they found out. Or how when her dad sent her away to an agricultural summer camp one year to teach her responsibility, she made out with the director's daughter behind the hay bales for two weeks straight instead of working, and they were "just glad their kid had finally made a friend."

Chloe likes to enjoy life and do what's fun and what feels good, and sometimes that's not enough. I had downplayed how much she "follows her bliss," as my mom politely describes her inability to stick with anything for longer than a month. And I overestimated how much my friendship meant to her. I thought they would balance each other out. Keep us on an even keel.

I was wrong.

"Sorry about your shirt," Chloe says, crumpling a napkin in her hand like it's taking physical effort for her not to resume blotting my clothes. "I liked that one."

"It's fine," I say, even though it really isn't.

She taps her hands against the steering wheel and huffs out a breath. "Welp, we're off to a fantastic start, aren't we?"

"It's fine," I lie again, gritting my teeth and forcing a smile.

"I know you won't believe me, but I kind of wanted this to go perfectly." She drags her hand through her hair. "You know this trip is either gonna untangle whatever knot we've tied ourselves into or make us hate each other forever, right?"

"It doesn't have to be perfect," I point out. "And we don't have to 'untangle any knots.' We just have to survive each other's company long enough to pull off the charity event."

"And then what?"

"And then nothing. We meet our parents in Dallas, and that's that."

"Sure," she says. "That's that."

"Why are you being so weird about it?"

"I'm not being weird!"

"You are!"

"Come on, didn't you see this playing out differently in your head?"

"Not really."

"Okay." She smirks.

"No, seriously. Sorry to disappoint you, but I definitely did not waste time daydreaming about something I already can't wait to forget."

That's a lie. In my head, I drove the whole time, even though driving the truck terrifies me. Chloe was impressed with my newfound confidence. She—

Chloe huffs like I just knocked the air out of her, and then doesn't say anything else. Did I actually hurt her feelings? Everything has rolled off her back since the day I met her; I didn't even think it was *possible* to get under her skin.

We make it another mile before my curiosity gnaws its way out from under my better judgment.

"Okay," I say, dragging out the word a little bit. "Enlighten me, then. How did you see this going?"

"You're just going to make fun of me." She scowls, clicking on the blinker before switching lanes.

"I won't make fun of you." We're on the highway now, finally. My mom's E-ZPass is already secured on the window, ready for tolls. We have hours and hours of driving ahead of us, and maybe Chloe has a point. Being bitchy from the jump isn't going to make things go faster. "Seriously, just tell me."

"I thought it could be fun if we both wanted it to be. Like, you would come in a good mood, and I would have the coffee waiting. I would drive the whole time so you wouldn't get all stressed out like you normally do whenever you have to drive the truck. It would be like old times. We would have killed to go on this trip together last year. I even found all these weird, like, tourist attractions for us to stop at, like we used to say we would do if you drove me out to college."

"But I didn't drive you out to college. You just left, remember? I didn't even take you to the airport."

She mumbles something that sounds a bit like "You left first," but when I press her on it, she just says, "You said you didn't mind when I texted you that day!"

"No, I said 'K.'"

"Is that not the same thing?" she mumbles, scratching the back of her neck before continuing on like I never said anything at all. "Remember how you used to say that you always wanted to see, like, 'the world's biggest chair' or whatever? It's coming up on your left in an hour. Okay, maybe it's technically not the world's biggest chair, but, like, it's one of them."

"One of the world's biggest chairs?" I ask, not exactly believing her.

"Kinda," she says, scrunching up her face, and oh, I've missed that. "It's a really big chair, okay? A really big wooden chair on the side of the highway. Look." She hits a button on the GPS, and it pops up.

"That's a really big chair," I say, trying really hard not to laugh, because this is ridiculous. This is all so ridiculous. I'm in a car with Chloe Shapiro. There's no one else around. It's the perfect chance to yell or talk or sort our shit, so of course, we're just talking about giant chairs.

"And we can take pictures on it!" she says, getting more excited. "There's a ladder to climb up and everything."

And it would be so easy to give in to this moment. To give in to all of it. To go and sit on a big chair just off the highway and take pictures together. To not hate her anymore.

To let go.

I can almost picture it too: the two of us sitting side by side, me leaning slightly into her, the heat of her cheek pressed against mine as she snaps a million selfies of us laughing and smiling and throwing peace signs. There's not enough phone storage in the universe for the number of photos we've taken over the years. Chloe, always on my right, her head angled to capture her features. Me, four inches shorter and always to her left, happy because she's happy.

And I wonder, *How much of our friendship was Chloe simply living her own life, with me on her left, following her lead, cheering her on?*

Well, I'm done with that.

I take a deep breath and lean my head on the window, letting my eyelids linger shut longer and longer with every blink.

"Are we ever going to *really* talk about this?" she asks.

"What is there to talk about?" I don't open my eyes. I can't look at her anymore, at least not for a while.

"I don't know, like why you hate me so much, and how long you're planning to keep it up."

I crinkle my forehead, because we both know what this is about. She has to. And I know, I know. You're probably thinking, *Why don't they just talk it out like the two adults they are about to be?*

How about this for a reason: I don't fucking want to.

I don't want to have to tell her what she did wrong or why it was wrong. I don't want to have to explain that you don't just have sex with someone and blow them off the next day via text. I'm done being her moral compass. *Done.*

"Fallon." She sighs. "I don't want the whole trip to be like this. College is wild, and—"

"Can you just drive?" I ask. "You're making this so awkward. I get that you want this to just be some fun road trip where we reconnect or whatever, but I don't want that. Okay? Can you respect that? For once, can you just respect what someone else wants?"

She stares at the road, her eyes hard like she's trying to

blow up the tractor trailer ahead of us with her mind or something. "You're seriously gonna be like that?"

"Don't worry about it," I say with a mean little smile. "It's not that deep, right?"

And when we drive by that giant chair, old and worn from the weather, perfectly welcoming on the side of the road in this dipshit town she found, on the secret route she mapped out and won't let me see, I swear I feel her speed up.

# ELEVEN

*Y*ou're really serious about this?" Chloe asks as I struggle to pull both tents out of the back of the truck.

"What?" I ask, batting my eyelashes in mock innocence.

She pinches the bridge of her nose. "Why are there two?"

"Two people, two tents. Here. You can use my mom's." I shove it into her arms, head to the opposite side of the site with my much-smaller bag, and get to work.

We're at a campground in Ohio. Well, an RV park, technically. Okay, fine, so it's more of an open field on the side of the road. I don't know why Chloe was so insistent that this was the one we stay at, but after about eight hours in the car with her, I'm ready for my own space. Plus, the sign was flashing VACANT, unlike those of the last three campgrounds we passed. It seems the great outdoors is popular around these parts.

I am not, however, entirely convinced that we aren't going

to get run over in the middle of the night by one of the mammoth RVs that keep showing up and parking near us every few minutes. Though, honestly, I might prefer it to another long day stuck in the truck beside Chloe. I welcome whatever fate has in store for me. Provided it doesn't actually involve the girl standing on the other side of the campsite.

It's only about five p.m., but we're both pretty wiped out. Unfortunately, that means we have way too much time to fill before sleep. My stomach grumbles hungrily. I haven't eaten a real meal since dinner last night.

Chloe offered to stop several times, but I didn't want to prolong the trip any more than I needed to, and god only knows how long the drive will take now that she's holding my "quickest route" plans hostage. I survived the day on the nuts and protein bars I had stashed in my bag for the trip, while Chloe seemed mostly content with her animal crackers and Diet Coke.

Can you believe she truly thinks animal crackers are a staple of any road trip, the ultimate car-ride nourishment? Apparently, this is something her mother mistakenly instilled in her from the moment Chloe had teeth. Animal crackers are for dipping in frosting, Dunkaroos style, not for munching on during long trips.

But still, there was a time—and by "a time" I mean last summer and every single summer before it—when *I* was the one hastily adding bags of animal crackers to our vacation shopping cart, just in case Chloe or her mom forgot.

There was also a time, again pretty much right up until

the end of last summer, when I would dig my hand into that shiny red bag right alongside hers, our fingers battling it out. We'd pull out an assorted shape, try to figure out if it was a rhino or a misshapen lion, and laugh our asses off when one of us inevitably suggested it could be both. A "rhion." A "lino."

I'd be lying, though, if I said I didn't get the tiniest thrill of satisfaction when Chloe narrowed her eyes and said, "Well, that's new," when she saw my almond-cashew mix.

*There are a lot of things that are new about me, Chloe,* I had wanted to say, *but you don't get to know any of them.*

Chloe sighs and shuffles behind me. I hear the unmistakable sound of her unzipping the tent bag and pulling out the poles.

Satisfied she's not going to fight me on this anymore, I pull out my own tent and shake it open about twenty feet away. I'd like to say it pops open on its own because it's a very sophisticated, classy, state-of-the art hiking tent or something. In reality, it just pops open all quick like because it consists of very, very lightweight tension rods and only a dash of nylon.

So, okay, maybe my tent is more of a "play tent" for kids than a "rugged, outdoorsy tent" made for camping in the wilderness, but still.

And I definitely hear Chloe stifle a laugh, no doubt having caught on that this "spare tent" I had lying around happens to be in the shape of a shark. Its gaping mouth forms the opening, and white strips of fabric meant to denote sharp teeth complete the look. I had originally bought it as a gag gift for

Jami during Shark Week last summer, but then her mom said they didn't have room for it in their apartment, so I brought it home and shoved it under my bed, where it was largely forgotten until last night. Lucky thing I remembered. Better to sleep in the belly of a shark than share a tent with the devil.

The laugh finally escapes her, and Chloe adds, "Nice tent."

I shake my head and shoot her a glare as I walk back to the truck to get my sleeping bag. Her tent is halfway up already and probably five times the size of mine, at the very least. It's sturdy and well made. Even the stitching itself is nice—a far cry from the fraying fishing line I think they used to make mine.

I carry my stuff back, crawling into the shark's mouth and spreading out my sleeping bag and pillow, frowning when I realize that I absolutely can't lay it all out flat. I try turning it in the other direction, but that proves even worse. I huff and move it back to the way it was before, the end of the sleeping bag dangling out of the shark's mouth like the remains of a fresh kill.

It'll be fine, I guess, as long as I keep my legs sort of curled up. I mean, honestly, the designers should have factored this scenario in. I'm sure there are some, like, five-foot-three toddlers running around avoiding exes too, and they deserve a tent they can sleep in.

I fluff up my pillow and carefully set the little green golf ball beside it. It spent most of the drive shoved in the side of my door, my fingers tracing its curves every so often—the memory of mini golf with Prisha and Jami somehow helping to keep me grounded. And I need its help now more than ever, when all the emotions surrounding this night with Chloe—

"There's plenty of room in this one, you know," Chloe calls, pulling me from my thoughts. I lean my head out and shake it again. She's got the tent up and is now assembling a little awning-type thing. It looks like a miniature covered porch. Even if it rains, she'll be able to keep the front flap down and not have to worry about getting wet.

Admittedly, it is a great tent, and there is plenty of room.

Too bad I have no interest.

I mean it. I'm never getting into a tent with Chloe again.

"I like this one better," I say as Chloe comes over and squats down beside the shark's mouth.

"Fallon, I don't think even my dog could fit in this one."

"Are you seriously comparing me to a dog right now?"

She rubs her forehead. "No, I'm *seriously* not. Will you calm down! This is ridiculous. This tent isn't safe! You can't even zipper it shut!"

"Safe from what? It's a tent. When's the last time a zipper ever stopped anyone from doing anything? Like, even if they don't want to waste time unzipping it, I'm sure your hypothetical bad guys who decide tonight's the night to loot an RV park probably have knives or guns or something, right? Tents are fabric after all."

"Fine," Chloe says, but her jaw twitches just enough to let me know it's not fine at all in her eyes. I can't deny that having her on edge for once is making me a little happy. Even if I do have to risk things that go bump in the night gobbling up my toes while I sleep. "What's with the golf ball?"

"Good memories," I say.

"You wanna share with the class?"

"Not particularly."

We return to working in silence after that, both of us trying and failing to pretend that the other one isn't there. She tries to talk to me a few times, but I make an excuse to head back into the truck and shut the door behind me.

I'm not hiding per se; I'm just making sure that the backup generators have kicked in and everything is staying nice and cool now that the truck is off. I'm not being a jerk; I'm being responsible.

So why do I have this sinking feeling in my chest that somehow now *I'm* the bad guy?

I can't help it. I want to be, I don't know, not friendly, but at least polite. It's just that sometimes when Chloe was picking up wood for the campfire or rearranging stuff around the site, the sun would hit her just right, and her smile would be a little too pink and perfect and inviting, her lip gloss glinting in the fading light. So no, it's not that I don't want to hang out with her—it's that I think I want to hang out with her a little too much.

My stomach rumbles, and I dig through my bag, uselessly searching for food. I ate all the nuts and both protein bars earlier. I glance around the truck, one step away from just saying *Screw it* and shoving my face into a vat of my mom's ice cream, when I notice Chloe's bag of animal crackers is right there, calling to me. I bite my lip. I swore to myself I wouldn't. But it's not like she's in here with me to see it—she wouldn't even know. Would it even really count?

Please ignore how kind of, sort of desperate it is to lock myself inside the back of an ice cream truck and secretly eat my ex-girlfriend's animal crackers. Especially when she's very clearly sitting out there, willing to share. This is not my proudest moment, all right?

I pull the bag open, the animals' shortbready goodness wafting toward me, before closing it with a groan. I don't need her delicious animal crackers or her perfect pouty lips or her comfortable tent, which is technically my tent, but still.

I pop open one of the containers beside me and grab one of the giant waffle cones inside. I know they're a big seller, and of all the things I could eat, it should absolutely not be one of Carmen's homemade cones. But desperate times call for desperate measures. This is simply the equivalent of eating a horse during times of war or whatever. Like, it's awful but also—

A knock on the back door pulls me from these just *slightly* dramatic thoughts. I shove the rest of the cone into my mouth and flick the lock, blinking in the sunlight when Chloe pulls open the door.

She frowns. "Everything okay?"

"Why wouldn't it be?" I ask, my mouth still full as I wipe some crumbs off my face.

"Okay, then." She laughs. "I guess it is. I was just making sure this was, like, a pouting thing on your end and not, like, an 'oh shit, the generators broke' thing. I'll leave you to it, then."

She pulls her hand back from the door, letting it fall shut, but oh, no. Nope. She is not getting the last word. Not again; not ever. I shove the door back open, but she's already made it to her tent, sprawling out inside, rubbing in my face how much room she's got.

She is, objectively, the worst.

I storm into her tent. "Where do you get off being so smug!"

She props herself up on her elbows with a grin, like she's *enjoying* this. "I'm the one who's smug? Me?"

"Yeah!"

"You're the one living in a shark tent to put me in my place and sneaking waffle cones instead of just admitting you're hungry! As the sole person here acting rationally, I think I could deserve to be a little *more* smug, don't you?"

I make this combination groan-growl scream and move to leave, but Chloe grabs my ankle, her fingers searing my skin and sending butterflies careening up my leg and straight into my stomach. It's been a long time since she's touched me, and I hate how much my skin misses hers.

"Wait," she says.

I turn to look at her, furious, but she looks so calm, so open, I hesitate. She starts to say something but then stops and lets go of my ankle. I step back and sit down, cross-legged, outside the opening of the tent.

"Why?" I try to sound hard, but it comes out plaintive, almost needy. I want to know what she was going to say; I need to know what comes after "wait." Is this where she finally tells me she's sorry for what happened? Is this when we—

No. Whatever she was going to say is gone. Her face morphs back into its carefully constructed, carefree smile as she sits up.

"Hey, did you notice where we are?" she asks.

"You mean besides some weird RV park in the middle of Ohio that you seem to be obsessed with sleeping at?"

"Yeah, besides that."

I look around the tent slowly, not sure what I'm missing.

"We're just outside Cleveland," she says. "That's why I mapped out the route this way. I mean"—she looks down, a little sheepish—"assuming you're still into that."

"Into what?" I am utterly confused. "Cleveland?"

"Creepy stone statues."

"Wait. *Cleveland* Cleveland?" I nearly shout as it all clicks into place. "Are we seriously near Haserot's Angel right now? I wasn't even thinking! Oh my god!"

She laughs at my reaction. "I'll take that as a 'Yes, I am still into that, Chloe. Thank you.'"

"Oh my god. Oh my god. I have to go," I say, standing up. "I have to go. Like, right now. They close at dusk, and I don't even know where to go!"

Chloe climbs out after me, brushing some nonexistent dust off her yoga pants. "I can show you."

And my stomach hits the ground. I've wanted to see Haserot's Angel forever. Well, for the last three years at least—ever since I saw the statue in *The Places We Lie*, Adya Mulroney's directorial debut, and found out it was a real place, not a set. Chloe and I probably watched that movie a hundred times together, utterly fascinated by the way Mulroney creates such a sense of dread leading up to that scene. It was almost a relief to finally see the terrifyingly beautiful statue in all its glory. Well, until the jump scare anyway.

Back in the before, we used to daydream about going together. But now the idea of seeing it with her feels wrong somehow. Too intimate.

Too much.

Chloe seems to read it on my face before I can even say anything. She rolls her eyes and goes back into her tent, zipping it shut behind her. I crouch down and attempt a knock, which sort of shakes the tent. I don't feel right just barging in. I mean, she zipped it. And I'm not a bad guy, no matter what she thinks.

"What, Fal?"

"Don't you have schoolwork to do after driving all day? My mom said you're taking your summer courses really seriously. Tutoring people, even."

"Something like that," she says. I see her shadow move away from the door and drop back onto her pillow, effectively ending the conversation.

And so I climb back into the truck, pull an address up in my phone, and drive.

# TWELVE

If there are weirder things in life than driving an ice cream truck through a cemetery, I am certainly not aware of them.

I creep up and down the rows, the bright white truck with its happy mural on the side in stark contrast to all the little gravestones and statues, until I find a suitable place to stop, a little pull-off beside a giant willow tree.

I had always imagined that when this moment came, it would be one of the best moments of my life. We would visit just before dusk, of course, on one of those weird days where you can see the moon even before the sun has set.

I would approach the angel slowly, much like the actress does in the movie, only the nearby bench wouldn't be empty like it is in the film. Chloe would be there watching me with that little smirk she always had when I was doing something nerdy. She liked to tease, but I could tell she secretly thought my movie obsession was cute.

Maybe she would even sneak around while I took everything in and pop out from behind a bush when I least expected it. I would shout and slap her arm before we both dissolved into laughter. Nothing would be awkward or weird. I wouldn't have a stomachache while wondering if ditching her tonight was the right move. And also, there would be one hundred percent fewer ice cream trucks involved.

I sigh and turn off the ignition, saying a silent prayer to whatever gods are listening that no one notices the truck and that none of the statues come to life—always a fear of mine; don't laugh. Then I pull my phone out of my pocket. I don't have Chloe, but I can have the next best thing. Jami picks up on the first ring, her face filling my screen as I get out of the truck.

"Hello from the magic forest," she says with a laugh. She pretends like she hates having to greet new campers like that, but I know she secretly loves it. It makes her feel like a fairy princess, I think, or someone in a Disney movie. "I just got off the phone with Prisha, so your timing is perfect."

"Oh yeah? How's she?" I ask as I wander around, trying to get my bearings. I have a general idea of where Haserot's Angel is, but they don't give super-specific directions, probably to dissuade vandals or because it feels too creepy to say, like, *Take a right at Marnie's grave and then a hard left at the broken headstone somebody tipped over as a prank.*

"She's good," Jami says. "Grossly in love, just like we left her. Kai was picking her up for a date and—oh! I don't see the truck, so does that mean you're at your first stop?"

"Yeah."

"Congrats! You survived your first day."

I laugh; I can't help it. I wish I could stuff her enthusiasm and positive attitude into my pocket like the little green golf ball.

"Wait"—she leans forward, squinting at the screen—"where are you? Is that a gravestone? God, you're such a tragic little goth sometimes."

"Ha!" I say. "This actually wasn't my idea."

"Okaaay," Jami says. "Please tell me how you ended up in a cemetery not by choice."

She shoves her iPad back and flops onto her belly on the bed. Senior counselors get private rooms, something she was really excited about. Her campers, however, pay two thousand dollars a week to sleep on tiny wooden bunks stacked three high. Jami claims "suffering is good for art" and all that other eyeroll-inducing stuff. But who am I to talk? I'm sleeping in a shark tent tonight.

"So, well," I say, hedging, not really wanting to admit the fact that Chloe actually did something really cool.

"Spit it out, Fallon."

"Okay, we did make it to the first stop. We're, like, camping tonight or whatever. Separate tents, don't worry," I add when she makes a face, but then her lips seem to almost pinch in disappointment, and I wonder if I misread her. "Anyway, so Chloe found this RV campground to stay at, and she was super insistent that we stay in this particular area. At first, I was like 'Wow, this sucks; there aren't even any trees.' But then she pointed out where we are."

I trail off, and Jami rolls her hand around like she's asking, *And the point is . . . ?*

"So, yeah, she sort of picked a spot that's right near that cemetery in Cleveland so I could see Haserot's Angel." I sort of whisper the last words, but it doesn't matter because she squeals before I even finish.

"*Haserot's* Angel? The one you've been talking about for years that you wanted to, like, take a pilgrimage to, except it was a 'you and Chloe' thing, which was the entire reason we had to switch our trip to Canada instead so you could look at some creepy horror-movie churches instead of creepy horror-movie cemeteries? *That* Haserot's Angel?"

"Yeah," I say, scrunching up my face. The sun is going down fast, and I know from the comments on a Reddit thread about the cemetery that the caretakers come and chain the gates at night. I pick up my pace, searching the field around me. "But you wanted to see those cathedrals anyway!"

She waves off this statement. "Given the fact that you're facetiming with me instead of talking to her, I'm guessing that you did not include her on the Trip of Your Lifetime."

"No, and that's the thing." I shake my head. "This is incredibly, seriously nice. But she's acting like we can just pick up where we left off. You know, before things happened. I think she thinks we're going to be best friends again by the end of this. It's like she can't even fathom WHY I wouldn't want that."

"Are you sure you *don't* want that?" Jami asks softly as I spot what could be the angel across the graveyard.

"Of course I am," I say, but it sounds like a lie even to me.

"You agreed to go on this trip with her, even though—"

"To save money for *our* trip," I say. "Remember? The one you used your book money for? Do you seriously want to start your freshman year broke and bookless?"

"No, but I hardly think that would have happened anyway, given all the extra hours you've been working."

"What was I was supposed to do? Bail on my mom when she needed me?"

"Of course not." Jami sighs. "But are we just going to ignore that you've been a massive sad sack all year without Chloe? Like, I know I've become your default best friend but—"

"That is not true! You've always been my best friend."

"Yeah, but not like your Chloe-level best friend."

I don't bother pointing out that no one could be my Chloe-level best friend, apparently not even Chloe herself.

"Fal, it was one night."

"I have to go," I say, feeling nauseated at the way everyone reduces what happened down to a handful of hours.

"Fallon."

"I have to let you go; I don't have good service here," I lie.

"Don't. Come on, wait."

"No, I get it," I say, rubbing my eyes. "Like, I get what you're saying, and I get why people think I'm being a drama queen or whatever, but it was a big deal for me. A really big deal."

"I know," Jami says. "I understand. It's just, you two were good together before you . . ."

I swallow hard and look up, hoping she won't finish that sentence.

"Holy shit." I almost drop my phone because there, right in front of me, is Haserot's Angel.

"Oh my god. Did you find it? I wish I could be there with you. I hate that you're finally there and you have to do it alone."

I smile. "I mean, I don't *have* to do it alone."

I hit the button on my phone so that the camera faces out, and slowly walk up to the statue. She's gorgeous, seated on a marble throne, her wings outstretched, an extinguished, inverted torch in her hands, black tears pouring down her face—okay, technically discoloration from being made of bronze, but who cares? She is stunning. She is—

"Yep." Jami laughs. "That's a creepy angel, all right."

♥

I STAY AT the cemetery for as long as I dare, filming video after video of the angel on my phone as the sun sets. None of them are as brilliant as the shots Adya directed, but still, they're mine. Proof that I was here, that this really happened.

When it starts to get dark, I climb back into the ice cream truck. I only swear twice driving back to the RV park: once when someone cuts me off and once when I accidentally cut off someone else.

I already flooded my socials with pictures and clips of the

Weeping Angel, or *The Angel of Death Victorious*, if we want to be more accurate. But even as the likes and comments stack up, I can't help but notice the ache that's growing inside me, like on the day after Christmas or my birthday or whatever. All that anticipation, and now it's over.

While I'm stopped at a red light, I notice that Chloe liked one of my posts, commenting a thumbs-up for good measure, and it makes my stomach hurt.

I take a deep breath as I finally pull into our site. My headlights dance over Chloe sitting underneath her makeshift tent porch. She's reading a book using her phone flashlight, and there are several take-out boxes set on a stump beside her. I walk over to her warily, as if *she's* the animal that's about to bolt and not the other way around. The whole thing feels horribly uncomfortable, like I'm intruding on a stranger—and aren't I?

"How was it?" she asks, raising her hand against the glare of the truck's headlights. They'll turn off in a second, and then we'll be left in the dark.

"It was amazing," I say, being honest for once. And I wonder, *Is it possible to miss someone when they're right in front of you?*

"Was it everything you hoped for and more?" She's teasing, but I can tell she's fishing for compliments. That she wants me to tell her that she did a good job. That I appreciate her. That I will take the olive branch and extend it back to her.

"For sure," I say, deciding that keeping things light, or trying to, is the best course of action.

Light is what we do best. Light is what we've always done

best. Maybe it's my own fault that I came to expect anything different from her.

"How's your studying going?" I ask.

"Well, you drove away with my hotspot, so I've just been doing the reading," she says, holding up her book. "So, boring."

"Sorry," I say. I hadn't considered that. And if I didn't feel like a complete asshole for leaving her behind before, I definitely do now.

"It's fine," she says, even though we both know it isn't.

"What are you majoring in, anyway?" I ask, trying to break the tension. But I also really want to know. I can't figure out what major would make use of both the paperback of *Dubliners* in her hand and the bio textbook beside her. Maybe she's just filling in her gen ed stuff? But still, it bothers me not knowing something so big about her. She still hasn't answered me, so I nudge. "Chloe?"

She shrugs. "I'm undecided."

Yeah, yeah, that definitely tracks.

"Oh," I say, and Chloe frowns.

The headlights finally click off, and we're left in darkness, the only light coming from her phone flashlight, a couple nearby RVs, and a tiny sliver of moon. Frogs and crickets chirp, and I suppose the comfortably warm night bodes well for my need to sleep with my feet hanging out of a tent.

Chloe scoots over, making room for me on the strip of fabric that serves as the floor. She even offers me her pillow to sit on, but for some reason my butt on her pillow seems like too much, too fast. Like once we had a friendship that allowed for sitting on each other's stuff, but now we're more like—I don't even know, but not that.

I drop onto the grass nearby, and I swear I hear her whisper, "Stubborn," but when I look, she's gone back to reading.

"What was that?"

She smirks and points the flashlight at the take-out boxes. "You hungry? Or did you eat all the waffle cones on your way back?"

I'm starving, and while I was willing to pretend I wasn't for the sake of efficiency earlier, my stomach is roaring loud enough that we both can hear it.

"I could eat," I say after a particularly loud gurgle, and Chloe smiles.

"I got spaghetti, of course," she says, as if it's a normal thing to get take-out spaghetti instead of pizza or a burger. But it's sort of my thing. Like, I don't know, one day when I was eight, my mom dared me to eat spaghetti in every state. I think it was just one of those desperate things a single mom says to make her kid eat on a road trip, but it stuck in my head, and now it's like this compulsive thing I have to do whenever I travel.

You're probably thinking, *What's the difference? Spaghetti is spaghetti whether you're boiling noodles in New York or Alaska.* But I don't know, man. I swear I can taste a difference with every state border we cross.

"I know you've already had the Ohio spaghetti," she says, dragging me back to my junior year when my dad had insisted on going to the Pro Football Hall of Fame as a family vacation. Another perk of divorced parents: Sometimes, when the money was okay, I'd get to go on *two* family vacations. As I had no interest in the NFL, I begged my dad to let me bring Chloe along. He hemmed and hawed and finally gave in.

The second night there, Chloe had asked me to sneak off with her.

I was scared and unsure, which was how most of my time went with Chloe. She broke the rules, and I followed them, but it didn't matter. We snuck out past my dad's bed after he fell asleep, and then we wandered around until we found the perfect all-night diner. It took three tries before we finally found one that actually served spaghetti.

Sure, when it came, it was cold in spots, like it had been microwaved from the day before, or maybe even the day before that, but eating cold spaghetti at a diner in Ohio with Chloe Shapiro sitting across from me wishing on straw wrappers? It made me feel infinite in a way you only can when you're young and nothing truly miserable has ever happened to you.

I blink hard, pulling myself out of the memory. "Uh, yeah, I have, actually."

"Which is why I also got you this," Chloe says, pulling out the box under it and passing it to me. "I figured you might be nervous after the quality of the Ohio spaghetti we previously found."

It's still hot somehow, the grease soaking through the bottom of the small cardboard square and warming my fingers. I pull open the lid and come face-to-face with the most perfect broccoli white pizza. It looks like it has extra cheese too, and I have to fight to keep from drooling.

I look up at her and smile, and she smiles back, and it's perfect.

Until I look away.

I know, I know. Why am I fighting this? Right? Why am I looking away instead of looking at her? Don't you hate when two people could resolve an argument if they'd just talk for once instead of being stubborn, pouty witches who traverse cemeteries alone and melt a little inside over the sight of a tiny pizza covered in broccoli?

But don't get mad at me. At least not yet.

I need you to understand one basic fact: I can never give Chloe Shapiro the chance to break my heart again. I can't. Because she will if I do, and I think we all know it.

I clear my throat, getting up and heading toward my tent. Her face falls, almost imperceptibly, but I catch it and feel guiltier than I probably should.

"Thanks for this," I say, holding up the box.

"You don't want to hang out?"

"Don't you need to finish your homework?"

"Yeah, but . . ."

I pause outside my tent, my shark, and look at her. "How

did you even find a place that would deliver here?"

"Uh, I didn't," she says sheepishly.

"Don't tell me you hitchhiked?" I shout, because Chloe has absolutely zero sense of self-preservation, and it's absolutely maddening.

"I didn't, I didn't," she says, clearly enjoying my moment of worry. And if that was her intention, to see if I cared even a little tiny bit, I'll need to make sure it doesn't happen again. "I didn't hitchhike, *Mom*, I swear. I walked out to the road and called an Uber. It was fine."

"Oh," I say, because that actually makes a lot of sense. "Well, let me know if you want any cash."

"I'm good," she says.

I crawl into the back of my tent as far as I can and devour the pizza like an absolute gremlin. I shouldn't care that she went into town by herself. I shouldn't care that we're in a strange campsite, in a strange town we've never been to, and if something had gone wrong, no one would ever even know where she went. It shouldn't make my chest feel tight just thinking about it.

But it does.

Halfway through eating my pizza, I hear a whispered "shit" right as her little phone flashlight goes dark.

I lean forward, just enough to see out of my tiny excuse for a window—the black mesh of the shark's eye—but Chloe's already gone inside. The old me would've run out, offering my own charged phone like I have a thousand times before. She could never keep hers charged to save her life. But I grab the golf ball instead and roll it around in my palm, letting its heaviness center me before I close the pizza box and drop my head to my pillow.

Chloe Shapiro's life is no longer my problem, and I need to stop letting it be.

# THIRTEEN

*I* wake up before Chloe, my socks damp from the morning dew. It was too hot to sleep inside my sleeping bag last night, so I slept on top, and apparently, the mosquitoes had a field day feasting on my ankles overnight.

I scratch at the little red bumps, cursing my lack of hydrocortisone and staring at Chloe's safely zipped-up tent. Do I regret the choices that led me to sitting here with wet socks and itchy ankles? Yes, yes, I do. Is it still better than sharing a tent with Chloe? Maybe, but—

"Morning!" she calls out through the window of her tent. Her hair is adorably mussed, and she yawns a yawn so wide it takes up her whole face. It reminds me of a kitten her mom fostered a few years back, snugglier and fluffier than it had any right to be.

I loved that damn kitten.

"Morning." I'm surprised she's up so early, but I don't let it show.

Chloe unzips the door and crawls out, taking a deep breath in the morning air. She raises her arms up in what looks to be a delicious stretch. I look away when her shirt rides up, just a little, over her hips. Instead, I watch a bug attempt to crawl up a stick, staring at it with a shocking intensity.

"Uh, Earth to Fallon." Chloe laughs, pulling the cover off the top of her tent and rolling it up. "You with me?"

"Yeah, sorry."

"We gotta hit the road. I have a lot planned for today."

"What do you mean?" I ask, following suit and disassembling my own sleeping quarters. "I looked up the map last night before bed, and if we hop on the highway, it'll have us back on my route in no time. We're a little behind schedule, but not too bad, and we can always—"

"Of course you did," she says, shaking her head in a way that makes me bristle.

"Is there something wrong with being prepared?" I ask, rolling up my sleeping bag, but she doesn't answer. "Besides, I'm driving today. This is important. Our parents are counting on us."

She doesn't reply. Good. Let her be quiet for once.

I finish packing up and then stand there awkwardly, waiting for Chloe to catch up, the shark tent slung over my shoulder, my sleeping bag bundled in my arms. When it becomes clear that the fight to disassemble her tent is one that Chloe absolutely is not winning, I set my stuff down and head over to help.

"Here, let me," I say, brushing her hand away from the knot she's been stubbornly trying to untie for the last five minutes.

She rubs her hand where I touched her like I burned her. Fine. Be that way. I dig my nail in between the nylon ties and work them apart. And I repeat for the next knot and the next and the next until the tent lies in shambles in front of us, just pieces of what it was only minutes before.

Because I guess the universe decided to punch me in the face with a metaphor this morning.

We make quick work of stuffing the tent into its case, putting it away, and guarding the truck while we take turns getting ready inside.

"Are you going to be weird all day?" Chloe asks when we're ready to take off, her voice neutral even though her words are not.

I frown as she hops into the passenger seat and digs out her animal crackers, flashing me a look that says she probably noticed they're not in the same place she left them yesterday.

I take my place behind the wheel and gulp down a big steadying breath. I hate this, yes, but it's better this way. With me in control of the route, I can get us back on track. The angel was nice, but no more detours. I set my little green golf ball in the cupholder—*please, Prisha and Jami, send me good vibes*—and fight the urge to scream.

"I'm not being weird," I say, starting up the engine.

She sighs the long-suffering sigh of a parent at the end of her rope. "Whatever you say."

"I'm not."

"Fine."

"Fine!"

"Look, Fal, like I said before, this trip is either gonna fix things between us or ruin them forever. And I'm not going to beg you, you know." She pops an animal cracker in her mouth, smiling as she devours a tiny lion.

*My mom needs us to do this. Do not jump out of this car, Fallon. Do. Not.*

"Beg me for what?" I huff, finally shifting the truck into drive and slowly maneuvering it through all the RVs.

"You're so determined to hate me. It'd be funny if it wasn't so sad."

"I don't hate you," I snap, but I instantly regret it. It might be true, but she doesn't need to know it.

"Prove it, then."

"I don't have to prove anything to you, Chloe. Let's just go." I kick up my speed a little, anxious to put a few miles between us and her last good deed. It feels suffocating being in this truck with her.

"We're stuck on this trip together, right? We might as well make the best of it."

I want to shout that there's absolutely no way to make the best of it so please stop talking, but instead I grit my teeth, keeping my eyes focused on the road.

"Look, I'm sure your route is super planned out and efficient, as usual. But I found a few cool places to stop at while still getting us there on time, in case you want to embrace the whole road-tripping-without-our-parents thing, like we used to always talk about doing. But you're *clearly* hell-bent on being miserable, so—"

I drop my head back and groan because, seriously, universe, did you need to stick me in a truck with literally the most annoying person in the world?

"We both know you hate driving this thing. This is ridiculous."

I shake my head. "Don't you have schoolwork you could be doing right now? Or anything—anything at all—besides harassing me for trying to get us to Memphis early?"

She sighs. "Maybe! But I'm just saying, stopping at minor roadside attractions that aren't really out of our way sure as hell beats the shit out of spending another day in awkward silence listening to your stomach grumble because you don't even want to admit that you're hungry."

"Hey, I didn't . . ." I trail off when she looks at me, and okay, yeah, maybe I did. "What kind of attractions? More giant chairs?"

"Oh, Fallon." She smiles, pulling her laptop out of the bag by her feet. "That chair was nothing. I'm just getting started."

# FOURTEEN

*W*e're an hour and a half into the drive—which Chloe has so far spent clicking away on her laptop with a determined crinkle in her brow that is *definitely* not adorable. Nope, not one bit, I swear. Her phone has charged up enough that I can finally plug mine in, and she immediately sets to work reconfiguring today's driving plan.

"Get off at the next exit," she says.

Part of me wants to protest—to keep driving straight on my perfectly mapped route, where I even marked restroom and coffee breaks, to get us as close to Memphis as humanly possible—but the other part of me is immensely curious.

If she opened with a visit to Haserot's Angel—go big or go home, I guess—what else could she possibly have up her sleeve?

I let my mind wander, choreographing the possibilities:

Chloe leading me through a stretch of roads, the houses getting older and farther apart. Chloe telling me to pull over and into a meadow full of wildflowers, where she pulls out a blanket and a picnic basket that she hid god knows where, a secret smile meant just for me crossing her face when I ask, "What's all this?" Chloe—

"Take this next left," real-life Chloe says, pulling me from my daydream as she slides in her earbuds and logs in to her bio lecture. I do, glancing at her screen, which fills up with other kids her age and a very tired-looking professor. So much for wildflowers and picnics, I guess.

Exactly fifty-seven minutes later, we arrive.

As I pull up to park in a dirt patch in front of a crudely designed T. rex statue made of plaster and wire, I realize that Chloe may have front-loaded the attractions she picked. It's not that I don't like dinosaurs. It's just that I should probably adjust my ideas accordingly, to be safe.

"Jurassic Adventures?" I say, reading the hand-painted sign leaning against the weathered porch of the house behind it. It looks like it used to hang from the rafters once upon a time. It also looks like "once upon a time" was at least a few decades ago.

"Yep," she says, popping the p as she pulls the keys out of the ignition and heads to the back of the truck.

I follow her quietly, letting her take the lead for our normal shutdown procedure. We check the coolers and make sure everything is on the up-and-up before we hop back out of the truck and lock it up tight. It dawns on me that if she's going through all of this right now, there is a zero percent chance this is a quick selfie-with-a-dino stop.

She walks over to a laminated piece of paper crudely stapled to one of the porch posts and then fishes out her wallet. I'm horrified to realize this sign lists tour prices.

"You can't seriously want to go in there."

"Oh, but I do," she says, walking backward toward the entrance with a gleam in her eye.

I have no choice but to follow her; she's taken my keys.

♥

"I'M NOT IN any way trying to question Martin's scientific accuracy here," I whisper to Chloe, gesturing to the tour leader as we make our way through the "jungle" over a wooden rope bridge. "But I do not recall there being gorillas in the Jurassic period."

As if on cue, a large animatronic gorilla pops up beside us and beats its chest, and I jump back, shaking the whole bridge. The whirring sound of the machine yanking the animal's arms around drowns out the jungle-noise soundtrack Martin has blasting all around us. I lean forward, trying to study the gorilla before it falls back down. I'm not always the biggest fan of animatronics—I'm more of a psychological-horror kinda gal—but I can appreciate good craftsmanship.

Unfortunately, this is not that. The velvety fur of the animal seems to have rubbed off in patches long ago, giving it a mangy appearance, the black color faded to a dull, lifeless brown from the harsh sunlight beating down on it for god knows how many years. But still, I wonder how many kids have jumped in this very spot. I wonder how many people on dates have laughed nervously and grabbed hands, how many have stood here and appreciated what it once was.

The gorilla will not be discounted, and that . . . ? That *is* interesting. I pull out my phone and take a quick recording, desperate to capture the animal in all its robotic glory. I'm leaning over the rail, searching for just the right angle, when I accidentally catch Chloe in the frame. She smirks, like she senses the exact moment it happens, and I smash the stop button with a frown. Chloe doesn't get to be in my clips. Not anymore.

Ahead of us, Martin, the owner and entrepreneur of Jurassic Adventures—which is not in any way affiliated with *Jurassic Park*, he was quick to point out—drones on about the various park highlights. I jog to catch up. He's in his late fifties, I think, and dressed in tan pants, a vest, and a little safari hat. His brown eyes glint from beneath big bushy eyebrows, surrounded by skin that's spent too much time outdoors for too many years.

I should be creeped out; I don't think many people would advise two girls to go wandering into an enclosed man-made "jungle" with an old white guy. But Martin's enthusiasm for the park is infectious, plus he gave us a discount, since there's a summer camp field trip arriving shortly and he'll need to cut our tour short to tend to them.

I smack a mosquito on my arm, rubbing off the red smear it leaves behind. Chloe asks Martin a million questions about dinosaurs and running this place, as if she's talking to a real paleontologist and not some random man with plaster and wire and too much time on his hands.

How smart were dinosaurs? (Very, for reptiles; not very, compared to literally anything else.) Why were they so *big*? (Evolution is a trip!) Were there more meat eaters or plant eaters? (Herbivores by a landslide.) Is it true they turned into birds? (Sort of.) How many teeth did T. rexes have, how big were their teeth, and does the sculpture out front reflect that? (About sixty, roughly the size of bananas, and no.)

"Well, I'll leave you two to it," Martin says the second Chloe finally pauses to think of her next question. "Make sure you head out back to the velociraptor pens before you leave."

"Wouldn't miss it, Martin," Chloe says, punching him gently on the shoulder like they're old friends.

"Clever girl," he says with a wink. Chloe laughs, and I swear I must be missing something.

"'Clever girl'?" I ask as soon as he's out of earshot. "More like 'creepy tour guide.'"

"You don't know 'clever girl'? From the original *Jurassic Park*? Are you being real right now?"

"Is that the one where they're all stuck in the hamster ball things?"

"Oh my god! How are you so obsessed with movies but you don't know the original *Jurassic Park*? How has life failed you so spectacularly?"

"I know of it!" I push back some leaves and keep walking toward the next rope bridge, smiling when I hear the unmistakable sound of the branch springing back to whap Chloe in the face.

"It's a classic."

"You sound like my mom. She thinks every movie from the nineties is a classic. Half of them don't hold up. There's a difference between being a classic and just being nostalgic for your childhood."

"Excuse you!" Chloe all but shrieks.

Which is the exact moment that an animatronic alligator jumps out of the water, full-on *Jaws* style, snapping its mouth at us, hard. I shout and jump back, losing my footing and nearly tumbling over the side of the bridge. It's not high—maybe two feet over the shallow pond—but still, I scramble to grab the rope and save myself the embarrassment.

Warm hands circle around my waist, pulling me closer and holding me steady. "It's okay. I've got you," Chloe says, pulling me against her.

And I can't breathe.

It's weird that we still fit together. My head on her shoulder, her face in my hair. It's weird to feel her smile again, instead of just seeing it.

But then the bridge stops swaying, and my feet are planted

firmly on the ground, and now we're just holding each other for the sake of holding.

I let go.

"Sorry," I say. She steps forward, and I step backward, trapped in this farce where maybe we can be comfortable together, but not too comfortable. Like, let's push ourselves to the absolute limit of what our friendship will bear.

Except our friendship didn't bear it, did it?

She leans over to look in the water. It's only a matter of time before the alligator pops back up, but this time we'll be prepared, I think.

"All right, Fal, you got me. Maybe it's not totally accurate," she says as a papier-mâché brachiosaurus leans down to sip from the same water the alligator hopped out of. Its gears stick a little, though, so it jerks on the descent, making the movement look more like an uncomfortable nod.

"How'd you find this place?" I ask when we're wandering through the snake house at the edge of the property. This part is creepily real, with actual snakes slithering around their enclosures, burrowing into their woodchips. But then a fake cobra pops out of an equally fake log in the corner, its hisses piped in through large speakers hung around the room.

"I don't know." She shrugs. "I'm kind of into dinosaurs right now."

"Don't most people go through a dinosaur phase when they're, like, ten?"

"I'm a late bloomer."

"I don't think that means what you think it means." I laugh, leaning my face closer to the glass. Inside, a small python writhes its way around a branch, looping itself over and over.

It reminds me of Mr. Trimple, who teaches film and photography at the high school. He was intimidating, always shouting at us to roll the cords the right way or we'd be replacing them. Maybe Mr. Trimple should have taught this snake instead. I think he would have preferred that to working with a bunch of teenagers.

I hope when I get to college it's different. I hope the professors are there because they want to be and not because they have to be. I hope they're passionate and inspirational, like all the college professors in the movies. But who knows if any of that's true to life, though?

Wait. Chloe does. After a year away, she must be a veritable college expert. And if I don't think too hard about what I'm really asking—*What was your life like without me?*—I can almost believe I just want to know if higher education sucks or not.

"So what's college really like?" I ask when I finally work up the nerve.

We've abandoned the snake house for a butterfly garden in the back. We're inching closer to the velociraptor pen, and I can already hear the children arriving on the other side of the park, their squeals of delight echoing through the entire "jungle." I wonder if they've gotten to the gorilla yet and how those camp counselors are going to explain the mishmash of chronology and geography to their students. I wonder if Jami ever has to deal with absolutely batshit field trips at her summer camp, but then I remember she doesn't ever get to leave.

"It's fine," Chloe says, watching a painted lady crawl all over her hand. I'm covered in butterflies myself now, their feet feather light as they cling to my skin.

"Just fine?"

Chloe shrugs. "What do you want me to say?"

And I'm not sure, honestly. I haven't really thought about it. I guess I always thought that we would experience it together somehow, so it feels weird to be so out of the loop, our one-year age difference never so apparent.

She bends down and picks up a little pink rock from the gravel path, shoving it into her pocket so fast, I almost think I imagined it. She looks at me, and I can tell she wants me to ask, but I don't.

"It's gotta be a little awesome, right?" I say, setting my finger against a strange blue butterfly on her head. I have to go on tiptoe to do it. I drop back down when it's securely on my palm, showing it to her.

I don't know why, but the thought of her missing the brilliant blue powder of its wings killed me. It was right there in front of her, and she couldn't see it. It wasn't fair. Chloe places her fingers against mine, and the butterfly walks over to investigate its new perch while I pretend this is fine. This is normal. We're just coworkers. This is for my mom.

"Some of it is awesome, yeah," she says, breaking the spell and pulling her hand away as the butterfly flies off. "But some of it sucks."

"Like what?"

She opens her mouth to say something, and for a half a second, I imagine what it would be like if she said "missing you" or something else equally cheesy and sentimental. Instead, she shrugs and says, "There's a lot more homework, for one thing." I pretend that doesn't bother me at all.

"Okay, besides the homework, though."

She seems to consider this for a moment, staring at a pale yellow butterfly resting on the stem of a nearby flower. "There's a lot of free time. Too much, maybe. And it's a lot of responsibility. Everybody expects you to know what you want to do and, like, to excel at your chosen major, even though just a few months before, you were begging high school teachers for a hall pass when you had to pee. You're just supposed to automatically know how to handle all that and adapt and everything . . ." She trails off.

"You said you don't have a major," I point out.

She catches herself, flashing me her patented Chloe smile, complete with finger guns. "You can't suck at your major if you don't have one."

"I don't think that's how it works."

"Come on," she says, ignoring me and heading for the door. "Let's go see what else there is here."

And when we get to the velociraptor pen and instead find flocks of chickens inside, their coop painted to look like a dinosaur's mouth and bearing a hand-painted sign that says, **CHICKENS: VELOCIRAPTORS OF THE MODERN AGE!** I'm not even a little bit surprised.

# FIFTEEN

*I*t's not that I want Chloe to suffer.

It's not like I want to make her fall in love with me the way I once fell in love with her.

But also, I would be lying if I said I'm not a little bit, sort of, you'll-see-it-if-you-squint delighted to find that she keeps sneaking glances at me when she thinks I'm not looking.

I don't hate it.

Because it's nice to feel desired, even if the door is closed and the bridge is burned. Which it is.

Obviously.

We grab a late lunch by the world's largest baseball bat and then do a quick drive past the world's largest sassafras tree. Chloe debates visiting the world's largest underpants but decides not to chance it after reading some reviews that say the exhibit is permanently closed.

Chloe takes over the driving, despite my weak protestations that she should be doing her schoolwork. She says she's all caught up, ahead even, and not to worry about it.

I'm instantly suspicious. I press her to find out how exactly this whole online summer class thing works, telling myself that maybe I'll want to do it in the future too, that it's good information to have, and that I'm not at all checking up on her.

"Only bio has a set schedule," she says. "English is mostly just reading and discussion boards and papers, with the occasional Zoom lecture sprinkled in for good measure."

I want to pry a little more—*What are these papers? Is that what you were working on before your Zoom today? Are you sure you're ahead?* But I stop myself. If she doesn't care, then neither should I, right? My days of organizing Chloe's schedule for her are long over.

I try to call my mom instead—twice—but she doesn't pick up. I pick at my nail, worried this is a sign the meeting went badly, until she texts back: **Out to dinner! Talk soon!** ♥

Dinner out means she has an appetite. And an appetite means things probably went well, right?

After overthinking *that* from every angle, I stretch an arm over my head, tucking my cheek against it and settling in. The air conditioner is on low, which means, for once, instead of freezing or melting, I'm the perfect comfortable temperature. Chloe plays the latest Taylor Swift album, and underneath it, softly, I can hear her singing.

You probably expect me to say that Chloe is some great

singer. That she sounds just like Taylor Swift or that the scratchiness in her voice gives her just the right hint of a sultry edge, like Janis Joplin on my grandma's old, crackling records.

That is, in fact, completely untrue. Chloe cannot, will not, and never has been able to carry a tune. Her voice is off-key, flat, the notes all wrong. She's the only kid probably to ever get a B in chorus even though she never missed a class. But somehow, her humming is mixing with the sound of tires on asphalt and the perfect-temperature air, and I feel this level of peace I haven't had in forever. This sense that everything is right in the world for this tiny moment and that I could do this, maybe: be her friend.

And I know, I know. You want to hear about the whole thing—everything in the before that tipped us straight into the after. But now's not the time for that. Now is the time for sleepy smiles and heavy eyelids and a familiar voice singing me to sleep.

♥

I WAKE UP when the truck stops moving and slide up in my seat, my bleary eyes trying to make sense of what's in front of me. We're in a parking lot that's more a patch of grass than anything truly identifiable as parking spaces, but there are other cars here too.

I roll my shoulders, coaxing the sleep out of them, and glance at the clock on the dash. It's six thirty; I've been asleep for two hours.

"Sorry," I say. "I guess I fell asleep."

"You must have needed it." Chloe shrugs, pulling the keys out of the ignition. "Maybe you should skip the shark tent tonight if you're not getting enough rest."

"I don't think the shark is the problem," I say, and her face tenses just for a second. She must think that I mean her, but this time, I actually don't. "I think it was more the mosquitoes and the dew," I clarify, and one side of her mouth quirks up into a smile.

Maybe this is my olive branch.

"I think the big tent is good for keeping both of those at bay," she says.

"Where are we?" I ask, searching the trees in front of us. A small but well-worn path cuts a ragged scar into the woods, welcoming and foreboding all at once. "Please tell me this isn't where we're camping." Suddenly, the idea of a slasher coming into our tents feels much more real here, and the shark not having even a flimsy zipper to delay it seems like begging for trouble.

"Yep," she says, hopping out of the truck with a smile. "Don't you love it?"

"Um . . . " I follow her, not really sure how to react. On the one hand, I'm not afraid of a nice little forest; on the other hand, this forest doesn't seem little or particularly nice.

"Relax, Fallon," she says, grabbing our water bottles. "We're not really staying overnight. Not that you'd have a say, though, since you forfeited your veto power."

"I did no such thing!"

"Um, road trip rules, remember? If you fall asleep on the driver, they get to decide where you end up."

I take my water bottle from her and squint down the path. In the distance, I think I can hear someone laughing. I narrow my eyes suspiciously. "And where exactly did I just end up?"

"The Forgotten Animal Forest." She grins, like that's a totally normal place to be, a perfect surprise, a delightful time to be had by all, and not truly creepiness personified.

"Wait, wait, wait! Why exactly are we at a forest again? And what sort of animals were forgotten?" Then I notice the stuffed animals littering the trees around us. Well, parts of stuffed animals, anyway.

"Don't ask me. You're the one whose dream it was to visit creepy cemeteries and churches. I thought this fit your aesthetic."

"My aesthetic is influential and inspirational movie locations, not decapitated stuffed animals."

"I don't think they're all decapitated, to be fair," she says as we start walking down the path. "At least, they weren't in all the pictures."

The trees are thick, and the fading sun struggles to illuminate the forest floor. Occasional bursts of sunlight manage to shove their way through the branches, but honestly, that only serves to disorient me more.

"Do you have, like, an actual, real death wish?" I ask, stepping over a fallen branch.

Chloe laughs. "I wouldn't have agreed to go on this trip with you if I didn't."

"Hey, I'm the one who agreed to go with you."

"Sure," she says.

We stumble into the first mess of stuffed-animal limbs, and I pull out my phone to start recording. A dozen stuffed arms and legs dangle precariously from a branch overhead. We have to duck to avoid hitting them as we pass.

"It's true!" I insist when she doesn't say anything else.

"Just like it's true you're the one who got me fired?"

I hesitate, our eyes locking.

She mumbles, "Don't lie."

And okay, looks like I will be editing the sound out of this clip as soon as I get home.

"I didn't get you fired." I push past her, because technically I didn't get her *fired*. Right? I just asked my mom to cut her hours. But Chloe's hours weren't even cut! And she ended up getting that tutoring job or whatever anyway!

There's a stream cutting through the path, and I hop-scotch over the rocks, cursing when my sneaker slips and I get a foot full of water. I shake it out and glance behind me, where Chloe is still standing on a rock in the center of the water, watching me.

"You're literally working right now, Chloe, and don't tell me your mom isn't paying you well to do this. I know you've always gotten a dollar more than me an hour."

"I'm a year older!" she says, like that matters at all. My

mom said it was because Chloe was going to college first, but I always suspected it was because she was better at flirting with the customers and getting them to buy more things.

"Okay, but then clearly you weren't fired."

"Technicality," she says, pushing a ropy spiderweb of stuffed animal heads out of my way and holding them up for me as I shove my foot back into my wet shoe. The stuffed animals' cold plastic eyes stare at me.

"Okay, that one's gross," I say.

"Gross like you trying not to ever work the same shift as me?"

I freeze because that part is true, and there's no denying it. I have enough sense to feel properly ashamed, and I guess I deserve it when she lets the fake spiderweb fall and knock against my shoulder. I stop recording and shove my phone back into my pocket, suddenly unsure if this is a place I'll ever want to remember.

"That's what I thought," she says, staring at me for a beat before turning and heading into a clearing off to the side. "Maybe you didn't actually get me fired, but you sure as hell made it feel impossible for me to come back."

"Sorry," I call after her, because what else is there to say? I surprise even myself with the sincerity of it. I really *am* sorry, and not because I've forgiven her for what she did, but because maybe it was a little messed up to screw with her hours when it's just as much her family business as mine. I don't want that red in my ledger. I want to be better than that. I hang my head. "I really wasn't thinking about—"

"About what?" she asks, her eyes cutting into mine as I follow her into the sun. We're in a little clearing now, one that, judging by the amount of graffiti, seems to get a lot of visitors.

And I knew she'd ask about this. I knew eventually we'd talk, that it was wishful thinking to believe that I could get through this entire trip avoiding it. But in all the random scenarios I imagined in my head—in a meadow or a bonfire or the ten million other places I dreamed up—I truly *didn't* expect that it would happen in the middle of a clearing full of stuffed animal heads, surrounded by rocks defaced by crudely drawn clowns and spray-painted penises.

"I didn't think about how it might affect you, or your mom. Like, me asking my mom to do that."

Chloe shakes her head and takes a seat on one of the large painted rocks, kicking her legs out in front of her. I stay standing, awkwardly, in the center of the clearing, pretending to be interested in a doll sculpture that looks remarkably like a tiny version of the human centipede from that awful movie Chloe made us watch once. Is art still art if it's gruesome and crude and hidden in a forest?

"Today was kind of cool, though. Right?" Her subject change is jarring, but maybe that's the point.

"Minus all the dismembered loveys." I smile, going along with it.

"I don't know. I think they're pretty great."

"Yikes." I flick a plastic elephant head away from me. It

swivels on its little string only to turn right around and swing toward me.

Chloe fights back a laugh and sighs.

"What?" I ask, perching awkwardly on a rock across from her, because her silence feels heavy now, and I'm not sure I'm ready for this conversation, as inevitable as it's seemed this whole time.

Chloe tilts her head. "So, this day wasn't awful for you, right?"

"Right," I say softly, suddenly feeling the weight of the eyes of a hundred forgotten stuffed animals upon me.

"If we still have the ability to have not-awful days together, then why aren't we?"

I would like to tell you that I haven't, in fact, ever imagined her saying this to me. That when she left, it was straight out of sight, out of mind. But I think we all know that would be a lie. Because the truth is . . . *the truth is* that you don't get to be as angry as I am at someone who used to matter to you if they don't matter to you still.

"What are you asking me right now?" I ask, and my heart jumps into my sinuses.

"I think I pretty much proved to you on this trip that we can still hang, right? I took you to see chicken velociraptors, many giant objects, your favorite creepy-ass angel." She stands up, gesturing around us. "I found you a thousand artistically placed stuffed animal parts in a beautiful natural landscape, because I thought it might in some way amuse or inspire you. But despite all of that, you still feel so far away. So tell me, Fallon. What else do I have to do to make you realize that I can still be your best friend? What other hoops are you going to make me jump through to get us back on track?"

I take a deep breath and lick my lips, trying to choose my words carefully. Half of me wants to hug her, and the other half wants to scream. I'm tired of being bitter and angry at her. I'm tired of all of this.

But she doesn't seem to get that the reason we can't be best friends isn't because I think we've grown apart or that we can't have fun anymore. It's because when I wanted more, she wanted less. Much, much less. How does she not get it? How does she not realize that we crossed a line that can't be uncrossed?

"Whatever you're thinking right now, tell me. Please," she says. "Put me out of my misery."

And that, *that* is the worst thing she could say. That makes the side that wants to scream punch down the side that wants to hug her.

Her misery?

*Hers?*

She's the one who went out and found a fantastic new life at college while I sat at home waiting for a call that never came. Do you know how hard it was to listen to Carmen going on and on about facetiming Chloe and finding someone else in her room? All the speculation and shipping between our two romance-obsessed parents, and I just had to sit and smile and act like I wasn't dying inside.

"Best friends aren't supposed to know how each other's tongues taste," I say, hopping off the rock and storming back toward the truck. "I thought we were just visiting random spots to break up the trip. I didn't realize this was all some game to . . . what? Make me fall in friend-love with you again?"

"Would it be so bad if it was?" she asks, chasing after me.

"Yes!"

"Why?!"

"Because!" I shake my head and keep walking. I knew this was a bad idea. I knew from the jump this trip was the worst idea my mom ever had. I should've gone alone. I should've insisted. I could've figured out the driving thing somehow. Even days of white knuckling a steering wheel would be better than this.

"Because why? Because we hooked up? Is that what this is about? You're willing to throw our whole friendship away over that? Just sex? Just one night of tent sex. Wow," she says, and I spin around in disbelief. *Just sex*. That's what she said. *Just sex*.

"You are unbelievable," I groan, but it comes out more like a frustrated shout.

"It's not that deep," she says, like I'm the one being irrational here. "Not enough to throw away our whole friendship! It felt good! We had fun, I thought. Didn't you have fun? Didn't you want—"

"I did," I say, because she deserves a lot of shit, but not the stricken look on her face right now that tells me she's scared maybe I wasn't completely on board.

"Okay," she says, sounding relieved. "Then why does that mean we can't be friends anymore? I don't get it!"

"No, you wouldn't, would you?"

"Fal—"

I huff out a disbelieving laugh and pick up the pace until I'm full-on running out of the woods. I don't stop until I'm in the truck, slamming the door behind me. I grab my golf ball out of the cup holder and squeeze it tight, wishing I was anywhere else.

Chloe climbs in a few minutes later, her hand on my arm, my name on her lips, but I pull away and shake my head.

"Just drive."

# SIXTEEN

*C*old rainwater drips down my arms as I wring out my sleeping bag. My soaked clothes are sticking to me, and one piece of my hair keeps flipping up no matter how much I pat it back down.

It poured last night. It turns out one of the *other* drawbacks of having no way to zip up the shark's mouth or cover the eye holes is that rain can literally drop on you all night long and there's nothing you can do about it.

Okay, fine. I know what you're going to say: *You had options, Fallon. Why didn't you suck it up and go into Chloe's tent? Or why didn't you sleep in the truck?*

Want to know why?

I'll tell you.

You probably think that frustrating, angry "just sex" fight was, like, the pinnacle of awkwardness, right? Wrong. It did not, in fact, get any less awkward on the drive to our next stop.

It turns out there is literally no way to make a statement like that from the girl you love(d) not feel like a hot-iron poker shoved under your ribs. Every breath hurt, every blink took effort to not just start crying, every swallow was me choking on the words I wanted to scream.

I knew it was useless. Our opinions and interpretations of that night were just too far apart. So I slunk down in my seat and watched the miles pass, wishing I was anywhere but there.

Whatever schoolwork Chloe was supposed to be doing was long forgotten as she pushed the truck to the brink. I thought about saying something, but I didn't. I just tried to shove it down, to ignore her. To get this over with. Even when she put on a song she knew I hated and kept looking at me, trying to get any kind of reaction. Even when she ate all the animal crackers right in front of me, without offering me any at all. She didn't even offer to stop for dinner when my stomach was grumbling, and I sure as hell wasn't going to ask.

I grabbed a bag of chips from a gas station when she stopped to pee, and managed to hold it together when my mom called to fill us in about the meeting. It went really well, but apparently now they have to go through a second round to finalize things starting today.

Other than that, I stayed quiet. Completely blank. An

empty pile of teenage girl stuffed into the seat next to Chloe.

Chloe, for her part, just kept driving. And whatever little detours she still had planned, she very deliberately deleted them from her phone. While maintaining eye contact with me.

At least now we're on the same page for probably the first time since last year.

At least now we both know it's over.

Around nine p.m. she started to drift a little in the lanes, her eyes looking sleepy no matter how much she fought it. I think she honestly believed we could drive straight on through to Memphis, even though we were still hours away.

"We need to stop," I said, because I was tired too.

If I'd had the foresight, I would have napped earlier so I could have driven all night. Never stopping, never pausing, making sure there wasn't any time to reflect on the fresh wounds we had inflicted on each other. We'd still have had one full day before FFAC, but we could have spent it in separate parts of Memphis if we wanted to. Other than the four hours that we're contractually obligated to spend standing next to each other scooping ice cream for millionaires, we don't technically need to see each other in Memphis.

Except I didn't think of that. I wasted the ride fuming.

Still, we were, comparatively, in the home stretch. Assuming we didn't crash.

She hadn't answered me, so I said again, "We need to stop. Now." And this time she did that little hum-grunt thing she does that's an affirmative.

Chloe gunned it to the first exit she could find with a campground logo on the "upcoming lodging" highway sign. Only the campground turned out to be, let's just say, less than ideal.

We followed a series of signs down increasingly unkempt back roads, to the point where I was triple-checking the GPS. At one point, the road switched from paved to dirt, and I looked at Chloe nervously, but she kept her eyes on the road, her hands tightening almost imperceptibly on the steering wheel.

We finally came to a stop in front of a rickety log cabin that had a flashing **VACANCY** sign with both A's burned out. A lone yellow light stood on the porch, highlighting the ominous front steps and mud-covered welcome mat. The sun had set long before, abandoning us for better places on the other side of the world.

I couldn't blame it. In fact, I wish it had taken me with it.

"I don't know about this place," Chloe said. She jumped as a bug zapper crackled and hissed somewhere to our right. Whatever that was, it was big. "Let's keep driving."

I shuddered at the thought of actually having to sleep here, but I absolutely was not about to get back into the truck.

"It's fine," I answered, my voice cold. "We needed to stop, and we're stopped."

"I wanted to stop somewhere safe and clean. This looks like where you go to be murdered by someone in a hockey mask."

"Then I guess we should have followed my route and pre-approved stopping points." I knocked on the door and wiped my shoes on the mat, probably making them even dirtier than they already were.

A kindly old woman opened the door, her permed silver hair shining gold in the yellow porch light. "Oh!" she said, likely surprised by the sight of a giant ice cream truck in her driveway.

"We need a site, if you have any available," I said.

"Of course. Come in, come in." The room was stifling hot, a fire burning brightly in the woodstove even though it's the middle of summer. "For ambiance," the woman said, as if she could read my mind.

The front room was all pine paneling, the coal-black woodstove sitting smack in the middle. On the wall, a bear head was caught in an eternal war, snarling into the air, its glass eyes fixed on nothing and everything all at once. I shivered.

"That's not from here, right?" I gestured to the bear head.

I swear Chloe rolled her eyes, but I ignored it. She could pout all she wanted, but I wasn't about to have my life ended in a shark tent in the middle of a forest by a freaky, large mammal that can climb trees.

"Oh no, dear, you don't have to worry about that. There are no bears like that around here. Layla caught that in . . . Layla!" she shouted. "Layla!"

"Huh?" A woman in her late sixties with short, cropped

brown hair and a fishing hat covered in lures leaned out of what was obviously their kitchen. In her hand she held a bowl of watery oatmeal. "What? Esther, I'm eatin' my night snack. Now speak up."

"She's a little hard of hearing," the first woman—Esther, I guess—stage-whispered to us. "Layla, where'd you kill that thing?" she asked, comically loud, as she gestured to the bear head hanging behind her.

"Hmm." Layla walked down the steps into the lobby-slash-living room we were standing in. She seemed delighted by the question. I braced myself for a long-winded one-sided conversation filled with her daring animal-murdering exploits, but instead she just shrugged and said, "I got that one a long, long time ago over in Virginia." She took another bite of her oatmeal. "But if you're looking to catch one yourself around here, they're pretty rare. I haven't ever heard of one in our neck of the woods."

"The opposite, actually," I said nervously, which made her laugh.

"Well, in that case, you're in luck. Certified bear-free camping up in these parts." She winked.

"Great, we'll take it." Honestly, I might have still taken it even if Layla had said it was a bear-infested woods and I'd have a bear helping me set up my tent.

"Is it just you two girls?" Esther asked in a way that made my skin prickle.

"Oh no, my parents are meeting us later on tonight," I lied. I hoped that would make it seem safer for us or at least like we weren't totally in over our heads.

Esther wrote us up a slip, which I paid: $15.50 plus tax for one night. Then she pulled out a small paper map about the size of a diner place mat, like the kind we used to get when we were little, you know, with the mazes and stuff on them? On it was a surprising number of labeled campsites.

She pulled out a broken red crayon and drew two circles. "This is where we are." She marked an X. "This is where you park." She drew a little car in the middle of the closest circle. "And then you walk down to here." She made a line connecting the two circles, and I had uncomfortable flashbacks to the stuffed animal forest. "This one here is where you camp. Site eleven. The nicest one we have open."

"It's not drive-up?" Chloe asked, sounding nervous.

"Not after the storm we had a couple days ago," Esther said. "At least not for big old ice cream trucks."

Chloe looked at me like I was honestly going to be the one to give us an out or veto the whole thing. But I just shrugged. Esther and Layla were growing on me. And besides, Chloe brought this on herself. Her words "just sex" still echoed in my ears.

"All right," I said, taking the map from Esther. Layla had already gone back to her oatmeal and stuffed herself into a big easy chair to watch the fire. She pushed up her flannel sleeves.

I guess she wasn't immune to the room's sweltering "ambiance," even if she lived there.

The walk back to the truck was quiet.

"I don't suppose you found this place on any of your maps of fun places, right?" I asked, but she shook her head. And okay, I knew that. Like, obviously, but after we were out of the warm glow of Esther and Layla's house and some of my anger had faded with exhaustion, the worriedness was coming back. I would have felt better if Chloe had come across it before—if this place had Yelp reviews and was easily googleable.

We made the short drive to the parking area and proceeded to close down the truck, checking the generators, making sure things were safe—the whole nine yards. And then we slid our sleeping bags and tents out of the back and locked it up tight. If Chloe was mad when I pulled the shark tent out right after she grabbed the big one, she didn't show it.

Cue a very long walk, three stubbed toes, one face-plant into mud, and the thunderstorm to end all thunderstorms, during which my entire tent got soaked and I spent the night shivering my butt off.

And now you're completely up to speed.

So you get it. There was no way I was risking that walk back during a thunderstorm, and *also* I was completely positive that Chloe was not about to unzip her tent for me.

Not that it matters in the harsh morning light.

I finish squeezing out my sleeping bag and work on my hair, thankful that the morning sun is already heating things up. I try to peek into Chloe's tent to see if she's even mildly awake, but all the windows are zipped up tight, nice and waterproof.

I fight the urge to scream at the idea of her nestled in her sleeping bag, cozy, warm, and most importantly, dry. Instead, I take to walking around the campsite, making as much noise as possible. Everything is too wet to sit on, and forget about starting a fire. Not that we ever gathered wood or even have breakfast food anyway. So I shake the water out of my tent, and when that doesn't work, I shake it again, this time significantly closer to her left-side window. With any luck, that's still the side she sleeps on.

This time, I hear her stir.

I make a big show of huffing and puffing as I fake struggle putting the shark tent into its carrying bag, trying not to seem so obvious. I hear the telltale sound of a zipper being unzipped.

Chloe crawls out, a cocky smile spreading across her face as she takes in my appearance. "Sleep well?" she asks, stretching languidly in her too-tight tank top and tiny sleep shorts with turtles on them. I don't recognize them, I don't think, and that thought makes the poker burn hot under my ribs again.

I used to know every pair of her pajamas inside and out.

We used to swap them like trading cards every sleepover. All those pajamas, carefully catalogued in my brain so I could remember to return them, belong to the before. These tiny blue-striped shorts with little green turtles on them? They belong to the after. To the other girls, the college girls, who aren't me.

"Perfect," I lie.

"Your clothes say otherwise." She laughs as I tug my still-wet T-shirt off my skin.

I huff, this time annoyed for real.

"You could have come in, you know," she says, walking over to my sleeping bag and unzipping it. She spreads it open wide in a particularly sunny spot. It lies there limply, like the flayed remains of my pride.

I want to say "I really couldn't," but I'm sure she already knows that.

"Want to go get breakfast?" There's no hint of teasing in her voice, and I think maybe she feels bad. "We don't have to check out until eleven, and it's only seven. I think I saw a bagel place in town when we drove through last night. Why don't we dry you off and go get something to eat, and by the time we get back, that"—she points to my sleeping bag—"will hopefully be dry. I don't know if you've ever been in a car with a damp, musty sleeping bag, but it is less than ideal, to put it nicely."

No, I haven't. And then I wonder when *she* was in a car with a damp, musty sleeping bag—if it happened while she was away at college or during that one week every summer she has to visit her dad.

Chloe's maybe tossing me another olive branch with this offer of breakfast. But I see it for what it is: a non-apology, a distraction, another way for her to force us back to what we were, to where "it's not that deep" and "just sex" fall from her lips so casually about me, about us, and I don't . . .

I don't know what I want anymore, I realize.

Because right now, with the soft morning light glinting in her eyes, she looks just sleepy and rumpled enough that I want to give her anything she asks for, and that confuses the hell out of me.

I have to get a grip.

If anything has become clear since yesterday, it's that I absolutely can't let myself get caught up in any of this bullshit. We are on two different wavelengths right now: She's a confused best friend, and I'm a scorned lover, and I don't know how to reconcile how different our interpretations of that night last summer seem to be. But I do know that I need to be here for my mom and Carmen, and that's what matters. If we screw this up with our drama, we could lose everything. Our moms could lose everything. *That* is where our focus needs to be.

Acting like an asshole to her, while warranted for sure, isn't going to help anyone with anything.

I finally settle on saying, "I could eat." Pleasant enough but not totally friendly.

"Come on, then." She tilts her head in the direction of the truck, an easy, warm smile on her face as she scoops up her hoodie and starts walking.

We're pretty quiet on the way back to where we parked the truck, other than when I occasionally point out a butterfly or she picks up a cool rock or two to add to the collection she's got going in the cupholder.

"What kind of rock is that?" I ask as she examines it in the light.

"I'm not sure. One I didn't want to miss?" She thumbs the bright green line cutting through the rough brown of the rock's exterior.

I wonder if it's a new thing, a college thing, like studying for classes on her own. Just another part of her that evolved while I was stuck at home.

We keep walking until I can't take it anymore. "So what's with all the rocks? You got geology on your list of majors you've yet to declare?"

"Just good memories." She's teasing me. That's the same thing I told her about my golf ball.

"Right," I snort. Because what good memories?

"I'm serious." She shrugs.

I chew on that for a while, wondering what it means exactly, until I convince myself that maybe, *maybe* I can do this. I can suck it up, and she can play nice, and maybe we won't be friends exactly, but I won't despise her anymore. And sometimes that's as much of a win as you can get. Maybe—

"What the fuck!" Chloe shouts.

I snap my eyes to her face, her eyebrows furrowed, eyes wide, mouth popped open in a little O. Then I follow her line of sight all the way to the truck, which is currently sporting a smashed windshield and has spray paint defiling the illustrations on the sides.

What the fuck indeed.

# SEVENTEEN

*I*'m so sorry. I don't know who could have done this!" Esther says, hovering around the truck.

Chloe is on the phone with her mom. Mine didn't pick up. Apparently, she's just gone out for a run and forgot her phone. I feel guilty that she's going to get back to the hotel room and learn about this nightmare.

Especially when she has another meeting today.

Another very important get-us-out-of-debt, keep-us-going, and probably help-me-pay-for-college meeting, and she absolutely doesn't need to be worrying about this mess during that. "Make-or-break, really" were the exact words she used last night.

I can't stop crying. Not sobbing, just constant, steady tears as I try to hold it together. I can't decide if this is all my fault or Chloe's. If I hadn't insisted we pull over, if I had refused to leave the truck, if she hadn't brought us on this ridiculous detour, if she hadn't picked a fight, if she hadn't said it was "just—"

Doesn't matter. Everything is ruined.

And the worst part is our parents were counting on me. I'm supposed to be the responsible one. I'm the one who knows better. Just because Chloe mapped a route to a dinosaur park doesn't mean I should have let her go.

Layla is patrolling the parking lot, an antique rifle strapped to her back, as if she's, I don't know, going to shoot someone for turning the woman licking an ice cream cone on the side of the truck into a woman licking, well, something else entirely.

"Where are you parents, dear?" Esther asks, and right, I lied to them last night.

"Uh, their flight was canceled because of the storms, so they got stuck in Dallas," I say, the lie rolling off my tongue so easily, it surprises me. Esther nods like that makes perfect sense—like it's completely normal for parents to fly in just to camp for a night. I wipe at my tears with my still-wet sleeve.

"Well, let's get you inside and changed out of those wet clothes first. Then we'll worry about patching up your truck."

Esther has become intensely invested in helping us with our predicament since Chloe and I burst through their door a half hour ago, unsure what to do but knowing we needed actual adults to help us. Sure, Layla rushed out ready to, apparently, defend us to the death, but it was Esther who told us where to find our insurance information and that there was a place in town that could possibly drive out and replace the windshield. She even called the guy for us, and he said he could be out this afternoon once we got the insurance all sorted. And it was Esther who told me I needed to get out of my wet clothes before I "catch my death," which seems unlikely in mid-June, but honestly, it's just nice to be told what to do right now instead of being the one having to figure everything out.

Why did I let Chloe get us off track?

"I'll be in in a second," I say, doing one more lap around the truck to survey the damage.

The front got the worst of it, with large cracks running down and across the length of the windshield and a dent in the bumper. The passenger's-side window was smashed in, presumably to unlock the door, which was left wide open when we got there. The rain got inside, but Mom had already waterproofed the seats, so they're just damp instead of totally ruined.

Most of our stuff was at the campsite with us or locked up in the back, but the vandals got away with a jar of change my mom always keeps in the front console, probably twenty dollars' worth of quarters, which is hardly worth the effort they put in.

When we first saw the truck, I was terrified they'd gotten into the back. It looked like they tried to pry open the serving window, and the handles on the back door were definitely messed with, but the intense industrial locks Carmen had insisted on—thank god for that—were still intact. We rushed to check that the generators and freezer and ice cream were all okay, but other than our shit being all over the place and a hefty crack on the screen of Chloe's laptop, everything else looked to be in good shape. Yeah, maybe I should have mentioned to Chloe that she left her laptop on one of the freezers last night, but I was expecting the battery to die, not, like, vandals to shake the truck so hard, it would fall.

No, we didn't lose the ice cream, but we also can't exactly pull up to FFAC or the food truck festival in Dallas looking this way. The tears start again. Even if it's technically partly Chloe's fault, it still feels like it's all mine.

"It's gonna be fine, Fal," Chloe says, shoving her phone in her pocket as she walks up.

"How?!"

"It always works out. It's going to this time too. Don't worry."

"It doesn't always work out," I snap. "And when it does, it's because I make it work out while you just sit there and—"

"You ready?" Esther asks, sticking her head around the back of the truck, stealing my attention away before I can finish my thought. I grab a handful of clothes from my bag on the ground and nod. I follow her to her house, through the sweltering living room, and down to what appears to be a guest bedroom with an attached bath.

The room smells like carpet spray, and there are vacuum lines dividing the floor into neat columns. It looks like the room doesn't get used much. And I'm not surprised. Rows of ceramic dolls stare at me from shelves and dressers. A large doll, nearly the size of a toddler, assumes a place of pride in the center of the bed. A bassinet beside the bathroom door contains a doll so realistic that I jump, thinking it's real.

"Oh, that's Dottie," Esther says, walking over and messing with the blankets to make sure the doll is perfectly tucked in. "She's one of those reborn babies, you know?"

"A what?" I clutch my clothes a little tighter against my chest.

"They're little dollies that look like real babies. This one looks just like my daughter, Charlotte, did, wherever she may be."

"Oh, I'm so sorry," I say, feeling like I'm intruding on something private, but then she gives me a funny look.

"What? Oh, it's not like that. Did you think . . . ? God, no, Charlotte's not dead; she's just a pain in my ass. Haven't seen her in years. And I didn't get the doll 'cause it looks like her. These here have excellent resale value. Picked this one up at a garage sale for next to nothing, got it and the bassinet cleaned up, and posted 'em both on eBay." I raise my eyebrows, and Esther taps her temple. "Always hustling."

"So you're, like, a doll flipper?" I ask incredulously.

"You say that like you're not on some wild ice cream truck adventure yourself." She grins, popping her dentures toward me before sucking them back into her mouth. "Who's the weirdo: me for making money off expensive dolls or the girl driving the ice cream truck into a deep, dark forest in the middle of the night?"

"You might have a point."

"You don't get to be as old as I am in this neck of the woods without always having a good plan and a lot of irons in the fire," Esther says. "But why do I get the feeling you've already got that part figured out?"

"That obvious?"

"Girl, you have 'life plan' written all over your face. I used to be like you; we can smell our own."

"Used to be?"

"Till Layla came along with her 'zest for life,' as she calls it." Esther rolls her eyes. "She made 'flighty' into a whole personality. I swear that one's gonna get us both killed someday. She never met a problem she couldn't fix by shooting at it or running away or coming up with some ridiculous plan that doesn't make a lick of sense."

"But you guys seem happy."

"We are," she says, like she's taken aback by the idea that they somehow wouldn't be.

"How can you stand it?"

"You love the person, not their bullshit. I call her out when she needs it, and I try to be understanding otherwise. You pick your battles. You love 'em for who they are, not who you want 'em to be. I'm surprised you and your girl-friend out there haven't worked that out yet. But you're young; you'll get there."

"Oh, we're not *together*." I swallow hard, because on the one hand, yes, that's excellent advice, but on the other hand, Chloe and I are not two people in love. We are a one-night stand that went too far. We are a drunken mistake. We are EX-best friends who shouldn't have ever tried to muddy the waters. We are—

"You know, if I could do it all over again, I would go along on more of Layla's little adventures. Sometimes what seems like a mistake can turn out to be the most fun you've ever had."

I look up at her, at a total loss for words.

"Well, I'll leave you to it," she says, turning to leave. "I'm gonna whip up some oatmeal for you girls. Y'all need to eat."

"Thanks," I say. But the door's already shut behind her. I stand there for a second, her words soaking into my skin and traveling to my brain, brushing feather soft against all the places inside me that light up whenever Chloe steps into the room.

And then I shake my head, laying my clothes out on the bed and pulling off my shirt, warm and still uncomfortably damp from last night's rain. I toss it over Dottie's face, not lik-ing the creepy way the doll stares in my direction.

I don't rush getting changed. I'm not ready to face Chloe or the truck or the realization that our decision to camp in this godforsaken place may have just screwed up our moms' whole lives.

But I can't let that thought linger. I can't. We have one day until the event.

We have to fix this.

♥

THE COP CAR pulls slowly out of the drive. Layla and Esther wave at the driver, a man who had introduced himself as "Sheriff Frank." The insurance insisted we needed a police report to prove we weren't scammers, which added another whole layer of stress to things.

"We've got to have him over for dinner," Layla says, adjusting her rifle on her back.

Beside me, Esther coughs, and I swear it sounds like "nope." I glance at her, but there's no sign on her face either way.

After multiple calls to our parents assuring them that we're okay, just a little shaken up, they calmed down. My mom was ready to spend the money to fly out, and Carmen offered to meet us in Memphis, but even if we did kind of wish we had one or both of them here right now, we knew they couldn't miss their next round of meetings. So we put on a brave face and told them we had it under control, and I prayed we were right.

I think it helped that Esther got on the phone too, her calming presence drifting through the cell towers all the way to Dallas.

The glass-repair shop that she called earlier said they're in fact happy to do drive-up service, and someone will be out later. Layla has now checked the truck inside and out and declared it perfectly drivable, with only minor dents and cosmetic issues. Apparently, she was a mechanic in a past life.

Chloe and I aren't really talking, a quiet sort of truce settling over us as we deal with what needs to be done.

Layla walks the campgrounds, asking if anybody heard anything, but other than a couple with small kids and two old men here for trout fishing, there's nobody else, and all of them seem like unlikely suspects.

"It was those Edwards kids," Esther says when Layla gets back. "I'd bet my life on it."

"I hate when you do that," Layla says. "Don't go betting your life on anything but me." She gives Esther a kiss on the cheek.

I would probably swoon if I wasn't just so over any thoughts of romance or love. Emotions got us into this mess; logical thinking needs to get us out. I can't let myself be distracted again.

"I'm right, though," Esther says. "Those boys are nothing but trouble."

"Probably," Layla reluctantly agrees. "Seems like their MO. Frank'll go talk to their parents, and if that doesn't work, I'll go talk to them myself. I'm sorry this happened, girls. They're new in town and a bit troubled."

"Troubled" is one way to describe the people who de-filed an ice cream cone on one side of the truck and painted SpongeBob doing . . . well, *that* on the other. Layla says she knows some spray that will take it right off, and she might even have some in the barn out back. She disappears for a minute and then comes back lugging a pail of soapy water, a plunger, and an armful of cleaners and sponges.

No matter how much we refuse their help, they insist on pulling up their sleeves and diving right in with us. So we all get to work and start scrubbing.

And if occasionally someone sprays someone else with a hose, or if I laugh a little too hard when Chloe accidentally gets some soap on her nose, it's probably fine.

It takes a while, but we're able to get most of the colors off. We legit all cheer when SpongeBob is finally gone and the ice cream cone becomes an ice cream cone again. But still, some of the dark black smudges remain stuck stub-bornly in place. My stomach twists knowing it's not enough. This needs to be perfect. We can't risk anybody complaining at FFAC. And what if the investors want to see us in action at the Dallas festival? We can't risk embarrassing our moms . . . or worse.

"What is wrong with those boys?" Esther grumbles, scrubbing a particularly thick streak of black paint. I think it was supposed to look like a beard. At least, I hope that's what they were going for.

"It could be a girl," Chloe says, and I scrunch up my forehead. Like, I'm all for gender equality, but no girl is—

"No girl is gonna do something this asinine," Esther says, nearly laughing out her dentures.

"Nah, this was those Edwards boys, and the next time they come over and ask if they can hunt for rabbits, they're going to get a boot up their asses for it." Layla laughs.

I smile politely and try not to let on how worried I am.

"Hey, we have plenty of time," Chloe says, resting her hand on my shoulder the third time she catches me checking the time on my phone. "We're ahead of the game from driving a little longer last night."

"None of this would have happened if I'd kept us on track. If we'd stuck to the plan," I say, my eyes watering. "This is my fault."

"No, it's not," Chloe insists. I look away, but she grabs my chin to stop me. "It's not just on you."

"I wasn't thinking clearly last night. I let my anger get the better of me and—"

"You have a right to feel however you want to feel, even angry."

"Remind you of anybody?" Layla asks, her plunger making a giant *FLUNK* sound as it sucks out the last dent from the side of the truck.

"Mm-hmm," Esther says with a smirk before leaning over to smack a cartoonishly loud kiss onto Layla's cheek.

Chloe looks at them for a moment, confused, but I shake my head, and we all get back to work.

"I'm gonna get us there on time, Fal," Chloe says just loud enough for me to hear. "I got you."

And her words are so sure, so strong, that my stomach flip-flops.

# EIGHTEEN

*T*hings calm down again after the glass guy goes, leaving us with sparkling new windows.

Esther and Layla help us finish washing off the last of the graffiti too. What we can't get off, we're able to touch up with some model-train paints Layla finds in their basement. Most of the paint is old and thick, but we figure it out. The truck isn't perfect—the dents are out, but you can still see the creases in the metal, and some of the texture from the paint is uneven. But it's leaps-and-bounds better than it was.

It'll do, I hope.

We may have slightly downplayed some of how it looked to our mothers during their repeated frantic phone calls, during which we pretended the signal wasn't strong enough for Facetime. I know they'll find out in the insurance paperwork and the police report, but hopefully that will be long after all their meetings are over and the investment deal is signed.

We're not lying so much as punting the worry down the road a little.

Esther and Layla load us up with snacks for the drive: homemade peanut brittle, piles of high-fiber granola bars, and weirdly, a massive pack of juice boxes—which sparks an argument between them over whether it came from Sam's Club or Costco, but it's quickly resolved when they notice a sticker from a restaurant-supply company.

I don't really ask.

Somewhere along the line, Esther ends up talking with my mom again, promising that she's looking out for us and sending us off comfortably. She says, "Don't worry one lick," and a million other platitudes, which makes me wonder whether Charlotte is missing out on a great mom by being a "pain in the ass." Like, maybe Esther deserves more than just a reborn baby doll and a bunch of ceramic faces staring at her from a guest room. But I guess that's not really any of my business.

As we pull out to the road, I almost think I'll miss them, this weird couple I just met. Like they had that big an impact or something.

I bet you're wondering, *How can you miss someone you don't even know? Someone you only saw for a few hours? And you spent the first part of those hours thinking they were creepy.*

The answer: *I don't know, but I know I will.* Especially as the miles pile up and I'm still chewing on the conversation I had earlier with Esther about how she wishes she'd gone along with things more when she was younger.

Chloe facetimes her mom once we're on the highway. I'm driving again in the hope that she can get some schoolwork done. She positions her phone in the center of the console so I can glance at it too—but mostly, I think, so my mom can see that I'm fine and hopefully stop worrying. Though she would flip her shit if she thought I was using the phone while driving. The school had us watch enough PSAs about kids who died while texting or playing on their phones for me to ever even consider it.

Chloe and Carmen chat for a minute before my mom takes over, like she's been sitting there gnawing on her fingernails, waiting to hear from me.

"How was your meeting?" I ask at the same time my mom panic-asks, "How are you feeling?"

I hate that she's worried about us when she should be worried about the company. She and Carmen had today's meeting with the investors while we were in the middle of the windshield replacement, and they have a final meeting scheduled over breakfast in a couple days. She needs to stay focused.

"We're good, Mom. But did it go well today?" I try again, hoping to set the tone for the conversation.

"It went fine," Mom says. "But really, are you sure you're okay? Maybe I should meet you in Memphis."

"We're fine, promise," Chloe says, sensing my frustration

in a way that only someone you've been friends with for an eternity can. "Tell us all about the meeting before Fal explodes."

Carmen pops onto the screen again, sitting next to my mom on the bed and leaning in. There's a smile on her face, too warm to be fake. "The meeting was great. Fallon, having your mom here has been a godsend. And yes, we get that you keep changing the subject because you don't want us freaking out about you and what happened to the truck, but we're your mothers, and worrying about you is part of the contract. So kindly stop trying to badger your mom into sharing more details about things and instead answer her questions. How's the truck driving? Are you sure we shouldn't fly out? We could meet you at the hotel in—"

"No," Chloe and I say in unison, and it surprises me how much I really don't want them to come.

I glance at Chloe right as a truck cuts me off, and I swerve, causing the phone to slide precariously. Chloe, thankfully, catches it and holds it steady, downplaying how much I just had to jerk the truck to miss the vehicle in front of us.

"What was that?" Mom asks.

"Nothing," I say, trying to be cool, like a tractor trailer didn't almost flatten us like a bug. "Just some crappy driver."

"Watch the road, girls," Carmen says sternly, as if she can read my mind.

"I am," I say, and my tone is just dismissive enough to

conceal how nerved up I really am right now. Tractor trailers, truck break-ins, a drive to Memphis, being way, way off schedule. If this day could just get a little less eventful, that would be swell.

"We'll text you when we get to Memphis, Mom," Chloe says. "I have to pee, and we're almost at a rest stop."

I scrunch up my forehead. She just went before we left Esther and Layla's house, and now that we're finally on the highway, she has to go again? Whatever. I click on the blinker and pull into the rest stop, finding a parking spot right as we're in the "love you forever" stage of hanging up with our mothers.

The second the call ends, I turn to Chloe. "We don't really have time to stop every five minutes," I say, the stress making me snappier than I mean to be. God, sometimes I annoy even myself.

"I know," Chloe says as she hops out of the truck. She runs around the front and pulls open my door.

"I'm good," I say, but she shakes her head.

"We've been friends long enough for me to know you're not. I'll drive for a bit. This day has been a lot already, and it's barely afternoon."

"What about your classes?"

"Let me worry about that," she says, but when I just keep looking at her, she adds, "Fine. The crack in my laptop's screen is driving me nuts, and I hate working on my phone, okay? I'd just be sitting there doing nothing anyway. So scoot."

"Wait, you don't even *have* to pee?"

"Nope, just wanted a way to get our moms off the phone without them getting worried. And to save you from being nerved up about all the trucks on the road right now."

Wow. I kind of love that.

*Like* that, I mean. In a very platonic, I'm-not-losing-my-focus sort of way.

"Thank you," I say instead of verbalizing whatever fuzzy thoughts are sliding around in my head.

And when I hop out of the truck and start walking around to the passenger seat, I hear a quiet "Welcome."

♥

THE REST OF the drive is blissfully uneventful. I spend more than half of it asleep. I always have the strong urge to nap whenever I get stressed out, although I guess in this case it could also just be that I'm absolutely spent from getting rained on all night.

Esther and Layla were even cool enough to let us use their dryer for all my gear, so we were in fact able to avoid the damp, musty smell that Chloe was so worried about. That was pretty great of them. My mom offered to Venmo them a bunch of money for all the trouble, but of course, they refused.

For whatever reason, I pretend to be sleeping long after I'm actually awake, smiling when Chloe curses over potholes and swerves through traffic. I've missed her foul mouth.

And yeah, maybe I'm a little afraid to see what would happen if I opened my eyes. If I sat up and tried to really talk to her. I'm afraid to upset this uneasy truce before tomorrow when we do in fact have to work together for hours—assuming FFAC doesn't throw us out for hastily painted-over graffiti.

No matter what happens with the distribution deal, losing this charity event would put us so far in the red we might never bounce back. And knowing Mom's back was so against the wall that she had to leave it in our hands? I won't let her down.

If we can just hold this Scotch-taped, faded friendship together until tomorrow night, I feel like it could all be okay.

For our moms, certainly.

And I don't know, maybe for us too.

"Wake up, Sleeping Beauty," Chloe says a little while later. She tucks a lock of my hair behind my ear, and I shiver in a way that's less than subtle.

I blink and sit up slowly in the waning sunlight, fully intending to pull off the façade that I'm, you know, just waking up and haven't in fact been low-key hiding behind my eyelids for that last half hour or so of the drive. But the gleam in her eyes suggests that she knows the truth. Still, better safe than sorry. I roll my shoulders and yawn, which earns me a raised eyebrow. So okay, maybe I'm overselling it a tad.

We're in Memphis now, right in the middle of the best

part, at a semi-cheap La Quinta that seems like a palace after a couple nights in a shark tent. We do a quick check on the ice cream—still good—and wheel our carry-ons into the hotel, our other bags slung low over our shoulders.

I am so excited for a hot shower, I can barely stand it. We'll have a bunch of truck prep to do later, but right now, *right now*, dinner and a hot shower are definitely on tap. Everything else can wait.

The desk clerk nods and asks for my ID before checking me in, handing me a little credit-card-looking thing to unlock the door and telling me I'm all set.

We ride up the elevator with matching smiles.

Because we made it.

We survived.

And truth be told, maybe going with the flow a little on Chloe's adventures wasn't so totally bad.

As the floor numbers tick up, I think about how we'll navigate this night. I'm sure we'll take turns taking scalding showers the second we're inside. Maybe Chloe will sneak in beforehand and draw a smiley face on the mirror. I won't notice it until I get out, wrapping myself in a towel as the steam reveals its secrets. It'll remind me of the mirror in my duplex and how much the smudges from Chloe's mirror drawings always annoyed my mom. Chloe kept doing it anyway, though, because she knew they made me happy.

Later, we'll curl up on our respective beds and watch a bad horror movie, occasionally tossing granola bars and peanut brittle at each other to up the jump scares. We'll be happy and content—old friends falling into old routines—if only for a little while.

I will do my part and whatever it takes to keep things good and light. Starting now. I slide the key card in and unlock the door, ready to flop across one of the nice, soft double beds I'm expecting to see, only to be met with a single queen bed in the center of the ice-cold room.

I flick my eyes to Chloe, who looks as exhausted I am.

She bursts out laughing.

And oh god.

I'm so screwed.

# NINETEEN

$S$o, it turns out maybe there is a limit to my going with the flow and doing whatever it takes to keep the truce going. *Whatever* is a big word. I meant more like whatever *within reason.*

"Okay, well, this isn't happening," I say, dumping my luggage onto the floor and marching to the phone in full let-me-speak-to-your-manager splendor. My mom says I must get that from my grandma, because god knows she never flips out on anyone but me. To the outside world, my mom is relaxed, so calm all the time. It's effective in a service-based business, sure, but I see how stressed and anxious she really is after a long day. It takes a lot of energy to act upbeat and pleasant sometimes.

The phone's ringing tone is loud in my ear. The person at the front desk picks up, and I quickly explain to her what's going on. Just one problem: Since I didn't actually make the reservation, and I don't have the card on file with me, she won't let me change it.

I hang up the phone with a groan, pull out my cell, and call my mom. Behind me, Chloe drags her carry-on inside, kicking the door shut before heading into the bathroom.

"Hello?" Mom says when she answers the Facetime. She visibly relaxes when she takes in the hotel room walls. "Oh, thank god. I was worried something else bad happened. I'm so glad you made it there safely. Thank you for letting me know."

"Well, that's the thing," I say, trying to figure out how to tell her that something bad is happening without sounding like a drama queen.

Like, I get that on a scale from "the truck you require for your livelihood was broken into and we could have lost everything" to "there's only one bed and please don't ask me why I care, because god knows we've slept in the same bed a thousand times together at various sleepovers," this rates very low. Not, like, zero low, just, like, small-potatoes low.

"There is one teensy, weensy issue," I say, scrunching up my face.

"What's wrong?" she asks, and I don't miss the way the worry pinches her face right back up again.

"Well, there seems to be only one bed, so, yeah."

"Oh," she says, and then her eyes widen. "Oh! Huh. Let me

call over there. There must be some kind of mistake. Carmen called it in with my card, but I know she asked for two double beds. Just hang tight; we'll get this all switched over in a jiffy."

"Thanks! Love you!"

We disconnect, and I sit on the edge of the bed, my body ramrod straight. I don't know what to do with myself while I wait for my mom to call back. Part of me wants to just go downstairs and start setting up the truck, but I also don't want to seem like I'm running away or hiding.

Even though I am, technically.

But even I recognize that I maybe can't pull that off immediately after getting caught faking a nap.

Chloe comes out of the bathroom looking marginally refreshed. She must have washed her face, but her raccoon eyes from wet mascara are making her look more tired somehow. Clearly, she didn't bring her makeup remover in with her. She walks over to her luggage and starts unzipping, pulling out pajamas and grabbing a towel off the rack.

"Do you want the first shower?" she asks when she realizes I'm looking at her like she has two heads or something.

"Um, no. I mean, you can go first, but my mom is trying to get us a different room."

"Oh, because of the bed thing?" she says, like she finds it a little bit ridiculous instead of painfully obvious and necessary.

"Yeah, because of the bed thing." I shift uncomfortably on the scratchy hotel bedspread. How does she not get this? "Mom's calling to sort it out, and then she's going to call me right back. I'm guessing we'll be switching rooms in a few minutes anyway. Probably not worth even taking a shower yet."

I swear she rolls her eyes as she turns around and starts shoving her clothes back into her suitcase with a huff.

"What was that for?" I ask, because I can't help it. I can't help how much it drives me nuts that almost nothing bothers her, like, at all, except when it comes to me. And even then, she mostly just seems annoyed that things bother *me*.

"What?" she asks.

And she's going to make me say it. She really is going to make me say it. Fine.

"You rolled your eyes," I point out. "And huffed!"

"Did I?" she asks, and I think she's really pissed.

Perfect.

Just in time for the big event tomorrow.

"I guess I just feel like this is all a little ridiculous." Chloe stands up with a shrug.

"All of *what*?"

She waves her hand, gesturing around the room like she means *All this.*

"I don't know, Fallon. This all just seems a little over the top. Like, we've had how many thousands of sleepovers in each other's beds, and suddenly now it's taboo for you? Why? Because we had sex one friggin' time? Is it seriously that big a deal to you? We can't be friends anymore because my tongue was—"

"Okay," I say, "I'm not doing this with you. We have an"

event tomorrow. So, please, if there's any way you could just stop acting like none of this matters and maybe even accept that to me *it does matter*, that would be awesome."

"But. I. Don't. Get. It! I spent this whole trip trying to remind you how much fun we used to have, but you seem determined to do everything you can to forget that. You faked sleeping the whole way here just to avoid me!"

"I'm not the one who forgot about us!" I shout.

"Really. REALLY?" she asks, raising her voice in apparent disbelief. "I left for college, and you stopped returning my texts."

"Give me a break, Chloe. That's not even remotely what happened. You had sex with me! We had sex with each other! And then—"

"And then you went home literally right after! I don't know where you get off acting like I'm the bad guy here!"

"I had a curfew!" I shout. "I couldn't stay! You knew that! My dad would have killed me! And maybe it was 'not that deep' for you or 'just sex' or whatever, but I never did that with any—" I shake my head. Nope, not going there.

"You never . . . ?"

"You know what? Forget it. It's not even worth talking about. We have to focus on FFAC and this business and not our bullshit."

"No, Fallon, finish that sentence. You never what?" she asks quietly, her eyes widening as the realization dawns on her. "Are you telling me now, *a year after the fact*, that I was your first? No. You dated people! You definitely acted like you had. I mean, we talked about it!"

"You assumed, and I let you," I say, crossing my arms, embarrassed for no good reason, feeling laid bare by the truth falling around us: Chloe was my first, and I had wanted her to be. I had wanted so much more. Everything was so perfect that night, exactly as I had imagined it ten thousand times that summer—right up until she stood me up at the diner the next day.

"Fal." She rubs her hands over her mouth and starts to pace. "Fallon."

"Don't," I say, swallowing hard. I turn around and stare at a generic painting of a sailboat above the bed, because I am definitely not about to let her see me cry. Never again.

"You can't just drop this on me."

"I'm not. I didn't."

"Why would you want your first time to be just some random hookup at a bonfire party? You're worth so much more than, like, a quickie in a tent! Why would you do that? It doesn't make any sense! You're so careful. You plan everything! Why would you just . . . Why?"

She doesn't get it. She still doesn't get it. And after all this, I'm not about to sit here and tell her how much I cared about her—loved her, even. How I didn't realize it was just a "random hookup" until the next day. How I really thought we were more than that. How I misread all the signs, deliberately or accidentally.

"So it was your first time, and then you just left right after? You let me think it wasn't a big deal to you! Why would you do that?"

"How could you possibly think it wasn't a big deal to me?" I ask. "And again, I had a curfew! It was my dad's weekend. I had to beg just to be allowed to go at all."

"You expect me to believe that you were honestly thinking about your curfew? No."

"Yes! I was worried about getting home. Not all of us are like you; some of us have to actually follow the rules."

"That is such bullshit, Fallon. Why would you even do that with me if you knew you had to leave?"

"Because I—" I catch myself before I make it worse.

"Because you what?" The bed creaks as she drops onto it. "I don't even know how to process this. I took my best friend's virginity, and she didn't have the courtesy to tell me or even stay the night. What the fuck? Seriously. How could you do that to me?"

And my eyes open wide, because *she's* not the victim. She's not the one who was wronged. And *she's* definitely not the one who's really going through it over this. Little Miss "It's Not That Deep" does not get to co-opt this revelation for her own self-pity.

"You didn't 'take' anything, first of all. That's so archaic."

I spin toward her, my sadness overwhelmed by anger. "And are you kidding me right now? You, like, basically dined and dashed my virginity, and now you're going to act like I'm the asshole for not telling you about it?"

"That is *not* what happened. If one of us dined and dashed, it certainly wasn't me." Her eyes narrow. "Were you ever going to tell me? This is so messed up. You can't just trick someone into sleeping with you! This is a big fucking deal."

"Trick you?! Trick you?!" I shout.

"You used me. That's what it was, wasn't it?" she says, and oh my god. Oh. My. God. What is happening right now? Seriously.

"I used you?" I say, utterly incredulous. "Did we just step into the Upside Down? Like, in what world did you get used?"

"What, did you plan it all out in your head with your little mind movies? Calculate the probabilities and decide I was your best bet for ditching your v-card before your senior year? It didn't even matter how I felt at all, did it? I was a just a safe, warm body in the right place at the right time for Fallon's optimal virginity-losing experience." She squeezes her eyes shut. "What is wrong with you?"

"Me? What's wrong with you?!" I shout.

"Wow." Chloe shakes her head. "This is unbelievably fucked up. And don't even get me started on the fact that we were supposedly super close, and yet you didn't even bother to tell me that, no, you didn't actually sleep with Sabine the summer after your sophomore year. You can't—" She hesitates, and I swear to god she looks like she is going to cry. "You can't just use people like that."

"Uh, you were very much into it," I say, like an asshole, because where does she even get off right now.

"Under false pretenses."

"Oh, what, does sleeping with a virgin go against your 'it's not that deep' fuckboy philosophy?" I sneer.

"It does when it's you!" she yells, wiping at her eyes. And she looks actually hurt right now. Like, kind of gutted, if I'm being honest. What the hell is happening? I don't get why she feels like this. I'm the one who got stood up afterward. I'm the one who got left behind.

"I . . ." I say, at a loss for words. "I'm going to go get the truck ready for tomorrow. I think I need a minute somewhere that's not here. With you."

"Good idea," she says, looking away.

"I'll text you when my mom calls."

"Whatever."

I stand there for a minute; I don't even know why. She just wraps her arms tighter around herself, staring at the wall like she wants to burn it down. Or, maybe, like she's going to fall apart if she stops.

I grab the truck keys off the desk, along with the key card. I don't *think* Chloe would lock me out of the room with my stuff still inside, but right now, I feel like I don't know her at all.

I glance back, but she's still in the same position, sniffling slightly, and then I push open the door and bolt to the elevator as fast as my legs can carry me.

♥

I'M ELBOW-DEEP IN counting waffle cones when my phone lights up with a Facetime from my mom. She looks grim, because of course she does. Why would anything go right on this awful day?

"What's up?" I ask nervously.

"Sooooo"—she draws out the word—"I tried to get your room switched, but because of Food for a Cause and your hotel being the official hotel for its vendors, they're completely booked up. I tried calling a few other hotels, and there are rooms available at some of them, but I just wanted to know how big of a deal this is."

"Uhhhh . . . ?" I'm not really sure what she's getting at here.

"Because without the event discount, we're looking at a pretty hefty bill for you guys to stay two nights somewhere else in the city. Is there any way—I know you aren't on the best of terms right now—but do you think you can make it work?"

I bite my lip. "Aren't on the best of terms" is the understatement of the century. But my mom looks so stressed right now, and I know how thin the margins are on this truck. I take a deep breath. I mean, the floor is free, right? As long as we don't have to share a bed, it should be fine. Maybe we could even alternate. Tonight, she gets the bed; tomorrow I do, or something like that.

"We'll figure it out," I say, not entirely sure how that's going to be true, but the relief that spreads across my mom's face makes me believe it.

"Are you sure?" she asks, even though the tone of her voice sounds completely and utterly like *Oh, thank god.*

"Yeah." I smile, my lips curving up like twin liars. "It's fine."

"How are things with the truck?" she asks, seeming to finally notice my surroundings.

"Great. I was just doing inventory for tomorrow. A couple of the waffle cone containers got knocked down, but we only lost, like, one or two, so there shouldn't really be a need for any of the plastic bowls and stuff unless someone specially requests it."

"And the ice cream? If the top—"

"The top didn't get melty," I say, and this time my smile is genuine. "But if it somehow randomly does overnight, I swear to god that we will scrape the tops off. I know it needs to be Love at First Bite quality at all times."

"We have a reputation to uphold." She smiles.

"I'm on it." And for a second, it feels like a little bit of weight has lifted off my shoulders.

After we disconnect, I text Chloe: **No other rooms unless we leave the hotel. Mom seemed worried about cost, so I said we'd make it work. If you're cool with it, then I guess**

**you can take a shower or whatever. Let me know if it's an issue.**

She writes back one letter. The dreaded **K**.

I stand there for a moment, waiting to see if she types any more, but she doesn't.

I finish up in the truck, trying to figure out what could possibly make me feel a little less pukey. I just need someone to help me figure this out, to talk me through the hurricane in my brain. Someone with a clear head, like I used to have. Someone like . . .

I hop out of the truck and lock it up, pulling my phone back out of my pocket, hitting Jami's name as fast as I can.

# TWENTY

*H*elp, help, help," I say as soon Jami's face fills the screen. "I screwed up."

My chest feels tight, like I'm caught in a vise that's slowly squishing the rational thoughts out of my body. I try hard not to move too much for fear they will all fall out.

I'm wandering around the streets of Memphis near the hotel, having abandoned the truck—parked under a lamppost and in perfect view of both security cameras and our hotel room window, of course. I'm taking no risks tonight.

"Hang on. I'm supposed to call Prisha. Can we make it a group call?"

"Yeah, obviously," I say. "I need both of you."

I wait while Jami gets Prisha on the line, walking faster and faster while my head spins out. The hot, sticky air makes my clothes cling to me in uncomfortable ways as I wipe the sweat from the back of my neck.

"Wait, calm down. What happened?" Jami says when I start to jog a little bit.

I just need to get away. From *her*. As far as I can get.

It's pointless, I know. I have to go back to the hotel eventually. We have to do the event tomorrow. I can't run forever.

But I can run away for a little while.

I slow back down to a walk and look at my friends, unsure how to answer. I don't even know where to start. But Jami and Prisha take one look at my pitiful face and say, in perfect unison, "You finally told her, didn't you?"

And I nod.

Jami sighs. "I wish I was there right now. Are you okay? What did she say?"

"I didn't tell her all of it," I answer, leaving out the fact that I didn't have time to before she got mad at me. "But I did tell her . . ." My cheeks grow so hot—hotter even than my eyes, which burn with unshed tears.

"Okay, well, you're going to have to finish that sentence so we can help," Prisha says, putting in her AirPods so Kai can't hear us.

Jami sits up and props her phone against something in front of her. The bed dips beside her, and I see her nudge something just off-screen with her foot and shake her head.

"Who's there?" I ask, wondering how much these eavesdroppers overheard. I don't think I said anything too embarrassing, but still, it's not something I'd want a little camper or Prisha's boyfriend to hear.

"No one." Jami shrugs.

"Did they seriously go back on their word of giving you a single room now that you're an employee?"

"No, I definitely have a single." Jami blushes, and I hear her door click shut. Whoever was there is definitely not there now.

"Was there a boy in your room?" Prisha grins.

And I'm grateful for the distraction from my own problems for once. It's a cool ice over my scorched nerves.

It's always been so simple for Jami to fall in love. She falls in and out of love like some people change their hair color. And Prisha? Prisha loves hard and fierce and forever. I wonder if they're ever afraid of it, like I always am.

"I'll tell you later," Jami practically squeals, and I can tell she's absolutely smitten.

"Is he hot?" Prisha asks.

"Like, burning," she says. "But this isn't about me. Fal, tell me what happened with you and Chlo."

I hate that she can call her "Chlo" too. That Chloe and I share all the same friends in our little hometown, even *my* best friend, Jami. But there's one difference between Jami and Prisha and every other friend we have in common: They're the only ones who know the extent of my feelings for Chloe. My real feelings, not just the angry ones. And they're the only ones who know that I hadn't ever had sex with anyone before Chloe. Well, they were the only ones who knew until tonight, I guess.

I shake my head. "I don't know." I veer into a park a few blocks from the hotel and take a seat on one of its well-worn benches. It's nearly dusk, and the sidewalks are full of people wandering around and laughing. Mostly tourists, probably, and a lot of people here for FFAC, which sort of takes over the city with all its spin-off events.

Tomorrow the streets will be even more crowded. And I'll be stuck in a little ice cream truck, working elbow-to-elbow with someone who seems to think that I'm the asshole, that I'm the screwup, and, god, what if I am?

What if I did?

Did I?

"Okay, that's a really nice cloud," Jami says, pulling me from my thoughts. "But we'd rather see you."

I paw at my eyes, hanging my head back and staring up at the darkening sky.

"Fal, what happened?" Prisha asks gently.

I take a deep breath and pull the phone up, letting them see my face, the pain etched across it, the tears threatening to fall. Because I don't know what I'm doing. I don't know what I'm doing at all.

"Chloe's really mad at me."

"She's mad that you caught feelings?" Jami asks.

Prisha looks annoyed. "What did she think was gonna happen? She was like a goddamn octopus on you all last summer, just glued right to your side, smacking kisses on your cheek all the—"

"I didn't tell her about the feelings part."

"Then why?" Jami asks, and her eyes widen as she realizes

what I must mean. "Oh god, did you tell her it was your first time, but not *why* you wanted your first time to be with her?"

I nod, rolling my eyes back, trying not to cry, because this isn't how any of it was supposed to go. None of it. *All of it.* From last summer falling for her, to thinking she liked me back, to losing my virginity, to detonating that fact like a weapon all over our hotel room floor tonight.

"And now she's mad because she doesn't get it," Prisha says with a frown.

"I guess," I say, staring at the sky again like I'll find the answers there. "She kept saying I used her, like it was some awful thing I tricked her into doing. It's gross. I feel gross about it now. I checked in with her the whole time! And she checked in with me! I didn't—*we* didn't—do anything that the other person didn't want to do. She was one hundred percent on board, and now she's acting like I did something wrong to her."

Jami studies my face, her arm muscles tensing like she's fighting how badly she wants to reach out and hug me. I'd give anything for us to be sitting together right now, face-to-face instead of screen-to-screen. If I ever needed a hug in my life, it's after this nightmare of a day.

"Do you think," Prisha starts to say, pinching her eyebrows together like she's still trying to make sense of everything. "Do you think maybe she misunderstood the whole scenario?"

"I don't know how you misunderstand me saying it was my first time."

"Well, without all the context!" Jami waves her arms in exasperation. And I know what she means; she means *my feelings*. She means the fact that I fell in love with my best friend, and maybe, okay, maybe that's all on me. It could be. But still. Screw my feelings. They don't have anything to do with this. Chloe doesn't get to know that. No one in this equation is better for knowing that.

"I'm not going to tell her that I fell for her when she's pissed enough about the fact we had sex in the first place," I say. "I just need to smooth things over so we can get through tomorrow, and then I want to go home and hide under my blankets until I leave for college."

"But that's just it," Jami says. "Without her knowing how you felt about it, I can see why she might feel used or lied to."

"Yeah, I'm trying to put myself in her shoes," Prisha says. "It's different for me because Kai and I were together for a while and we were each other's firsts, no matter how much he tries to brush that off. But if I were in your situation, I can see how she would feel used. Like, the assumption would be that you were just trying to have sex for the first time for the sake of having sex for the first time. I would feel lied to, I think."

"But how would her knowing my feelings change that? In what world does that make sense? It's just going to make things more complicated."

"Because she wouldn't feel like she was just a body to you," Jami says. "You know how some people act like if you haven't lost it before graduation, you're, like, a reject or something?"

"We all know that's bullshit," I say. "There's not a time limit on something that!"

"I know; thus me still not getting any yet. Although . . . " Jami smirks.

"Oh my god, are you going to bang at summer camp?" Prisha laughs. "You are such a cliché!"

"Says the girl literally wearing her boyfriend's varsity jersey right now, with his number painted on her cheek."

"The baseball team's throwing a bonfire tonight. One last hurrah before a couple of them head to college early to start practicing with their new teams." Prisha flips her hair in pretend annoyance. "And I need to show my support. Also, I may have lied and told my parents it was actually a late-night rec game so they'd let me go. *Kai got a te-ent.*" She sings that last part.

"Get it, girl!" Jami laughs. "I hope to be having a, um, 'bonfire' of my own pretty soon."

"You already like this guy enough that you might go *there* with him?" I ask. "You haven't been at camp very long."

"Maybe," she says. "Probably not. But I do think trying some other stuff would be pretty awesome."

"Just be safe, okay? If you're going to, you know, experiment with other stuff."

"Oh my god, yes, Mom!" she says, looking mortified. "You know, for someone who's only had sex once in her entire life, you sure seem to know a lot about it."

"I did get an A in health," I remind her. "Given that they were wildly heterosexual textbooks, I'm way overprepared in the event a penis is ever involved. God forbid." I fake shudder. I don't hate guys or anything, and yeah, as you know, I've dated a few, but it's not usually my preference.

"Oh, right, I did get a C in the class." Jami snorts. "So I defer to you."

"Maybe if you didn't fall asleep all the time?" Prisha helpfully suggests.

I wait for the teasing to die down, for us to mostly catch our breaths, and then I hang my head. "So what do I do?"

"I think you need to talk to her," Jami says.

"She hates me."

Prisha shrugs. "Fine, then I guess just spend the rest of your life on a park bench in Memphis hiding from her."

"Don't tempt me. It doesn't sound like the worst idea, compared to the alternative."

"Yeah, and then your drama ruins Love at First Bite's chances of ever getting booked at FFAC or any other high-end events again."

"Okay, that actually *would* be the worst."

"Yes, yes it would, and that's why you should be having this conversation with her and not with us. I think you'll feel a lot better just getting it out there. And if she really does have it in her head that you used her, then I think she'll feel a lot better too."

"Can I just remind you that she's the one who didn't show up to the diner? She blew me off. Why didn't she call me after when I was clearly upset?"

"I don't know, but I think it's time for you to ask her that question instead of us."

"I can't."

"You can; you just don't want to," Jami says, frowning. "Look, I know I've only known him like a couple days, but Hideki doesn't take any of my shit. Like, we talk to each other. He makes me say what I feel, and there are no games or bullshit. It's nice. Ten out of ten, would recommend."

"Hideki? Is that your new boyfriend?" Prisha teases.

"Hopefully!" Jami says. "But stay on topic!"

I roll my eyes. "Okay, so you guys talk, but like, what does that mean, really?"

"You can't be serious. You suddenly don't know how to talk?"

"I mean, does he know that you haven't ever been with anyone before? Does he know that you're already thinking about it?"

"Kind of," she says. "I mean, I haven't said I want to screw his brains out under the stars when all our campers are asleep, if that's what you're asking. But we've kissed, and I've definitely told him that I've never had sex before and that I don't know how far I want to go."

"But if you knew you wanted to, if you were both sure, would you still feel like you *had* to tell him that you hadn't yet? Like, if you knew you were gonna, and he hadn't, you'd want to know?"

"Well, it's kind of a dick thing to spring on—" She stops

when she sees my face. "I don't mean you're a dick for not . . . I just mean, like, I'd want to know. I'd want to make it mean something or be careful or check in more. Like, I wouldn't be so—"

"So what?"

"I wouldn't rush into it. And maybe that's why she's mad. Maybe she would have done things differently. Taken different precautions."

"I was a virgin. I didn't have an STI or anything for her to worry about!"

"I meant emotionally, but whatever. I'm just saying, that's probably why she's upset about it."

I bite my lip. "So how do I fix this before tomorrow?"

"You go back to the hotel, and you ask her if she wants to talk, and then you very carefully, honestly, *finally* explain to her exactly what you've been moaning to us about for the last year," Prisha says. "It's time. You know it is."

And yeah, as much as I'm dreading it, I know they're probably right.

# TWENTY-ONE

*H*ey," I say quietly when I step into the room.

Chloe is sprawled out on the bed in her pajamas, her hair wrapped up in a plush towel. She's eating the last of the peanut brittle and doing schoolwork. She glances up at me and then goes back to glaring at her cracked screen as she types away.

"Hey," I say again, because she's barely acknowledged I'm here at all.

"Hey yourself," she finally says back, sitting up and shutting her laptop. She presses her lips together, hard, like she's fighting the urge to say anything else, and I don't know what to do.

"Um," I manage to say, but she just looks at me expectantly.

Tilting her head.

Waiting.

So, of course, I chicken out.

"I'm going to take a shower." I grab my suitcase and drag

the whole thing into the bathroom, locking the door behind me. Then I turn on the faucet, letting the water drown out every single thought in my head.

I'm hiding again.

And I know Jami and Prisha are right: I need to talk to Chloe. Really talk to her and not just put a Band-Aid on our relationship or try to patch things up. It's clear the revelation that it was my first time really shook her up or whatever. And as annoyed as I got that she was mad, maybe my friends have a point about how Chloe might be feeling too.

I drop onto the closed toilet, letting hot steam fill the room and trying to figure out where I go from here. I know I owe her an explanation, but what if this just messes everything up even more? We have just over thirteen hours before we need to head over to FFAC. Is now really the time to profess my undying love?

Or, I guess, my dead love, since it's over now.

Unless . . .

Nope. Not going there.

*Okay, think, Fallon. Think. If this were a movie, if you were directing it, what would you do?*

I shut my eyes and imagine the camera zooming in on my face in the shower. I'm nervous and cautious and practicing saying just the right words as I lather myself with soap. I stay until the water runs cold, because apparently, even in my "mind movies," as Chloe called them, I'm just as nervous as I am in real life.

"We should talk," I'll say when I step out of the bathroom in my cutest pajamas, and Chloe will nod and scoot over on the bed.

I'll tell her I'm sorry. She'll ask me to explain, and I will, skirting over the feelings part, but getting across that I didn't use her in any way.

Then she'll say she's sorry in that tone she only uses when she really, really means it.

Afterward, we'll both feel better. We'll share the bed but sleep head-to-foot, like we did when we were ten.

Tomorrow morning, we'll devour the hotel breakfast and head to FFAC. The event will go perfectly. At the end of the day, we'll high-five a job well done, get some sleep, and then wake up ready to head to Dallas, where we'll leave each other on good terms. And then I guess I'll probably see her around town all summer, and we'll smile and wave at each other, maybe even take a moment to catch up. Not best friends, but not enemies either. It'll be fine.

It's what I should want, and I know it. It's the best thing for both of us. But then why, as I sit here letting the steam rise around me, does it feel so, so wrong?

I blink a few times and let myself imagine something else. In my head, I watch myself turn off the water and run out to tell her the truth—to tell her how much she meant to me then, how much she means to me still, if I'm being honest. I picture her smiling. There are tears, maybe a kiss, maybe more.

My eyes bolt open. Is that something I want? I don't even know.

I sigh and peel off my clothes, desperate to buy myself some more time to figure this out. The water pours over me, rinsing away the grime and dirt of the past few days, and exhaustion settles into my bones.

I sit in the tub, letting the droplets fall into my hair and slide down my back, the hot spray calming me. I just need a minute, a second even, to think. I can't hide in here forever, and I know that. You don't have to tell me. But maybe, maybe I *can* hide for just a little bit longer.

WHEN I'VE STEELED my spine enough, I finally get out of the shower. The words "I loved you once, you asshole" are clawing their way up my throat faster than I can stop them, refusing to be swallowed for one second longer, my need for Chloe to know that she got it wrong—*so wrong*—blinding me to any possible consequences of my forthcoming confession. The idea that she honestly, truly thinks that I used her to get off or to "ditch my v-card," as she put it, when that's not even close to the truth, makes every cell in my body hurt.

But when I step into the room, she's gone.

My confession sits like bile in my throat. *I loved you.* Past tense. That's all we could ever be, and she's not even here to hear it. A missed opportunity then and now.

I change into my pajamas and pull my fuzzy socks out of

my suitcase, adrenaline making my hands shake, because I was so ready, so sure about telling her the whole truth about last summer. That it was "that deep" for me once, even if it won't ever be again. That I don't want to hide it anymore, because if I think too hard about the hurt on her face, the betrayal for not telling her about my virginity, for *using her*, as if I ever could, I think I'll explode.

I sit on a little chair in the corner for a while, not daring to touch the bed, comforting myself that there's no way she'll be gone for long. She probably just ran down the hall for ice or to hit up one of the vending machines or something, right? God knows the stuff in the mini fridge and the little snack bar are ridiculously overpriced.

But then I realize her sleep shorts are tossed onto the other side of the bed, partially hidden under a damp towel.

I used to hate that so much. She used to burst into my room after a shower, her super-long hair wrapped up, using two towels every time like she was at some kind of luxury hotel where time to do laundry was infinite and towels were always plentiful. And then, when she got tired of the weight on her neck, she would unwrap the towel, gently squeezing the water out of whatever hair she could reach as she went, and toss the towel onto the bed, where the cool water would soak down into my comforter.

I used to think it was the worst thing about her. But now as I stare at it, sitting there in a spot where other towels have probably been tossed a thousand times before, I catch myself wanting to smile. Because at least that hasn't changed. At least that's one part of her I still know and understand.

Maybe I've been trapped in the after so long, I've completely lost sight of the before. Chloe wasn't wrong; I did have fun on this trip. There were moments where I nearly forgot our whole tangled history and it felt almost like it did before. But maybe it was all just wishful thinking. Maybe there is no "before" for us to get back to anymore, just a string of after and after and after, dragging us through time until we're all stretched out and worn thin like a favorite T-shirt we can't bear to toss.

I would cry if I let myself, but I can't. I won't.

And if Chloe doesn't want to talk, if she wants to run away the same way I've been running this whole trip, the way she did after that night in the tent, and the way I have been ever since, then maybe I should let her.

I try to calculate in my head if I can do this alone; if I can handle the event tomorrow by myself; if I can get the truck to Dallas to meet our moms; if I can keep pushing the "after" forward for the both of us. But as sure as I was about things before we left, I'm unsure now. I'm trapped in a time loop of bad decisions, and I don't see a clear way out.

At a loss for what to do next, I tear open the closet door and dig out the spare blankets and pillows. I've been to enough hotels to know that housekeeping usually leaves a ton of them for people who need to hibernate in a pile of blankets and build themselves a little nest, strangers' skin be damned.

I wonder what it must be like to be so comfortable with yourself that you can make your home anywhere, at any time. Even in a cold, clinical hotel room like this one with its cheap still lifes hanging in little glass frames, like a person actually painted them and not a computer. Like they're something valuable and precious and not a photocopy printed on too-cheap paper that will crinkle and fade in the sunlight as surely as my friendship with Chloe did.

I almost laugh at the sight of her clothes, hung neatly in the closet, her pants folded up on the little shelf beside them. She was never the neat one, ever, and I wonder if she was at just as much of a loss about what to do earlier as I am now.

Who is she hiding with? Who does she facetime when things get hard? Someone from college, most likely. A new, better best friend or a partner worth more than "just sex." Jealousy simmers beneath my skin.

I take what I need and slide the closet door shut, feeling like I've seen something I'm not supposed to. I inspect the carpet carefully, and seeing no suspicious stains, I spread out the thinner of the blankets—more of a fuzzy sheet, really. I set my pillow on top and hit the lights before lying down and arranging the other blanket over me, pulling it up to my chin.

I don't know how long I lie there. I watch the shadows passing in the hall through the little crack between the door and the floor: strangers stumbling to their rooms, laughing and having fun, enjoying the hot Memphis night. Someone starts crooning Elvis songs. I roll my eyes, because seriously, man? But then I hear someone else with them: A boyfriend? A husband? A one-night stand? That other person laughs a big belly laugh. The shadows of their shoes collide in what I can only assume to be some sort of epic make-out session.

Which is when I decide to pull the blanket over my head.

The sweaty humidity from being trapped under a blanket in summer, despite the freezing air-conditioning piping into the room, is preferable to the idea that people are happy and kissing just on the other side of the door.

♥

"WHAT ARE YOU doing?" Chloe asks, the light from the hallway spilling in through the open door and painting her in stark relief. The couple, whoever they were, must have moved on at some point. She flicks the switch on as she shuts the door, her broken laptop tucked under her arm. I pull the blanket down and blink against the harsh overhead light.

"I was trying to sleep," I mumble halfheartedly. My heart picks up to double speed because she came back. She. Came. Back.

"On the floor?"

"You were gone," I answer, like that means anything at all or even remotely addresses the "why the hell are you on a thin blanket hugging a lumpy pillow when there is a perfectly good bed right next to you?" question in her voice.

"Yeah, because I had to finish this paper that was due today, and this laptop keeps crapping out. I went down to the business center and used one of their desktops like a caveman. I figured you were just going to go right to bed anyway. I didn't want to bother you."

"Oh," I say, trying to process the fact that she didn't run away. She was being courteous, although it's safe to say that her decision not to disturb me flew out the window when she noticed me on the floor. It's almost unfair how the universe gave me the ability to figure out almost anyone in life, to see their thoughts and motivations as clear as day, only to stick me straight in the path of the most confusing person to ever breathe.

I glance at the clock, which reads 12:30 a.m. "Did you get it done in time?"

"On time-ish," she says, setting her laptop on the desk. "Close enough, I hope."

"If you had a paper due today, why did you drive? I could have made the trip, and you could have been working on it all day."

"It's not a big deal." She shrugs.

"Well, it seems like a big deal if you had to stay up until midnight to work on it."

"Will you just worry about your own life, please?" she says, and *that*? That hurts.

"I'm not trying to, like, pry or anything, but I'm just saying—"

"I don't think I really need to take advice from someone sleeping on the floor."

I sit up, the blanket pooling over my lap as she comes to stand over me. I feel small and confused, even though she's not really doing anything to make me feel like that.

She crouches down, rocking back a little on her heels with a frown. "You're not really staying down here tonight, are you?"

"I mean, yeah," I say, gesturing to the pillow and blanket.

"You are so stubborn." Chloe shakes her head and stands up. She goes to the other side of the bed, her side, and I look away as she pulls off her leggings and slides her pajamas on. She sighs and then throws back the covers, making a big show of snuggling in and humming happily against the pillow. "Oh my god, this bed is so SOFT," she says. "Feels so good after all that camping." And then she hums another little hum of contentment before the room goes silent.

I slide back down, thumping against the hard floor. This is fine. It's fine.

I stare at the ceiling, praying that sleep comes for me. That anything comes for me. Maybe a friendly local boogeyman will stop by on its way to some kid's bedroom and put me out of my misery.

"Chloe?" I finally say, not sure what will come after.

"Yeah," she says a few seconds later, with a little sigh, and my terror that she was already asleep melts away.

I swallow hard and take a deep breath. "I just wanted you to know that I didn't use you the way you think. I didn't."

"But you did use me some other way?"

"No! That's not what I meant," I say, slapping myself on the forehead. "I didn't, like . . . I wasn't trying to just get it over with. You weren't just a warm body in the right place, and I'm sorry that I made you feel like that tonight. I don't want you to feel like that. Ever. It's not true."

She's quiet for a minute, and then she rolls over to the side of the bed closer to me. I can almost make out her face in the shadows, but I can't decide if I'm imagining her little-bit-sad, kind-of-hopeful expression. Wishful thinking, probably. A reflection of what my own face might look like if I could see it.

She pulls the covers away a little so she can see me better. "Then why *did* you keep it from me?"

"I don't know. I was embarrassed?"

"Why would you be embarrassed?"

"Because you have more experience than me?"

"Fallon, come on. That's bullshit."

"Fine." I take a deep breath. "I just, I liked that you thought we had that in common. I liked that you thought people would want to . . ." I trail off, not wanting to admit how pitiful I am.

"People would want to what?"

"That people would be into me that much or whatever," I mumble. "But I'm sorry that I didn't tell you. And that I let you think circumstances were different. I didn't think it would even matter. You're the queen of 'it's not that deep,' right? I guess I don't entirely understand why you're mad, if I'm being honest, but I do understand I shouldn't have kept it from you. And I'm really, truly sorry."

"Thank you," she says. "But I'm mad because you deserve better than getting taken advantage of in some shitty tent in the middle of the woods!" Her words are so fierce, so firm, that I jerk my head back and sit up.

"There was definitely no one taking advantage of anybody that night! We both wanted it, I thought. I wanted it. Didn't you? You said you did!"

"Of course I did!" Now it's her turn to sit up, tugging at her hair. "But is that why you've been so weird to me? Because I was your first? Or is it because you regret it? Or was it not good for you? Because I didn't know. And I would have done things so, so different," she says. She sounds desperate and scared, and oh, I hate this.

"You stood me up! I didn't want . . ." I trail off again when her pain overwhelms me, because if I'm the bad guy here, and I'm willing to concede that maybe I am, I'm definitely not the only one.

"I had to leave for school the next day! It was my going-away party! What was I supposed to do?"

"You were supposed to meet me at the diner. I was waiting for you. I was supposed to drive you to the airport. I was going to—" I shut my mouth before the tears make me choke. Nobody says anything for a minute, and I desperately try to pull myself together. "You weren't supposed to disappear."

"Fal," she says.

I wipe at my eyes. "Why didn't you meet me that morning?"

"Are you sure you want to know?"

"Yeah." I let out a watery laugh. "Not knowing hasn't worked out very well for us, has it?"

Chloe sighs. "Would you believe me if I said I didn't want to face you?"

"Wow, it was that bad?" I ask, automatically thinking the worst.

"No. No!" she says more firmly. "You're getting me all wrong. Again." She huffs. "I didn't want to say goodbye to you. I didn't know how, especially after how we spent our last night together." She rubs her hands over her face. "I was so scared about leaving for school, but I was trying to be so cool about it. And then it was confusing, what happened between us. I didn't know what it meant. And then you immediately acted like it wasn't a big deal, so I tried to just go with it."

"Me?!"

"Yeah, you left, like, right after, like it was any other night where you had to get home." I open my mouth to protest, but she holds up her hand. "I know you had a curfew. And yeah, your dad probably would have driven up and dragged you out if you missed it. But that's the thing. You just slipped back into regular, reliable Fallon. I was trying to follow your lead. But then I just couldn't. I didn't know how I felt, but I knew it wasn't nothing to me." She takes a breath when her voice cracks. "It sucked to have to get on a plane the next day, you know? To think of you at home with our friends and with that guy, Syed. You said he was cute at the beginning of summer, and then you two were talking the whole night at the bonfire. I saw the way he looked at you, and I knew as soon as I left, he would ask you out. And he did. He did! Tayshia told me. You can't blame me for—"

"What are you saying? You were jealous of some random boy? What, did you like Syed or something?"

"Oh my god. Yeah, that's it, Fal. You figured me out." She shakes her head. "What is wrong with you? Seriously? Is that what you think of me?"

"You had sex with me and then ghosted! What am I supposed to think of you?"

"I didn't ghost! I texted you!"

"I was already there! I was so excited to see you!"

"What did you want me to do, Fallon? I had to go anyway, and you had to stay. Even if I did show up at the diner, it would just have been delaying the inevitable. It was going to suck no matter what. And yeah, it was shitty. I can see that now. But it's not like there ever could have been a good outcome between us anyway," she insists.

And my heart spills to the floor, like a marionette with its strings cut. The realization that this whole future for us that

I made up last summer was so utterly one-sided kills me. I lie back on my pillow, trying to remember how to breathe.

"Come on, if you really thought it was this big, epic thing, I doubt you would have rushed home right after, curfew or not. Maybe I didn't handle it gracefully, but I swear to god I was doing my best, Fallon, and you've been punishing me for it for a year."

"I'm not punishing you. I'm pissed at you."

"What's the difference?"

I rub my hand over my eyes. "You know my dad. If I was even a minute late, I wouldn't have been able to see you the next day, and I wanted that so bad—you and me alone before you left. I couldn't risk being grounded! Not that it ended up mattering anyway," I say, my voice coarse.

Chloe drags her hand through her hair. "Fuck. I didn't realize. I wasn't thinking about it like that. I was just focused on being in the moment, and when we were, you left first."

"Would you have preferred that my dad caught us? That he dragged me out of your tent?"

"Maybe!" she says, and she sounds frustrated. "At least then I would have had some fucking context. Given what happened, I honestly thought giving us some space to reset was the right move for both of us."

"Did you? Or did you just think it was the easiest choice?"

"That's not fair."

"None of this is fair. But maybe if you weren't so worried about 'giving us some space,' we could have talked through

it the next morning and still salvaged a friendship or something."

I swallow down the words I had been so ready to confess
only a little while ago. I realize now this isn't the time for
hands pressed close and whispered declarations of love, past
or present. This is the time for cold hotel floors and truth
exploding into the night sky and drowning out my every
thought.

"Oh, really? Like we talked about it when I got home this
summer? Or even last winter?"

"It was too late by then," I say, and we lapse back into
silence.

"Is it still too late?" she asks.

And I don't say anything, because I don't know.

Chloe sniffs. "I knew this trip would make or break us. At
least we had a little fun tearing it all the way down, though,
didn't we?"

"Yeah," I say quietly, because now I really get it. Now I understand that the entire relationship I built up in my head only
existed in that one moment, in that one tent, and was lost the
second we unzipped it.

It's just sometimes you don't understand that you've lost
something, or that you're in that one final second before it all
goes to shit, until far, far too late.

I wonder what I would have done if I'd known what was
coming for us. I wonder if I'd have kissed her still, just to see
her eyes widen, to feel her mouth shift from surprise to desire.

Would I have gone into the tent if I'd known where we would be a year later?

I want to say no, that I'm better than that. But I think I still would have. And maybe I wouldn't have ever left. Maybe I would have given Chloe that "context" she needed, and everything would have been different.

"Tomorrow's a big day," she says. "I think we should get some sleep."

"Yeah," I say again, not wanting the conversation to end, but also not sure what else there is to say.

"Are you seriously staying down there?" she asks, leaning her head over the edge of the bed so her hair tickles my forehead.

"Yeah, I'm good. It would be weird if we slept together. Not like—I didn't mean *slept together* slept together—I just . . . You know what I mean. You take the bed."

And oh my god, just kill me now.

"Suit yourself," she says. She lies back, and then the room goes silent again, my thoughts swallowing me up.

Approximately five minutes later, Chloe groans. "Oh my god. You are so stubborn." There's a bunch of rustling as she presumably sits up. "Fine." There's more rustling, followed by a swooshing sound as she climbs out of the bed and rips the comforter off. She stomps around the bed close to my spot on the floor and throws down a pillow—a respectful distance away—before lying down in a huff and rolling herself up in the blanket. She has full-on cocooned herself in the comforter, her back to me so I can't even see her face.

"What are you doing?"

"I'm not going to be the asshole who takes the bed."

"What?"

"If you sleep on the floor, then I sleep on the floor."

"You're being ridiculous."

"So are you."

"You can't be serious."

"And you can't be this obstinate, but here we are," she says, freeing one of her arms just long enough to gesture how annoyed she is. She rolls over and studies my face, and I almost, *almost* think she might kiss me. But instead, she shakes her head and flicks me on the nose.

And for a second, she's my old best friend, guiding us out of the danger zone and back to where it's safe. To where we can both pretend things are okay, maybe even long enough to get through the next day. A day we both really, really need to go well.

And I don't know what to do. We do need to talk more, I think. Part of me still wants to tell her exactly how I feel and felt that night.

But not tonight. Not when we just hurt each other in ways that neither of us thought possible. Not now that I know the reason I've been hurting for the last year is because she was hurting too.

And wasn't I the one who kissed her first? The one who leaned her back in the tent, hovering over her until my hair fell around her face, tangling with hers when we brushed noses, once, twice, three times, before pressing our lips together? My guard dropped when she rolled us over, her eyes darker, her lopsided grin changing into something wilder, something hungry that sent a shiver ghosting over my skin when I said, "Yes, yes, like that."

And she's right. Curfew or not, I was the one who left that night and left this night and left so many nights in between.

But I can't say any of that when she's lying there wrapped up like a burrito in someone else's blanket, in someone else's room, begging me for a laugh, waiting for me to say that we're okay—that we can be okay. That we're in the after now, but maybe the after doesn't have to be so awful.

Tomorrow is a big day, the biggest, and I owe it to my mother and Carmen to do my best, and so does she. And so I laugh, loud and fake, but hope it doesn't sound that way to her.

# TWENTY-TWO

*I* nuzzle against the body beneath me, a smile spreading across my face. I shift slightly, greedily inhaling the familiar scent of Chloe's sleep-warmed skin, snuggling in a little bit more before my brain catches up to my body.

I jerk back, wide-eyed.

A laugh rumbles up from Chloe's chest, an easy smile on her face, her hands tucked carefully behind her head on the pillow, like she's worried about touching me or maybe fighting the urge. "Morning," she says when our eyes meet.

"Oh my god, I'm so sorry." I wipe at the wetness on my cheek, and it hits me with a stomach-sinking realization that I drooled on her. A dark patch, no doubt soaked with my saliva, stains the shoulder of her shirt where my head once rested. "That's so gross. I did not mean to do that."

"It's not a big deal. You were sleeping."

"Why didn't you shove me off?" I run my hands through my hair, trying to untangle it. "This is so embarrassing. Oh my god."

"Oh my god yourself," she says. "This is hardly the first time I've had your spit on me."

I know she's talking about the billion times she's made me spit out my drinks over the years, timing her jokes and tickling me just right so that I spew Hi-C or shoot chocolate milk out of my nose. But right now, staring at her sleepy, cozy face, all I can think about is kissing.

What is wrong with me? And can it be fixed?

I look away before I do something I regret.

Yeah, yeah, I know. You want me to tell her right now that maybe my feelings are not completely gone. Or maybe you think this is some kind of simple, easy love story where morning breath and real-life consequences aren't a thing and I should pounce on her, kiss her, pull those hands from behind her head. But you gotta know I can't. Not really. Definitely not now.

We're not a simple, easy love story. And I still need to brush my teeth.

But then her eyes snag on mine, like a magnet to metal, like we're on a collision course, ripping through time and space—screw making logical choices; screw "it's not that deep." Her brow furrows, and I wonder if she feels it too.

But it's also possible she's just wondering why I'm still staring at her.

My phone lights up and starts buzzing on the floor beside me, yanking me out of whatever moment-slash-memory I was trapped in. It's Mom.

Chloe purses her lips and lets out a sigh. "You should probably get that." She hops up, kicking her blankets off. "I gotta pee."

I close my eyes, trying to shake it off, trying to erase the scent of her skin from my brain, trying to erase everything because—

"Today's the day!" Mom says cheerily when I click on her call. And it's waaaaaaay too early for this.

"Hi, Mom," I say, stretching wearily and rolling my shoulders. My back feels stiff, my legs aching from yet another night spent on the ground. Waking up next to Chloe wasn't exactly the worst thing, though. But I definitely could have done without the drool.

"Are you guys up? Don't tell me you were still asleep!" Mom says incredulously.

It's only eight a.m., and check-in doesn't even start until eleven. It's not like we're behind schedule.

"Yeah, it was a late night." I leave out the reason why and the fact that we both ditched the expensive hotel bed in favor of sleeping on the floor. "We got in late, I mean, after setting up the truck and taking inventory and stuff," I say, correcting myself. I don't want her to worry. I want her to know I'm taking this seriously. I *am* taking this seriously.

"Mm-hmm," she says, like she doesn't quite believe me. I'm sure whatever she's imagining—hitting the minibar, going out and trying to find a place that would let us in without IDs, or I don't know, streaking through the streets of Memphis while setting off fireworks—is way more fun than the reality of awkward conversations and sleeping on the floor.

Switching gears seems appropriate. "What's up? How are things in Dallas?" I put her on speaker so I can start to get ready.

"They're good," she says, brushing me off. "Have you checked on the truck yet this morning?" And ah, that's what she's worried about: a repeat of the other night. I don't blame her.

I walk to the window, pull back the curtain, the harsh morning light streaming in, and peer down at the parking lot. The truck, completely unscathed, is right where I left it, beside the trusty lamppost.

"It's good," I reassure her. "I can see it from here. We're just getting dressed, and then we're going to go finalize all the pre-event stuff. I got everything counted and organized last night before bed, so we're in good shape and ready to go. I definitely have this under control," I say, letting myself feel good about that, even if "current waffle cone inventory" is the *only* thing I have under control.

"Good," she says. "And Chloe?"

"Yeah, she's got everything under control too."

My mom laughs, which makes me feel like I'm missing something. "I'm sure she does. But I meant how are things with you and Chloe?"

"They're fine," I say, not sure how else to answer.

"Fine is a huge improvement," she says. "I knew this trip would be good for you two."

♥

EVEN THOUGH THE event doesn't start until one p.m., we have to be there two hours early for check-in and location assignment.

I told Chloe I didn't mind driving. I told her it was fine if she just read her book on the way and let me handle it.

I lied. I've done FFAC before with my mom, but even so, I'm a jumble of nerves. The sigh I let out when I finally ease the truck up to the first checkpoint outside the gates is loud enough to make Chloe shut her book.

The guard at the table gets up off his chair and gestures for me to put down my window. He's a squat white man, probably in his late forties or early fifties, complete with a rent-a-cop mustache and a tan uniform that I can tell makes him feel like a tough guy. He's even got a little metal badge that glints in the sunlight. I wonder if this is part of the toxic masculinity starter pack or if you have to level up to get it.

"Vendor?" he asks, as if the name isn't printed in giant letters all over the truck.

"Um, Love at First Bite ice cream truck," I mumble.

He rolls his eyes like I said something ridiculous and marks it down. "Yeah, I figured." He waves his clipboard at the side of the truck as if he wasn't the one who just asked.

I slink down in my seat a little as he radios the second checkpoint, the one where we'll get our location assignment for the day, and then he walks back to the table to get a packet and some lanyards.

"You're all set," he says. "Drive up to the second table. You got ten minutes there before you need to clear out so I can send the next one down. You got any questions for the organizer, ask them quick. Guides and rules and maps are all in this packet, along with your passes. Don't lose them. They aren't replaceable, and if you get caught without them or an entry bracelet, you'll be removed, no matter how much you beg."

*Bracelets. Right,* I think. I remember last year when some local jeweler was a sponsor. Instead of the traditional neon wristbands, everybody got a little silver bangle. They must be back this year. Mom says the point is to make these rich donors feel like they're doing a good thing, while still having something to show for it. Does charity even count if no one sees you do it?

I take the packet, and now it's my turn to roll my eyes, trying really hard not to think about the fact that this so-called charity event costs eight hundred dollars for a pair of VIP tickets, hands out jewelry like candy, and pays my mom a ridiculous amount of money for a single day's work.

I pass the folder over to Chloe, who sets to work trying to get the VENDOR tag clipped onto a delicate lace lanyard while I drive down to the back of the lot. A second table is set up there, with a harried-looking volunteer posted behind it. She doesn't look that much older than us, and I realize it's Delilah. I knew she would be here, since her mom is the organizer; I just didn't think she'd be working it.

"So, you got roped into this too, huh?" I ask, and Delilah looks up from the papers in front of her, startled.

"Fallon?!" Her face breaks into a grin. We may only see each other once a year or so, and we may suck at keeping up with texts, but whenever we're together, it's like we never missed a beat.

"Hey, D!"

"Oh my god, check-in is the worrrrst," she says, walking over with her clipboard, a glittery pink affair. "Is your mom here?"

"No, just us." Chloe leans over, reaching her hand over me to try to shake Delilah's. "I'm Chloe," she says, "co-owner."

Wait, is she jealous?

"Kid of the co-owner," I clarify. "And Chloe, this is Delilah."

"Ohh, Delilah," Chloe says, recognition dawning on her face, because, of course, I've mentioned her before. "I've heard sooooooo much about you."

"Only good things, I hope," Delilah says, her hostess training kicking in.

"I wouldn't go that far."

I smack Chloe's arm, and Delilah flashes her a look before going back to only addressing me. Her hand rests on the side of the truck, over the unrolled window, her fingers lightly brushing my forearm as she flips through the maps. "Right, um, if you're not too slammed later, Fal, maybe we can sneak out for—"

"We'll probably be extremely busy," Chloe says, but when I shoot her a look, she adds, "but, uh, if you really want to go, Fal, then whatever."

I turn back toward Delilah. "I don't know how today'll go, but maybe. It would be fun to catch up."

"Don't we just have ten minutes here?" Chloe asks, batting her eyelashes innocently—or as innocently as she can when it's blatantly obvious that she's being a brat.

"Um, right," Delilah says, looking back at her clipboard. "Okay, well, you're at E6. Do you have your map?"

Chloe fumbles with the folder, pulling out the map with a flourish. "Right here. You know what they say about me. Always prepared."

"No one has ever said that about you, but thanks," I say, passing the map to Delilah, who takes a bright red Sharpie and draws an X over a spot. It's a great spot; I'm positive Delilah's mom, Clare, made sure of that. It's right in the middle of the busiest part, but far enough from the art displays that people won't skip us for fear of dripping all over something expensive.

"I'll come by when I'm done here, if you want?" Delilah asks almost shyly.

Beside me, Chloe chokes on her coffee, and I pretend not to notice.

"Yeah, that would be awesome."

"Cool," she says, and then we both just stare at each other for a second, not sure what else to do.

"Well, we should go set up," Chloe says, leaning over to pull the map out of my hand.

"Right," I say, shifting the truck into drive. "I'll, um, see you later?"

Delilah smiles. "Definitely."

# TWENTY-THREE

*S*o, *she's* in love with you, obviously," Chloe says after we've parked the truck and climbed into the back to get organized.

"Oh my god, she is not." I'm arranging the sprinkles display station on the counter and setting out the menus. "It's definitely not that deep," I tease, but that just makes Chloe's scowl deepen.

"Not funny," she says.

We check the freezers next, dropping scoops into each fresh bucket of ice cream and triple-checking the quantities in storage. Mom and Carmen are heading to a local creamery in Texas today to get the flavors set before the Dallas festival, so we're free and clear to use up everything here without worry. If we had to save enough ice cream for Dallas, it would mean turning away a lot of unhappy customers at the end of the day.

"We only have two buckets of Blueberry Burning Love!"

Chloe says. "It's the special! I thought we had three. Shit."

"Check under the extra All Shook Up sprinkles. I know it's there," I say. "And trust me, there's nothing between me and Delilah. I've known her since we were kids."

"Found it!" She shuts the freezer and adds a tally to the inventory notebook before sticking the pencil behind her ear. "And what does that matter? You've known me since we were kids too," she says, and we both stare at each other with wide eyes.

"Okay, new pact," I say, sticking my pinkie in the air.

"New pact?"

"Mm-hmm," I say, blushing furiously. "We are not going to talk about what happened last summer or last night. Please?"

She huffs. "Ever?"

"No," I say, clearly frazzled. "We're sticking a pin in it until after . . . I don't know. Just not now or at this event. Deal? We can't screw this up, and I can't be freaking out about . . ."

"About?"

"Please, Chlo. Deal? Just for today?" I extend my hand for the ultimate of promises: the dreaded pinkie swear.

"Fine," she says, hooking her pinkie with mine as she looks me in the eyes. "Till after. But are you hanging out with that girl later?"

"Why, you jealous?" I tease.

She freezes for a second before letting out a little laugh. "Nope, not talking about it," she says. "Consider it part of the pact. Subsection A." And then she goes back to setting up the toppings station.

"Subsection A?" I ask, but she doesn't answer.

I bump her with my hip to wipe the tense look off her face. Today is supposed to be light. Today *needs* to be light. Today is about scooping ice cream and being, well, friendly. Whatever feelings we're catching or caught or lost or found again will have to wait. Possibly forever, depending on how emotionally constipated we both want to be about this.

Chloe bumps me back, and we both erupt into giggles, pushing and shoving right as Clare walks up. I haven't seen my mom's old college roommate since last year, and I'm worried this is maybe not the best impression to be making on our first solo trip.

"Girls," she says, smiling warmly, but there's a hint of something in her eyes. Mistrust, maybe? Worry we'll ruin her event or ruin Mom's reputation? Or maybe even all of the above? Sure, she let us come without our moms, but that was a favor.

Chloe and I straighten up fast.

"Clare," I say, hopping out of the truck and smoothing my apron. "How are you?"

Clare air-kisses both of my cheeks, and I try not to squirm. She's done that as long as I've known her. My mom gets a kick out of the Ohio farm girl who made some cash and started air-kissing people like a European model or whatever, but I never liked it. It feels fake. I clutch her arms, weakly moving my head from side to side, and I paste a big, fake grin on my face when she leans back to get a look at me.

"My, you've grown so much this year," she says. "College this fall, right? I can't believe it."

I nod, and she turns her attention to Chloe. "And you must be Carmen's daughter," she says. "So nice to finally meet you. I've heard a lot about you."

Chloe blows her a kiss and then curtseys, which seems to puzzle Clare, and I fight off the urge to laugh. Chloe has never been one for honorifics or fake niceties. But our moms need this money, so I stand a little taller, prepared for whatever hoops Clare may require us to jump through.

"Are you ready for today?" she asks. "I promised your mothers I'd be keeping an eye on you both, and I'll be sending Delilah over frequently to see if there's anything you need."

"Great," Chloe mumbles behind me.

"Your moms reviewed the setup with you, right, Fallon? The patrons paid in advance, so there won't be any money exchanged, but we do encourage cash tipping. Be sure to keep your jar out, and empty it regularly. People are less likely to tip a too-full jar. But too empty, they'll think you haven't done anything worthy of a bonus. They're also allowed to leave ratings and electronic tips on our app, which will be directly deposited into your moms' business account. You two don't need to worry about that at all. I'll text your mother the statement tomorrow morning so she knows what to expect. Final payment to bring our balance current will process at the end of next week, assuming there are no issues today."

I don't miss how pointedly she says that last part. "There won't be, I promise," I say, the thought of Mom not getting the second half of the payment making my stomach churn.

"Excellent. And we've advertised the exclusive flavor that your mother made for us, Blueberry Burning Love, correct? I would expect a major run on that."

"Oh yeah, it's phenomenal," I say. "I helped her taste test it when she was still developing the flavor. You won't believe how good it is."

"Now that you mention it, I barely had breakfast today." Clare smiles.

"Yeah, you should totally come get some later."

Clare looks at me as if she's waiting for something. I smile politely.

"Here you go," Chloe says, carrying a scoop of ice cream in a perfect chocolate-dipped waffle cone to the window. She adds an extra splash of All Shook Up sprinkles and presents it to Clare with a smile. "Breakfast of champions."

And okay, maybe I'm not the only one willing to jump through hoops for the sake of our moms. I smile at Chloe, relieved, as Clare takes it. I can't believe I didn't pick up on that.

"Thank you," Clare says. "I make it a point to sample all the exclusive offerings that are here today in advance, but ice cream is obviously much harder to ship. I've been dying to try it." She takes a bite and lets out a groan of delight, which she promptly looks embarrassed by. "Heavenly, as always," she says. "Your mothers never disappoint." Her phone buzzes, and she checks the screen. "Oh no, there's an issue at the pancake truck. I have to go." She hands me her card. "Call my cell if you need anything. And like I said, Delilah will be on hand all day, eager to help with anything. Feel free to text her as well."

"Will do!" I smile as she walks away.

"So eager to help *you*. With *anything*," Chloe teases when I climb back into the truck. "I bet she would service you any way you—"

"Okaaay." I laugh, snapping a towel at her. "Come on, let's finish setting up."

♥

IF I'M BEING honest, in all the times that I've choreographed what FFAC would look like for me and Chloe in my head, it was never like this. I was sure it would be tense, awkward, horrible, the worst time with the worst person. Best-case scenario? We would tolerate each other long enough to pull it off. Worst-case scenario? You don't even want to know. Think lots of yelling and waffle cone throwing.

But as we finish setting up and the first customers start to trickle in around one p.m., I realize it might just shape up to be something else entirely. Something not just different, but better.

We're situated in the center of the event space, so it takes a minute for people to start getting to us. It's lunchtime—well, more or less—and they seem to have come hungry, their silver bangles glinting on their wrists, a tiny "admit one" charm dangling off each one. Again, I try not to think too hard about where all that money could have gone instead. I glance at Chloe, her elbows on the counter and a scowl on her face, and I wonder if she's thinking about the same thing.

Probably.

She catches me looking at her, a small smile pulling at her lips when we make eye contact. "What?" she asks, scrunching up her face.

"Nothing," I say, pretending to wipe up a nonexistent spot on the counter.

"You're such a weirdo." Her voice is soft, and even though her words are jokey and teasing, it feels like she's saying something else entirely.

"Can I get the, uh, Blueberry Burning Love," a man says, and we snap to attention. Our first customer. We want to set the bar high.

I pull out the chocolate-dipped waffle cone while Chloe pops open the freezer and drags the cold metal scoop through the ice cream. She deposits the perfectly round scoop into the cone. It looks like something in an ad. She adds a second scoop on top, and then I add the sprinkles.

The man takes a taste and then pops a ten-dollar bill

into the tip jar before disappearing into the quickly growing crowd.

The first hour continues on like that, people coming and going, their bedazzled wrists shining in the sunlight. The tips pile up. Some people put in twenties, and many people put in fives and tens. One person even puts in a hundred-dollar bill, and my eyes nearly bug out of my head. "Enjoy, kid," the woman says before drifting off, and I practically faint.

"Let me guess," Chloe says, her hip against the counter, the faintest sheen of sweat on her face after we work our way through a particularly long line of customers. "They're letting you keep the tips in exchange for putting up with me?"

"As a college present," I clarify, even though she doesn't look convinced. "Same as you."

"I didn't get the whole tip jar. My mom was afraid I would blow it all."

"Oh," I say, like I'm surprised. Chloe can barely remember to keep her phone charged. Trusting her with hundreds of dollars right from the jump probably wouldn't have gone well at all.

"Well, maybe they'll do that to me too," I say. I don't know why. We both know they won't.

"Are you honestly telling me they didn't bribe you even a little bit to work with me?"

"I thought we weren't talking about it," I say, even though that's not an answer. I realize too late what I've implied.

Chloe's lips quirk to the side with a little nod. "Am I really all that bad?" she asks, but before I can answer, Delilah appears at the counter.

"How's it going?" Delilah looks around, taking in our temporary break from customers. "Has it been this quiet? Do you need me to funnel more people over here?" But then she notices the money in our tip jar, which is nearly overflowing. "Guess not."

"Nah." I scoop up the jar to take care of it, remembering Clare's warning to not let it get too full. "Just a few minutes' break right now, thank god."

"Yeah, thank god," Chloe echoes, coming up behind me. "Or you two wouldn't have time to talk." She takes the jar out of my hands and carries it over to the cashbox, unlocking it and dumping the money in without even attempting to sort it.

"And wouldn't that be the worst?" Delilah says. I think she's trying to be funny or suggestive, but it falls flat.

I'm grateful when a customer appears and breaks the tension. I move to take her order, but Chloe lightly pushes me aside. "I got this," she says. "Enjoy catching up with *Delilah*."

There's an edge to that last word—a bitterness that makes me want to grab her and yell, "I like you, you absolute dipshit." But I can't do that. Not in front of a customer anyway, and definitely not in front of Delilah either. Maybe not even in front of Chloe. What am I even thinking?

Chloe takes the woman's order. The Elvis Special. Again.

Very on theme, very predictable, but what else do you expect from people with this much money and time to waste?

"How long are you in town?" Delilah asks.

I swear Chloe scoffs beside me, but I suppose it could have been a coincidental clearing of the throat that happened to occur at the exact second Delilah was dancing around her cute little remix of "you come here often?"

"Just for the night. Tomorrow we have to move on to meet our moms for the Dallas Food Truck Festival. We only have one day between events. They're already there, so we kind of have to rush."

"Mom said you're going to UT Austin in the fall, though, right?"

"Um, yeah." I nod.

"Me too. Well, near there. I'm right at Southwestern. We'll practically be neighbors."

"Oh cool," I say, glad that I'll at least know *someone* around there.

"Yeah, so we should definitely catch up. If you're free after cleanup, I could show you around town. How the locals do it. We could figure out some plans for fall too. It's going to be awesome!"

Beside me, Chloe shoves the freezer lid open so hard, it slams. Her customer and I make eye contact, and I hope she catches the apology in my eyes. All I need is one of Clare's clients to give us a low rating or complain.

Chloe mumbles an apology for startling the customer but steadfastly does not look my way. I can tell by the pink of her cheeks that she knows I heard and knows I'm looking at her. My eyes catch on her biceps as she scoops the ice cream from the barrel, flexing and relaxing as she scrapes and tugs and finally drops yet another perfect scoop into the cone in her other hand.

I'd be tempted to whip my phone out and start filming, if it wouldn't make me a grade A creeper. Pull it together, girl. Now is not the time to be mesmerized by—

"Fallon?" Delilah calls, and I snap my eyes back to her.

The customer stuffs a five-dollar bill in the now mostly empty tip jar and scurries off, leaving the three of us alone again. *Wait,* I want to say, or *Take me with you.*

Because Delilah is cute. Cute and uncomplicated. I could spend this night having fun with her, and it would be easy. It would be so easy. And I'd be near her in the fall, instead of separated by multiple states. It would be so much easier than whatever this is with Chloe, who has moved on to sulking on the far side of the counter, as far away from me as she can get without physically removing herself from the truck.

"You can bring your friend," Delilah offers, her eyes flicking between me and Chloe. But before I can answer, her phone goes off in her hand, signaling a flurry of new texts. "Shit, it's my mom." She frowns. "I guess there's some drama near the cereal truck. I have to go help, but seriously, let me know? I'd love to take you out."

"Yeah," I say, wondering what kind of drama there can actually be by a cereal truck. Did they run out of milk? Did someone leave out an empty box? I open my mouth to joke about it with Chloe, but a sudden rush of customers keeps us taking orders and scooping and sprinkling as fast as we can for the next hour.

The mood in the truck has quickly gone from friendly to strained, whether because Delilah came to visit and not-so-nonchalantly asked me to go out with her tonight or because neither of us slept well, I don't know. I have my suspicions, though.

"Excuse me," Chloe says, leaning over to scoop in front of me. She goes out of her way to make sure her bare arm brushes right against my hand, her hot skin pressing against the backs of my freezer-cooled fingers, and damned if all common sense doesn't fly right out of my head. There's that bicep again—that goddamn bicep flexing, and, wow, I need to get a grip.

The smirk on her lips tells me that she knows exactly what she's doing.

I wait until a few minutes later, when she's busy helping another customer and least expects it, to brush my hip against her as I squeeze past to get to the Pink Blush whipped cream my mom makes special for the I'll Have What She's Having split.

Chloe freezes, her entire body going tense for one glorious second as she stumbles over her words, mistakenly saying "I'll Have What She's Hot" instead of "I'll Have What She's

Having" while running through the list of available flavors with a customer. So awkward. I try not to laugh, spraying extra whipped cream with a little smirk.

Exhausted, we finally get another blissful break from customers, and I resist the urge to collapse on the floor. My fingers are freezing, and my hair is coated with a sheen of sweat under my little serving cap-slash-hairnet. Thank god for industrial-strength deodorant. Chloe leans against the counter while I sit on one of the boxes filled with spare napkin inventory. One of us always has to be up front, per the written rules in the FFAC packet.

Chloe stretches out her shoulders. "I'm gonna go get some food while it's quiet. You want anything?"

"I'd love . . ." I say, sniffing the air. Because I don't even know—Italian, Mexican, both? "I'd love to cross Tennessee spaghetti off the list, and if it's not too much trouble, a chicken taco."

She looks at me weird—I know, my cravings make no sense—but then grabs her vendor pass lanyard and yanks it over her head with a determined look. "Sure, one spaghetti and one taco coming up."

Chloe has barely been gone fifteen minutes when Delilah comes back, her grin ratcheting up when she sees we're alone.

"Where's your friend?" she asks.

"Getting us food."

"I would have done that for you." She laughs. "It's literally what I'm here for."

"No worries," I say.

Which is the exact moment Chloe returns, looking so cute with a container of spaghetti from Scola La Pasta and a giant bag from Guac and Roll. Her face falls when she sees Delilah.

"Hey," I say, trying to break the tension.

Chloe nods and gets into the truck, heading to the back to set up the food and plasticware. "Got your lunch," she says sheepishly.

"Have you two given any more thought to going out tonight?" Delilah reaches for me as I turn, her fingers rubbing circles on my hand. "Come on. We'd have fun."

But before I can answer, Chloe's behind me, handing me a napkin, which is weird because I already have a pile next to me. She whispers fast and hard in my ear, "Don't go with her. Go with me."

And thank god for that second napkin, because I immediately knock over the ones beside me.

Chloe walks back to her food like nothing happened, and if it wasn't for the look on her face when I say, "Sorry, Delilah, I kind of have plans with Chloe already," I would have thought I imagined it.

Delilah, to her credit, only looks a little put out, and she covers it well as she turns to leave. "Too bad, but at least I'll have you all to myself this fall."

Chloe watches her go before gesturing for me to come over, opening up my container of spaghetti and pulling out my taco with a little smile. We eat in a comfortable silence, taking turns inhaling our food and serving customers, everything light and smooth.

I had forgotten how easy it could be with Chloe sometimes.

But I'm starting to remember.

# TWENTY-FOUR

*B*y the time the event starts winding down, I'm already a jumble of nerves wondering what tonight will bring. And by the time the gates close and we're actually deep into cleanup, I swear to god I have manifested into pure electricity.

I think Chloe feels it too, the way our hips keep sliding and bumping against each other as we work. The way she puts her hand on my lower back whenever she has to get by. Every touch a zing of nerves, every smile a hard-won victory, and every time our eyes meet? Forget it.

It grows inside me, this joy and *wanting*. I feel tense and tight, like a weighted branch about to snap, thrilled by the little bit of jealousy and the way the words "go with me" sent chills all the way to my toes. The anticipation feels toe-curling good but also sort of makes me want to scream. Because what happens when we're alone, finally, away from this place and

Delilah and Clare and all the Elvis superfans asking for extra Blueberry Burning Love?

What will it mean?

And if it means nothing, if it's just another bubble in another place and time that we won't escape from unscathed, do I even care? Maybe one more perfect moment can be enough if we both know the rules from the jump. A do-over on my own terms doesn't sound so bad. It doesn't have to be a happily ever after; sometimes closure is enough.

"You ready?" Chloe asks, her eyes soft as she pulls off her little Love at First Bite hat. She unpins her hair, which falls in loose waves around her face. My own hair is a jumble of frizz and knots after being trapped in a hairnet all day; I've never had the patience for bobby pins. But somehow, despite all that, she's looking at me the same way I'm looking at her.

Like it feels so good and hurts all at once.

I rub my lips together, because this is it, and I know it. This is me giving in, giving up. This is me falling under her spell again, utterly, even if only for a night.

I could fight it if I wanted to. I could go back to the hotel and go to bed. I could remind her she's behind on her schoolwork. She would look hurt, and I would feel sick, but maybe we could go back to being ex-best friends and friendly coworkers. Maybe we could swallow down the electricity between us, grounding it beneath the soles of our comfy old sneakers.

Maybe.

Chloe waits, not pressing, letting me decide.

And when I say, "Yeah," her face spills into the most beautiful smile I've ever seen, and all I can think is *Finally, finally* and *What if one more moment isn't enough, could never be enough? Screw closure, I—*

Chloe's smile falters, and I snap my head in the direction she's looking. Delilah and Clare are standing at the counter, looking friendly and normal and as unobtrusive as possible for two people who've just inadvertently walked up on what is potentially the moment to end all moments.

"Just wanted to check in and say good night," Clare says cheerfully. "Thank you so much for coming today. I know it was hard with your mom stuck in Dallas." She sounds sincere, apologetic almost, as if we were doing her a favor rather than the other way around.

I realize with a start that maybe we were. That maybe Mom's truck is getting so much traction lately, getting so revered in little hipster food circles, that having us come here—even the B-team crew—was some kind of status symbol for her. Maybe putting us right in the middle of the action wasn't because she was doing us a favor but because we were a draw. And god, I want that so bad for my mom and Carmen. They deserve it. I really hope we made them proud today.

"Did you girls need anything before you head out?" Clare

asks, and the lights from a departing food truck make her hair look like a halo.

"No, we're good," I say. "We're just about to leave ourselves."

"You sure I can't show you around, Fal?" Delilah asks, but Chloe interrupts, stepping forward a little and sizing Delilah up.

"We're gonna get some food, and then I've got a lot of schoolwork to do tonight," Chloe says, like that explains why I can't come out either. Delilah just flicks her eyes to mine.

"I'm just going to hang out with her," I say. "We've got a long, early drive tomorrow."

"How responsible of you," Clare says fondly before nudging her daughter. "It wouldn't hurt you to take things a little more seriously too."

Delilah rolls her eyes. "Sounds boring, but have fun, I guess."

♥

OUR CURRENT PLAN, per Chloe, is to go get cleaned up back at the room and then head out. But now that we're almost there, now that it's just us, I'm worried some of the spell has been broken. Not enough to keep me from desperately hoping we can still spend time together, but enough that I realize if she's got another paper to do or something, we can always make out later.

*Hang out* later! I meant *hang* out. God, you people.

Still, I would like to hit the shower and brush my teeth before we do either. I really, really regret eating that garlic breadstick that came with my spaghetti now.

"Do you really have a lot of schoolwork tonight?" I ask.

"Nothing that can't wait," Chloe says, pulling into the same parking spot we used last night. Well lit, visible from our room, security camera pointing right at it. Take no chances.

It's kind of wild to think how it was only yesterday morning that we were scrubbing stuff off the truck and arguing.

Only yesterday that Esther hinted I should go with the flow a little more.

"When's it due?" I ask, the tiny voice in my head saying that she should be taking her classes more seriously.

"Don't worry about it."

"One of us should, though." And I mean it in a light-hearted way, but her eyes go hard. I've struck a nerve. "Sorry," I say, not wanting to ruin the mood. "I was kidding. Sort of. But if you need to get something done, like, if you have something due for one of your classes, it wouldn't be the worst thing. I could wait for you to finish, or we could get takeout. We don't even have to go any—"

Her warm hand pressing against my lips cuts me off. I think about biting it. And then I think about kissing it. And now it's just all jumbled up—fighting and kissing and being confused—the way it's been with us for nearly a year.

"We are going out, and we are having fun," she says, her voice steady. "It's our last night in an awesome place without our parents. I'm not spending it doing homework."

She pulls her hand away, a stern look on her face that gives way to a smile. I laugh and shake my head, trying to push down any doubt, any worry about her and her grades, about anything but the here and now.

I'm trying to be present.

To go with the flow.

To "it's not that deep" all over the place with her.

"Are you sure?" I ask again on the elevator ride up to our room. Just one final time and I'll stop, I swear.

"I'm sure," she says as we walk to the door.

Chloe inserts the key card, glancing up at me, and whatever she sees in my face makes her annoyance give way to something softer. Much softer.

"Fal," she says quietly. "I don't want you worrying all night about my homework. New deal: We go out tonight, have fun for a little while, and then tomorrow, we get up early, and I'll let you drive while I do my homework. I promise nothing will be late, and I'll get it all done, as long as you give me this night. Okay?" She holds up her pinkie.

"Okay," I say, linking mine with hers and feeling about one thousand times lighter.

We make quick work of getting showered and ready and calling our moms to spill all the details and let them know tomorrow's ETA. It's a short call but a good one—everyone's feeling really great about how the day went; Clare even called Mom already—and before I know it, we're in an Uber heading downtown to some club Chloe found that's eighteen and over.

Some country band I've never heard of is playing their hearts out up on the small stage. The music is loud, and it's hard to breathe with the smell of everyone's sweat and cheap alcohol mixing. It's too hot and too sticky, and I'd hate every second of it if I wasn't with *her*.

But I am with her, and I'm living in the moment—trying to, anyway. Because I don't want to be like Esther; I don't want to have regrets about the adventures I never went on. Even if Esther did end up in a good place, what did she miss along the way?

And Chloe's making plans and being responsible—trying to, anyway.

Isn't that just what we both wanted for each other all along? We can never go back to the before, but maybe our after can be even better, because *we're* better. And if that's true, I don't want to miss a thing.

Chloe's dancing behind me, and before I can stop myself, I spin around and reach out, my hands on her hips, moving us in unison. She tips her head down, studying me, still dancing to the music, before pulling me close. Her cheek glides up into a smile against my temple, a smile that I put there. And if I just tilted my head the slightest bit, and if she just turned hers . . .

But instead, we dance.

"**What are you** going to do with all that cash you got to-day? Save it for textbooks and, like, responsible khaki pants?" Chloe teases as we walk back to the hotel. It's only six blocks, so the idea that we wasted money on an Uber earlier has low-key bothered me all night. I'm relieved that she agreed we could walk back.

"No khakis, but definitely textbooks and living expenses." She nods as if to say, *I told you so.*

"*But* I'm also going on a trip with Jami. A big part of why I agreed to do this was to pay her back. She fronted all the money, so I was pretty screwed for a minute there. We're going to go check out the cathedrals in Montreal. You know, where Adya Mulroney filmed—"

"*Too Dead to Die.*" Chloe laughs. "Look at you, letting loose."

"Something like that." Although I'm not entirely sure that a field trip to Montreal to visit cathedrals and stuff really counts as letting loose, even if they *are* filming locations.

"I knew I'd rub off on you," she teases. "Finally. Part of me was worried you were going to say you were saving the money for retirement or something."

"That's not a bad thing," I snort. "You could stand to be a little more like me sometimes too. Admit it."

"So my mom always says."

I don't know what to say to that, so I don't say anything. I was just joking, but the look on her face makes me feel like I've walked onto a land mine.

"Well, she's gotta be happy you're taking things seriously now," I say, and Chloe looks at me, confused. "Getting a jump on summer classes and stuff? Tutoring people, even! That's pretty cool."

"Yeah, so," Chloe says nervously, "the truth is, I'm not getting a jump on things. I actually kind of messed up."

"Oh," I say softly. "How? I mean, if you want to tell me."

Chloe rubs the back of her neck and looks away. "I need those summer classes; they're not extra. And I'm not tutoring people either. That's just what I wanted you to think. I'm the one getting extra help. I have to retake both of the classes I failed last semester to have a chance at saving my GPA. It's kind of a nightmare."

"You failed?" I ask before I can stop myself.

"Technically, I withdrew at the last minute, so I have a W, not an F in one of them, but yeah, not great."

"What happened? Your mom always made it sound like you were doing great."

"Biology was just really boring, so that's on me. But the other I had to stop going to."

"Because?"

"Okay, so there was this guy I hooked up with who thought one night after a frat party meant we were, like, married or something. We had English together, and it was way too weird. He acted like I did something horrible to him when—" She looks at me then, my eyes wide. "Shit."

I huff out a little sigh and keep walking. It's all I can do.

"It's not the same thing. That's not like . . . That wasn't how I felt about you!" Chloe grabs my arm, spinning me around to face her. "It wasn't like what happened with you, I swear."

I open my mouth to say something—*It's fine,* maybe? I don't even know. But then she keeps talking.

"I've been thinking a lot about what we talked about—and in no way am I trying to let myself off the hook; like, I'll happily apologize forever for what happened between us. But do you think it's possible to be hurt by something even if it doesn't necessarily mean the other person did something to hurt you?"

She looks at me, so lost, so sad. And I don't know what to say. *Yes? No? A little of both?* We screwed this up in so many ways that I don't know what the right answer is, but I know what I want it to be right now.

"I think yeah, maybe," I say, and a relieved breath whooshes out of her, like I absolved her of her sins or something, but I'm not done. "But I also think that you have to consider other people sometimes, and our feelings. Maybe you don't owe everyone that—I don't know what the deal was with that guy in your class—but I think there are definitely some people that you do."

*Like me,* I want to scream. *I should have mattered. My feelings should have been considered when you bailed on me. You shouldn't have just decided for the both of us that what we needed was space.*

*Just because you were the center of my world doesn't mean you were the only one who mattered.*

"I'm so sorry," she says, her breath coming out a near whisper as she wraps me in a tight hug. "Fallon, I . . ."

I hesitate but then hug her back.

I was always going to.

# TWENTY-FIVE

*T*he ride in the elevator back up to our room is tense. We both keep looking at each other, daring the other to make a move with our eyes.

My head is a tangled mess of threads, and if I tug too hard, I'm worried it'll all come crashing down. But I know, right now, in this moment, what I want. Without a doubt.

I want Chloe. In a no-strings-attached, on-my-own-terms kind of way. Full circle but better. If this is our one moment to do it over, I want it, even if it all fades in the light of morning. And I'm sure it will. This is me choosing the tent all over again, even knowing the outcome.

Judging by the way Chloe slides her gaze over me, sending shivers over my skin, I think she feels the same. Every cell in my body is urging me on, searching her face for the green light. Chloe leans against the elevator wall, a little pout on her lips that she wipes away with a swipe of her very pink tongue, and then raises her eyebrows like *Game on.*

And that's all it takes for me to pounce, landing in her arms, feeling her laugh as I kiss her, as her hands squeeze anything they can reach.

The elevator dings, and we stumble past a scandalized old white couple. I just kiss her harder against the wall, swallowing her laughs as she walks me backward, presses me against the door to our room, and shoves in the key card. It takes three tries with trembling fingers before it finally unlocks, and we fall into the room, laughing so hard we lose our balance.

I climb onto the bed, eager—so eager. Nobody's sleeping on the floor tonight. She tosses the key card on the desk and stalks toward me, my toes curling in anticipation.

Chloe jumps onto the bed, caging me between her forearms and dipping her head onto my shoulder. She takes a few heavy breaths, the air tickling my neck, and then she sits back onto her knees.

Her pupils are dilated, her cheeks flushed, her hands flexed and ready to go, but her face is tentative. I sit up, fully ready to kiss that look right off her face, but she gently presses me back down.

"What is this to you?" Chloe asks, her voice quiet, huskier and more breathless than normal. And I love, love, love that sound. I want to live in that sound forever.

"Whatever we want it to be," I say, and I absolutely mean it. I don't know if tonight is a "hello" or a "goodbye" or what she's thinking, but I know I want this either way. That this is my decision.

I'm here. Now. My eyes are open.

Tomorrow, we could get to Dallas and go our separate ways. Or we could not. But either way, it's okay. It will be okay. A grand finale to the joy and pain. Better than anything I could have invented in my head.

"I don't want to hurt you again. And I don't know what you're thinking right now. I—"

I move to sit up again, and this time she lets me. I brush some of her hair out of her face, tucking it behind her ear. "Make or break, it's not that deep," I whisper, and she takes a shuddering breath, tracing her fingers over my hip. "It doesn't have to be."

"What if it is?" she asks, her eyes blazing, her fingers tightening on the edge of my shirt.

"Then it is," I say, like it's the easiest thing in the world. "But we don't have to know that right now. We can just have fun blowing it all up. See where the pieces land another day."

Chloe lifts my shirt enough for her fingers to brush the skin on my sides, and then she stops. My breath comes out all trembly and weird, excited, embarrassed. She searches my eyes, tracing circles on my skin.

"Is this okay?" she asks, watching for any hesitation.

"Yeah," I say. "Yes. Completely."

"Are you sure?"

"More than I've ever been," I say, and my eagerness forces a small laugh out of her.

"I want this to be good for you." She looks away. She sounds nervous.

Hold up. "Do *you* want to do this? Because we don't have to. We can take a breather or stop or whatever." I tip her face back toward mine, and now it's my turn to check for any hesitation.

"I do." She nods so fast, her hair tips into her face. "Yeah. Yes."

"Then it'll be great, no matter what," I say, and we both smile, relieved. "This isn't like the last time. I'm not worrying about our future or planning next steps. There are no secrets between us. I'm here. With you. Right now. Will you be here with me?"

She licks her lips, and I swallow hard, and this time, when she pushes me back, she falls with me.

♥

I WAKE UP to the smell of fresh coffee and sugar, roll over to nuzzle Chloe, and find an empty bed instead. On the nightstand is a still-steaming cup of coffee and a giant chocolate muffin dusted with enormous sugar crystals. And oh my god, I want to kiss this girl all over again.

The shower is running in the bathroom, and I take a minute to drag my fingers through my hair and wrap myself in a sheet before climbing over her pillow to attack my breakfast. Chloe comes out a few minutes later in a pair of cozy yoga pants and a form-fitting tank top, her hair wrapped in a towel high on her head.

"You're getting crumbs everywhere." She laughs. She walks to the closet and pulls out her suitcase, beginning to toss her neatly folded clothes in all haphazardly. A little *too* fast, I think. I gulp down the coffee, suddenly worried that things are going to be weird.

I hope she's not worried about me.

"Fallon." She turns to me, looking serious. "We need to talk. I—"

"Don't sweat it. I feel good about last night," I say, which makes Chloe freeze for a second before going back to pulling her shirts from the hangers and balling them up. No, no, no, I don't want this to be weird. I need to reassure her. "I don't expect you to, like, marry me now or something, if that's what you're stressing about."

"Right, no," Chloe says, her voice a little strained.

"I think we both just needed closure, right? Fun, *really* fun, closure," I say, trying for cheerful but landing somewhere a little closer to awkward. I force a smile to try to cover for it. "I don't have all these expectations. It isn't like last time. Relax, you're off the hook."

"I'm gonna . . . I have to . . . I forgot something in the truck."

Chloe pulls the towel off her head and tosses it onto the end of the bed.

"We'll actually be in the truck in, like, a half hour," I say, trying and failing to sound lighthearted. "I need to take a quick shower, but then we can hit the road."

"Right, but, um, I just need something to get ready, and it's in the truck." She shoves her feet into her flip-flops and disappears out the door before I can stop her.

Okaaay. That was definitely weird. Did she not hear my speech? Or did she not *want* to hear my speech? No, she would have said something. *Just go with the flow, Fallon,* I remind myself. *Go. With. The. Flow.*

I cross over to the window, waiting for her to appear below, wondering how far she's going to take this ruse of "forgetting something in the truck," but my phone buzzing on the nightstand pulls me away. It's Jami, facetiming.

"How did the charity event go?" she asks the second her face fills the screen. "Did you and Chloe kill each other, or does the truce prevail?"

"The truce prevails," I say, blushing.

Jami's jaw drops just a little bit as she leans closer to her phone, her eyes squinting. "Is that a hickey on your neck?" She squeals in delight.

"What?" I throw my hand up, trying to cover it, but she just laughs.

"Oh my god, did you hook up with some rando last night in Memphis? Tell me everything."

"No, god. I didn't. Come on, you know I would never—"

"Then who?" she asks, and then her face gets scary serious. "No, no, no, no, no, no, no. You didn't."

I look away, biting my lip.

"You did." She sighs to herself, burying her face in her hands.

"It's different this time. It was like, I don't know, closure or something. For both of us."

"Closure? *You* hooked up with Chloe for 'closure'? Sure, that sounds like you."

"I did! We talked. Seriously, we did."

"I see that," she snarks.

"No, before that. We talked about last summer, and she gets now how it made me feel, and I get why she was mad I didn't tell her about never doing that before. I don't know. It felt right last night. I think this was a good thing. It was everything last summer should have been. Now we can go off to our colleges and—"

"Are you trying to convince me or yourself?"

"Ha ha," I say. "I mean it. This is me being mature about it. I'm going with the flow."

"Yeah, right," Jami says. "And where's Chloe now?"

I drop my head back. "She just ran out of here, saying she forgot something in the truck, even though we're literally packing up to go to the same truck."

"So she's the one feeling emotional whiplash this time?"

"I think she's probably worried I'm going to be mad again or get all caught up in my feelings."

"Are you sure you're not?"

"The timing's all wrong." I shrug. "We're going to colleges in different states. She's gotta figure a lot of stuff out, and I need to focus on freshman year. Even if I did have feelings, *which I'm not saying I do,* I get why it wouldn't work out."

"What if she doesn't?"

"What?"

"What if Chloe isn't looking for closure? What if she never was? God, Fal, for someone who's spent the last year being pissed that she didn't seem to care about your feelings, it sure seems like you didn't consider hers this time. You two need to talk, like now, before you waste any more time dancing around each other."

"What's that supposed to mean?"

"It means maybe she's not being weird because she's worried you weren't just looking for closure. What if she's being weird because you said that's all it was." She huffs. "Which, by the way, is basically how you two got yourselves into this mess in the first place! You're killing me! Please! Talk to her, or I swear to god—"

"No, that's . . . No," I say, because that can't be right. Chloe isn't like that. Chloe being "not like that" is how we got so off track in the first place. No matter what she says or does in the moment, I know she doesn't want anything real. Like, it's not even worth giving it brain space. "Trust me, she doesn't want anything serious. That's so not her MO."

"Have you ever considered that maybe you're not the only one realizing stuff right now?"

"Cut it out," I say. "We already talked about it! We're on the same page, I promise. Besides, if we were really meant to be, don't you think we would have been by now? We aren't. I don't want that. *She* doesn't want that." And suddenly I don't know if I'm trying to convince Jami or myself.

"You know the timing is also awful for me and Hideki."

"And?" I say, not quite sure where she's going with this other than proving that both of us are disaster daters.

"Annnnnnd"—she laughs—"we're taking it day by day and figuring out our feelings as we go. Is bad timing always a deal breaker? We're not letting it be. Besides, there's a lot of summer left to figure stuff out."

"I don't—"

Chloe walks back in, the door banging behind her. She's carrying a broken waffle cone in her hand, one of the rejects we tossed aside yesterday to be squished down for crumble topping.

"You forgot a waffle cone?" I ask, and she holds it up like a prize.

"Breakfast of champions, right?"

I glance down at my phone. Jami makes an awkward face and mouths "talk to her" before ending our call.

"Yeah," I mumble, "breakfast of champions."

# TWENTY-SIX

*T*he ride is quiet, but not horribly so. We both have plausible reasons for our quietness; at least, we do if you don't look too hard.

Chloe keeps her head down, buried in her books. Her laptop is pretty officially dead, the cracks growing in intensity every day, with a little black splotch added in now for good measure, so she's switched to using to her phone. She grumbles every so often about how bad the discussion board interface is on iOS, and I just agree politely that it sucks, because I don't really know how to fix that.

I don't know how to fix any of this, really, but I know things are quickly slipping back into the awkward tension that last night was supposed to have ended, and I hate it.

At one point Chloe even tries to move to the back of the truck under the guise of "spreading out," but I convince her that it's probably not safe while the truck is in motion. So she remains, buckled safely, biting the end of her pencil, rolling the rocks she's picked up on the trip around in her hands, and frowning intensely.

Every so often, I catch her glancing in my direction, and my cheeks heat, the hickey on my neck burning like fire.

For my part, I'm quietly mulling over Jami's words in my head. Is it possible that this awkwardness is because Chloe does have actual feelings for me? Or is it more likely that she's just desperately trying to run away again? Probably the latter. It has to be the latter.

And I'm strangely at peace with that.

I know Jami thinks it's ridiculous and that I'm lying to myself—that getting close with Chloe again could never mean anything except more confusion and heartbreak for me. And well, maybe it will. But maybe it won't.

Because the truth of the matter is, even though I think there's a significantly greater than zero chance that Chloe is getting ready to act all flighty again, it's honestly fine. Last night was nostalgia and loneliness and happiness, and yeah, okay, maybe a little bit of hopefulness, all rolled into one. But if it *was* goodbye, the send-off wasn't bad. Like, at all.

I know you don't believe me. I get it. I know you're thinking the same thing as Jami, and I'm not going to do you the disservice of actually lying to you. I don't know what this is between me and Chloe anymore. I don't know what I want it to be either, or how I'll feel a week from now, a month from now, a year. But at least things are better than they were, and I'm not going to be the one rocking the boat right now.

Besides, even if we did both want something more—which I'm 99.9 percent sure we don't—the idea of being with Chloe seems just as complicated as not being with her, and what am I supposed to do with that? Logically, we don't make sense. What I'm telling you is that I got my logic about this girl back. Finally. Somewhere on this trip, the fog and hurt finally cleared, and now I can look at things as they really are.

We'll be in different parts of the country for school soon. She'll be a sophomore, probably, and I'll be a freshman, and everything is going to change really, really fast. Nobody stays with their high school girlfriend, and may I remind you that, technically, she never even *was* my girlfriend. So, yeah.

As cheesy as it sounds, knowing that we had this one awesome week together, that we pulled off a big event without our parents, and that we went out and saw a new city together with no one else around, it feels good. No matter what happens with us or even with Love at First Bite, this trip wasn't for nothing.

As if on cue, my phone buzzes with a Facetime from my mom. Chloe closes her book and answers it, positioning the phone so my mom can see me. I don't take my eyes off the road for one second, though, not wanting to get yelled at again.

"Hiii!" Mom's cheery voice cuts through the quietness.

"Hey, Mom," I say at the same time Chloe calls out, "Hellooooo."

"I see you girls are on the way." She sounds so excited. "Are you still on track? What time do you think you'll get into town?"

"A few hours or so," I say. "We're making good time."

"I can't wait to see you, baby bear! I've missed you so much!" she says, and if it was in front of anyone but Chloe, I would be mortified. Thankfully, Carmen is just as bad when it comes to embarrassing pet names.

"Miss you too." I check the time. It's after ten a.m. "Mom, it's Friday! I thought you had a breakfast meeting with the investors today," I say, worried she somehow forgot.

A nervous look flits over her face, or maybe I'm just reading into things too much, as hyper-focused as I am. I can't ignore the ache in my stomach, though—the one from wondering if she's not talking about the deal because it fell apart. If she's shielding me the way I tried to shield her after the break-in.

"Oh, oh!" she says. "No, um, it got rescheduled."

I furrow my brow. This was supposed to be the last meeting. How long are they going to drag this out? "Rescheduled? Rescheduled for when?"

"Uh, soon," she says in a voice that definitely sounds off. "Lunchtime."

Chloe seems to be thinking the same thing, her pencil

now tapping gently on the back of her book. And now I'm sure of it. Something has gone really, really wrong.

I swallow hard. "Why do you sound weird? What's going on?"

"Oh, you know, we just get so nervous before these things," Carmen says, taking the phone from my mom, who looks slightly panicked. "Hi, Chloe, did you get your homework done?" Her voice sounds weirdly high-pitched.

Chloe turns the phone to face herself and gives her mom a little wave hello. "What's going on with you two? I know *you* always freak out about business stuff, but I thought Maggie was always cool as a cucumber. Did something happen?"

"That's just what Maggie wants you to think." Carmen laughs, and it sounds just genuine enough that I relax. It must just be nerves. Please let it just be nerves. "Everything's fine. Tell me about school."

Chloe reassures her mom that the meeting will go great and rattles on about her assignments as I drive. But the more they talk, the more I get a sinking feeling. I think I'm going to be sick.

"Do you think our moms were kind of off?" I ask a little while after Chloe ends the call, because if we have to sit silently any longer, I'm going to lose it.

"Probably just nerves."

"I guess. But what if the deal fell through? What are we going to do? My dad's not going to keep paying my mom's rent, and she'll be all alone! What if—"

"Fal." She puts her hand on my arm. "Deep breath. They said they would have the meeting soon. Why would they lie?"

"I don't know, but—"

"Let's just see what happens when we get there, okay?"

I scratch the back of my neck. "Yeah. Yeah, okay." I take a deep breath, eyes on the road. Chloe watches me for a minute and, seemingly satisfied with whatever she sees, goes back to doing her work.

The ride passes by in silence, and I try to distract myself from worrying about my mom. I go back to thinking about what Jami said. No, not the thing about Chloe maybe having feelings for me—the thing about how she doesn't know where things are going with Hideki but she doesn't mind because there's a lot of summer left.

Could that maybe work for Chloe and me too? There are so many days left between today and us leaving for college. Could we have a blast together the whole rest of this summer and part as friends at the end of it?

I sigh loudly, and Chloe taps her pencil on my knuckles. I drag my eyes from the road just long enough for her little smirk to make my belly flip-flop. She licks her lips, and I blush down to my toes. She turns and looks out her window, her smirk giving way to a full-on grin reflected back at me. She mutters something that sounds suspiciously like, "Yeah, I thought so."

"What was that?"

"Nothing," she says, looking back at me coyly. "Can't I look at you?"

Before I can answer, she snakes her fingers through mine, both of our hands dangling off the edge of the armrest.

"It's okay, Fal," she says, studying my face, probably trying to gauge my reaction, and I flash her a smile. Because whatever this is, it feels good; it feels natural.

And for the first time, I think maybe Jami could be onto something.

# TWENTY-SEVEN

*D*riving through Dallas in an ice cream truck is, well, terrifying.

Between the streets that make no sense, the massive highways, and the whiplash of going from flat farmland as far as the eye can see to this ridiculous city congestion, I'm about to lose it.

I'm trying so, so, so, so, so hard to go with the flow here. But it would be easier if the flow wasn't a backed-up four-lane highway where everyone keeps cutting me off.

"Pull over," Chloe says as I white-knuckle my way to exit the highway.

The hotel is barely a mile away, but for some reason, the GPS says it's going to take us approximately twelve eternities to get there. *Why? Why are you all on the road right now? Please.*

I hope Austin isn't this busy. I guess I never really considered that part of it. I visited the campus once with my mom a few months ago, but we flew in and out—tickets courtesy of my dad—and we didn't really get to explore too much. I didn't want to spend a lot of money, nor did I want to waste my time. It didn't matter what the world around it was like; I just knew that was the college I'd be going to. End of discussion.

But this? This is overwhelming. I thought Memphis was busy, but this is Memphis times a million with a hefty dose of zooming trucks.

"I can do it," I say, because I don't want to seem like a baby. "We're almost there."

"Okay," she says with a little shrug, like she's not going to press the issue. "But just know you don't have to."

And for some reason, that makes everything relax inside of me. Maybe going with the flow doesn't always mean fighting against my basic instincts. Maybe there's a middle ground. There's a gas station up ahead, and I signal to get over, grateful to be out of the hustle and bustle of traffic. I pull up next to a fuel pump and drop my head to the steering wheel. I've never been so happy to not be in a moving vehicle in my life.

Chloe puts her hands on my back, sliding them up to my shoulders and giving me a quick shoulder rub that I start to melt into—before remembering that we're at a gas station in the middle of Dallas, and I probably can't, like, make out with her right now, even though I'm sort of, confusingly, dying to.

I know, I know. I'm not making any sense anymore. It's just that I've spent the last couple hours holding her hand and imagining what it would be like if we just went for it. Chloe even teased me, tapping my temple and saying she wished she could see whatever movie I was writing in my head right then. And I wondered if she would like it, because it wasn't about us just being friends. It wasn't about closure or endings or any of that.

Chloe seems to sense the shift in my thoughts and, without another word, hops out of the truck and begins to pump the gas. We have plenty to make it to the hotel—we fueled up not that far from Dallas—but it doesn't hurt to top it off and leave our moms with a full tank.

I drop my head back against the seat and try not to wonder what it's going to be like after this—after we get to the hotel and the adventure as we know it is all over. Somehow, I'm more confused than ever. That logic I thought I found? I think I lost it again around mile marker five million on this roller coaster of a trip. Did we find our way back to each other? Or did we just give ourselves an epic send-off?

Chloe brushes some hair out of her eyes, leaning her hip against the truck and watching the numbers on the meter tick up. As if on cue, she blows a bright pink bubble with her gum and sucks it back in. It's one of those moments that punches you right in the face with how perfect it is. The sun hitting her

Bubble Yum smile, her very white sneakers and long tan legs, her short shorts, and that tank top. She is the epitome of summer in still life. The girl everyone wants, and the girl I have. Had? Still have?

A knock on my window makes me jump. It's Chloe, standing by the driver's-side door with a puzzled expression on her face. I pop the door open and hop out, rushing around to the other side and climbing in.

Chloe pulls her stones out of her pocket, rolling them around in her hand a few times before dropping them into the cup holder beside my bright green golf ball. I tap my finger against the door, my nail making a clicking sound as my thoughts spiral out in a thousand directions. It was a lot easier to live in the moment an hour ago, when the moment seemed equal parts inevitable and eternal. But now that we're a mile from parental supervision and the end of the trip, it feels like—

"You're making a lot of noise over there," she says, pulling out of the gas station.

I freeze, sheepishly pulling my hand into my lap. "Sorry."

"I didn't mean your nails, although now that you mention it, that was *really* annoying, so thank you for stopping."

I look at her, confused.

"You're thinking so loud, it's giving me a headache. What's up?" she asks, so casually, like she's not the one who ran out this morning pretending to have forgotten a broken waffle cone.

I just shrug. I don't want to sound too clingy, but I don't want to sound too aloof either. I'm searching for the perfect response but coming up short.

"If you want to talk about—"

"I don't," I say, because I need to sort out my own feelings first.

Her face shifts a little, like a cloud's passing over that perfect summer day. "Okay, then."

"Maybe I do. I don't know. I just mean, like, I know last night wasn't supposed to be something serious. I don't want you to be scared that I'm going to turn into some clingy bog witch or something."

"Are bog witches clingy?" She laughs.

"I have no idea," I say. "I don't even know why I said that."

"It's okay. But how do you want to play this? You keep saying you 'know' this or that about what last night was. But maybe . . ."

"Maybe what?" I ask, my heart picking up just a little.

But she ignores my question, staring straight ahead before mumbling, "What happens now, Fal?"

I don't know the best way to answer. I don't think I even know what the answer is. I look out the window, hoping that she'll say something else, that the clarity will come from her this time, but she just takes a deep breath and keeps driving. Maybe she doesn't know either.

Could we be okay not knowing? Could I?

Far too soon we're pulling into the hotel, our moms waiting out front with giant excited smiles on their faces.

"Girls!" they shout, running toward us the second we're stopped.

We each hug our respective mother, both of us grunting when they inevitably squeeze us too hard. No matter how much I pretend, though, I really don't mind. I missed this, and I don't even want to think about how much I'll miss these hugs when I'm at college.

"How was the lunch meeting?" Chloe asks excitedly. "Tell us everything. Did you close the deal?"

Carmen and my mom look at each other the way I think only people who have been friends as long as they have can. It's like they're having an entire conversation between themselves without saying a word. My mom nods, almost imperceptibly, and Carmen turns back toward us.

"Actually, there wasn't a meeting today," she says.

"Oh no!" My eyes go wide. "Did they have to reschedule again?"

We only have two days left here, and if they can't close the deal, I don't know what will happen. My chest feels painfully tight.

"No," my mom says, squeezing my hand excitedly. "We actually finished negotiations early!"

"Oh my god, so it's really happening? For real?"

Our moms nod, and we both squeal excitedly, smashing in for a group hug.

"Oh my god, oh my god, oh my god, oh my god," I say,

jumping up and down. "You guys did it! You really did it!"

We're on our third giant hug, my head still exploding with excitement and relief, when Chloe leans back, looking at her mother. "Wait, then why did you say you had a meeting today?"

Which is when Carmen makes a face I've never seen on her before.

"Well." She hesitates. "We actually wrapped up negotiations the day after your mom got here."

I tilt my head, positive I've heard her wrong. "But that was—"

"Days ago! Why did you say you hadn't?" Chloe asks.

Our moms look at each other again.

"We just wanted you girls to spend some time together. We knew if we could get you talking again, you guys would work it out," my mom says cheerfully, like this is a fun ending to one of her romance movies, where we all laugh and live happily ever after or something.

This is decidedly not that, though. This is my *life*. What the hell?

"Wait," I say. "You set us up?"

Chloe and I look at each other, and it feels like the floor just dropped out from under me. This is Dallas traffic multiplied by a graffitied truck increased by a factor of, oh, I don't know, *infinity*? I'm gonna be sick.

"We didn't set you up," Carmen says. "Don't be so dramatic."

Chloe looks pale beside me, which makes me twice as furious. "Did you even need my mom to fly out?"

"Well, yes," Carmen says, "that part was true."

"What part wasn't true, then?" Chloe asks, her voice hard.

"We both understood we were either going to close at that next meeting or were going to lose the deal," Mom says. "It's not like they would really keep meeting with us over and over. It was our one shot, and I did need to come out here to help secure it."

The realization hits me like a slap to the face. "But you didn't need me and Chloe to run the charity event. You could have flown out and met me almost from the start, or we could have even left a day or two later if we alternated driving. You knew you only needed to be in Dallas for one day."

My mom and Carmen look at each other, and my heart sinks. Did my mom seriously just screw with our emotions like this? I . . . we . . .

"You didn't even really need me on this trip, did you?" asks Chloe. "Fal could have brought one of her friends for company, and you two could have worked the Memphis event with her." Chloe's voice trembles, and I want to reach out to hug her and to squeeze her hand. But I don't.

"Girls," Carmen says. "We just wanted you to—"

"What the fuck, Mom?" Chloe says.

And yeah, what the fuck indeed?

# TWENTY-EIGHT

*O*ur moms usher us into the hotel dining room, which is blessedly deserted, considering the time of day. We find a little booth in the way back and all sit down, Chloe and I on one side, my mom and Carmen on the other.

I know Carmen has to go drive the truck to the festival site, where it'll be locked up safe for the night after setup is done, and then she'll need to Uber back to our hotel, but this seems more important. This can't wait.

"Chloe," Carmen says, but Chloe just narrows her eyes and snorts. Her arms are tightly crossed, and her leg is bouncing. It's not often that I see Chloe mad—really mad—and this is totally beyond even that. This is next-level, scary mad.

"I don't want to hear it," she says.

"I kinda do," I say, surprising myself. Not because I think

what they did is fine, and definitely not because I'm over it, but just because I really, really want to hear about the extent of their fuckery and how this plan all came about.

"You do?" Chloe asks, raising her eyebrows.

"Yeah, I want to know exactly how long you both lied," I say, turning back to our moms and leveling them with my stare. "Like, at what point did you decide you were going to mess with us? Was it, like, before Carmen left or after?"

"Fallon!" my mom says, and I can't help but shrink a little bit. Talking back to my mom or being rude in general isn't really something that's tolerated in my house. Even now, when I think she probably really deserves it, it feels wrong. Like I'm going to get grounded for it even though I have the moral high ground.

Carmen sighs and looks at my mom, and they do that pseudo-twin-speak-look thing again before my mom turns back to talk to us.

"Fallon, you were so miserable," Mom says.

"And so were you, Chloe, sweetie," Carmen says.

"Do not call me that," Chloe snaps.

"We knew—well, we had a hunch anyway—that if we could get you two together, you would work it all out. And look, it clearly worked. You guys were all smiles yesterday when we facetimed, and we group hugged when you pulled in! That would not have happened last week."

"You risked losing your biggest contracted event on a

hunch? What if we blew it?" I shout, because, to my logical brain, this sounds incredibly risky.

"The event was never in jeopardy." Carmen rolls her eyes like that should have been obvious. "One or both of us would have flown out to meet you if it seemed like things had gone off the rails."

"I almost did when the truck got broken into," Mom says, "but Carmen convinced me you guys could handle it. Clearly, she was right. I was keeping tabs on you the whole day, and if anything went wrong, Clare was fully prepared to hop in with an assist. We wouldn't put the business at risk."

"Besides, you knocked it out of the park," Carmen says. "We're so proud of you. You made it here. You made up, and everything is great. I don't know why you—"

"Everything isn't great," Chloe snaps. "I can't even believe you, Mom! I told you I wanted to stay out of this. I told you I just wanted to lay low after the schedule thing, and I wasn't messing with any more of Fal's drama this summer."

"You did?" I ask, because Chloe seemed enthusiastic from the start. It never occurred to me that maybe she wouldn't have chosen to go either if things had been different. And if she wasn't eager to make up, then where does that leave us now? "I thought you wanted to go. I thought you wanted us to be friends again."

Chloe pinches her nose. "My mother was counting on me, or so I thought. I didn't realize that she was reverse

Parent Trapping us or whatever you want to call it." Chloe looks at me. "I knew we needed to work together, and I knew that we needed to sort out our friendship stuff before we could do that, so I put on a happy face."

"Put on a happy face?" I say, my stomach in free fall. I don't know why this feels like it changes everything, but it does. All along I thought that Chloe was so desperate to get our friendship back, but she was just manipulating me too. Trying to make it seem like she was all about it but really just trying to save the event and help her mom.

"Fal." Chloe sighs. "I told you up front I thought this trip would make or break us."

"Yeah, I guess I just didn't realize you didn't have a preference." I slam my hands on the table. I may have been acting like a petty monster this whole time, but at least I was being honest. I was mad when I was mad, and then I was . . . something else entirely later. Was any of this real, or was Chloe just as full of shit as our mothers? "Excuse me," I say, tapping her shoulder until she slides out of the booth so I can escape.

I rush to the bathroom, not sure if I want to cry or throw up, but knowing that whatever it is, I don't want to do it with an audience.

I storm into a stall, grateful that the bathroom is just as abandoned and empty as the hotel restaurant, and slam the lock shut behind me. I take a second, just breathing. Because what does this all mean now? It was easier, this idea of going with the flow, when I thought I knew what the flow was. But now? This feels more like being caught in the undertow.

Look, I'm not saying Chloe lied to get me into bed or that this changes anything about that. She might still be mostly an enigma, but I know she's not a terrible person. I don't regret what happened last night, which was super consensual and a lot of fun, but it does change everything before and after. It does change the emotions surrounding it, the linked pinkies, the walls falling down, all the what-ifs.

Because I thought she wanted us to make up the whole time. I thought she was eager for this road trip, her little detours an attempt to prove to me how much I meant to her—to prove that things could go back to the way they were.

But now that I know she dreaded this as much as I did, that she was putting on a happy face, I don't know how to feel about any of this. Instead of being a natural evolution, this whole trip now just feels like we fell into a trap.

Would we have ever talked again if our moms hadn't arranged this little setup? Maybe. But maybe not! And rather than feeling grateful that it worked out this way, I'm left feeling ripped off. I know we got there. I know we made up and moved on during this trip, but does it even count if it was all under false pretenses? We were robbed of our own resolution. The idea that this is closure—that it could ever be with this new context—feels laughable at best.

The bathroom door opens and shuts, and I peek through the sliver of space between the wall and the door. It's Chloe.

I sigh—I can't avoid her forever, clearly—and flush the toilet, pretending I was in here for a better reason than to maybe cry. Chloe eyes me warily as I walk to the sink.

"Here," she says, and she holds up a key card that looks remarkably similar to the one that we had at the other hotel.

"Thanks." I nod, taking it from her when I finish washing my hands. She leans her hip against the sink, and it looks like she's not any more sure of what to say than I am.

"Our moms left to take the truck to the staging area and get it all settled and stuff. I guess check-in ends in a couple hours or whatever." Chloe sniffs, and I wonder if she's on the verge of crying too. "I hope you don't mind, but I told them to go and said I would give you your key. I didn't think you were really in the mood to keep talking. I know I'm not."

"Thanks," I say again, because I don't know what I'm in the mood for right now, but talking more to our moms is definitely not on the list.

You probably think I'm being harsh. But I don't really care.

"I'm 212 and you're 208," she says. Which means there's a room between us. Maybe there will always be something coming between us. It feels fitting in a really awful way.

"Cool," I say, suddenly cognizant of the fact that we're standing in a hotel bathroom and anybody could walk in at any time. Not to mention the stench of liberally sprayed disinfectant and too much humidity is giving me a headache.

"Look, I didn't have anything to do with this." And she looks so serious, like she desperately needs me to know it's true. And I know it; I can feel it deep down. I never suspected her for a second.

But I wonder, if she had, would I feel differently right now? Would I be mad at her the way I'm mad at my mom? Would I still be standing awkwardly in a hotel bathroom, just utterly drowning in waves of disappointment? Would anything—or maybe everything—be different?

"I know," I say finally. "I never thought you did."

♥

I TAKE A shower and then spend the next half hour in my hotel room trying to facetime Jami and Prisha over and over and over while clutching my golf ball like a lifeline, but neither of them pick up. I imagine Jami making out with Hideki, and Prisha curled up in the bleachers, watching Kai swing his way to the majors. The jealousy burns.

What is it like for it to just be simple? You like me; I like you; how about we kiss without drama?

God. So much drama. I'm exhausted just thinking about it.

On the one hand, Chloe and I got to *wherever* we are right now with each other in the end. We had to talk; we had to sort it out. Does it really matter so much that our parents interfered? Isn't the real question still *Where do we go from here?* and not *What's wrong with how we got here?* Isn't focusing on the *how* instead of the *now* what got us into this mess in the first place?

Maybe.

But maybe there *is* something to be said about the false pretenses. Sure, we slowly glued together all the pieces of our shattered friendship as the miles piled on, but can it really mean anything if the whole foundation was built on a deception, even if neither of us was the deceiver?

I flop back on the bed. Funny how they managed to book us double rooms this time. I know Mom doesn't know why Chloe and I ended our friendship. I have to imagine she wouldn't have pulled the "only one bed" stunt if she did. I bet she just thought it would be good for bonding and bring back memories of the thousands of sleepovers we used to have.

Screw it. I can't just sit here and spiral. I need to get out. To go for a walk or something, even if it's just wandering around the hotel grounds or down the street. I won't go far, but I can't stay here.

I shove the room key into my pocket, slide my feet into my ballet flats, and pull my hair up into a ponytail. It's hot out, sweltering even, and I'll probably regret going for a walk when it means yet another shower, but I don't even care.

I fling open the door, ready to march straight to downtown if I have to. To march every thought straight out of my head.

But there's Chloe, standing in front of me, her hand poised to knock, her mouth popped just slightly open in surprise in a way that looks so utterly kissable. I press my lips together, praying I don't say anything I'll regret.

"We need to talk," she says when I just stand there, staring. "Can I come in?"

I blink, trying to buy myself another second before I have to hear whatever awful things she's going to tell me, like *I don't want to be friends anymore now that I know our moms set us up* or *I regret last night.*

"Yeah," I say, stepping back. "Come on in."

# TWENTY-NINE

I perch on the edge of the bed as Chloe paces the room. She's keyed up beyond belief, opening and shutting her mouth like she's trying to figure out just the right place to start. It's making me nervous.

"Fallon," she says, and then paces some more. "Fal," she starts again, this time even raising her hand quickly before swallowing her words again.

I realize that she's probably just as confused as I am about this whole thing. We hooked up. And thanks to our moms, it wasn't really the fresh-start, going-with-the-moment type of thing we both thought it was. (And also, if my mom finds out that I hooked up with her BFF-slash-business-partner's daughter, she might kill me. Sorry, Mom, but just because you *wanted* Chloe and me to be like sisters doesn't mean we are.)

"Last night was . . . And then to find out that our moms were . . ." She huffs and shakes her head like she's over-whelmed and sorry all at once.

I want to put her out of her misery. I want to put us both out of our misery, to stop delaying the inevitable, and to make this awkward moment as unawkward as possible.

"It's fine," I say, throwing her a life raft, because she looks like she's drowning. "I get it."

"You do?" Chloe takes a step toward me, and I pull my legs in a little tighter. She stops, her once-animated arms falling to her sides. She tilts her head, and I'm scared she can see straight into my brain to where all my secrets live.

I don't want her to see the truth. I don't want her to know how much shit this stirred up for me or how much I *feel* right now. *Closure*, I remind myself. *This has to just be for closure. Right?*

"Yeah, I do," I say. "And the fact that our moms had to in-terfere like this just to get us talking again? I didn't realize that you didn't want to go on the trip either. You're a lot more *dip-lomatic* about things than I am, I guess."

Or maybe she's just a better liar, but it hurts too much to think about her like that now. I think the last shred of anger I had for her dissipated somewhere between Chloe whispering in my ear that I should explore Memphis with *her* and Chloe asking me if it's possible to be hurt without someone hurting you.

"Yeah," she says, tucking her hands into her pockets. "Yeah."

"We were both manipulated here, and I know that complicates pretty much everything. I don't regret what happened between us last night, at all, and I promise I'm not gonna get all weird on you or anything, so don't worry."

"Fallon—"

"No, I know," I say, scared to let her finish. Scared that if she squashes whatever this is between us before I can, it'll somehow be worse than the first time. "You don't have to say it. I know you're not looking for anything with me. You didn't even want to come on this trip! If we were meant to be something, we would have been already, right?" I ask, voicing my biggest fear—the one that up until now I could only say out loud to Jami, and only because I'd hoped she would tell me I was wrong. It wasn't lost on me that she didn't.

Chloe doesn't say anything for a long time, and I pick at a loose thread on my jeans, my entire focus narrowing down to the little piece of cotton. The truth of the truth is that I desperately want her to say something, anything, to challenge me.

I shut my eyes and imagine what the next few minutes could look like. Her dropping in front of me, telling me I'm so wrong, that she doesn't care how we got here, she's just happy we did. That just because we haven't happened yet, doesn't mean we can't, doesn't mean we never ever will. She'll tell me that our feelings are *our* feelings and that they have nothing to do with forced proximity or what our moms did. She'll take my hands and look into my eyes and tell me that she always did have a preference, that she still does, and that she's sorry she made me think otherwise when we were arguing with our moms.

I open my eyes, my whole body practically begging for it to come true—for it be a premonition instead of just my imagination. But Chloe doesn't do any of that. She doesn't *say* any of that.

"Yeah, probably," is what comes out instead, her voice sounding strangled somehow, like she has to force the words out.

I flick my eyes to hers, hoping to see something there— regret for agreeing with me? Disappointment? I don't know. But she looks the same as always standing there. She looks like regular Chloe. Like she's ready to coast on to her next adventure.

I can't blame her.

I can't blame her for any of this.

I knew what I was doing last night.

"I mean, the timing is so obviously off." I laugh, and it's a bitter, sad sort of thing. "Like, even if we wanted to. Which obviously neither of us do."

"Right," she says, furrowing her brow. "It wouldn't make any sense. You're going to be around here for college, and I'm gonna be in California. Nothing has really changed, I guess. I'm just glad that we're talking again."

"Me too," I say. "Like, we have to be reasonable, right? Logical. We had our chance. Not just last summer but all of high school. If we were supposed to be together, it wouldn't have taken, like, Jurassic Adventures and Delilah and, ugh, even our moms to get us together. We hung out almost every day of our lives!"

And I don't know who I'm trying to convince or who I'm trying to reassure, but every lie falls like acid from my tongue. But she's not burning. She's not. She looks perfectly fine now. She's not even pacing anymore. Jami was wrong, clearly, and I shouldn't have gotten my hopes up. But that's on me. I let my emotions temporarily get the better of me, but I can get us out of this mess. On my own. And no one has to know, especially not Chloe.

"I still want to be friends, though," I rush to add, because the thought of losing her, really losing her, the way that I did all last year, hurts too much. "If you want to, I mean."

"Yeah," Chloe says. "I missed you. I don't want to go that long without talking again."

"Then it's settled. We're friends. Like you always say, it doesn't have to be that deep."

"No," she says slowly. "It doesn't *have* to be."

"Exactly!" I say, forcing cheerfulness even though I feel like throwing up.

I stand up like, I don't know, I'm going to hold out my hand and make her shake on it or something. Another pinkie promise to the seal the deal? I don't want her to disappear on me again. Except now we're nearly face-to-face, just twelve inches of space between her and me, and if I lean forward, just a little, and she does the same, we'd—

"Fallon," she says, tipping her head just slightly, her lips parted, like she's daring me to close the distance.

God, I want to. I want to so bad. But what if I'm just seeing what I want to see? What if I'm reading this all wrong? What if I make an ass of myself? Again. Our tenuous friendship, patched together with string as fragile as a spiderweb, would never make it through another epic misunderstanding. And that's a risk I'm not willing to take.

"Friends, then," I say, swallowing hard and holding out my pinkie.

Except she doesn't take it. Instead, her eyes shut for the briefest of moments, with an almost imperceptible nod.

"Friends," she says finally.

And then she's gone.

# THIRTY

*I* open my eyes the next morning to find a note from my mom scribbled on hotel stationery. She left it on top of my phone, and honestly, I don't know why she didn't just text me. The note says she went down to the truck early to get ready for the crowds and not to forget my vendor pass, which she left for me on the dresser. Apparently, there's complimentary breakfast down in the lobby, and Chloe and I should make our way to the truck once we're up and showered. Normally, they would expect us there bright and early too, but I guess our moms messing with our heads bought us some time to sleep in.

I fire off a text to Chloe to let her know I'm up, assuming she got the same note I did, and wait for her to respond. She doesn't, and I try not to let it bother me. I am more than capable of getting my own Uber if she left earlier to head over to help or whatever or if she's decided to sleep until noon.

I just thought sharing a ride would be a friendship kind of thing to do.

I take my time getting ready, savoring the hot spray of the shower, and then head downstairs to devour the breakfast bar. A kind server behind the buffet sets out a fresh pan of cinnamon rolls, the icing still gooey and warm. She boxes up two for me, and I smile. One for me, one for Chloe, if Sleeping Beauty ever wakes up. Friends get each other cinnamon rolls, right? A nice, platonic cinnamon roll to start off what no doubt will be a super-awkward day.

I turn to leave, the Uber app already up on my phone. Which is when I notice Carmen sitting in a small booth in the corner, rubbing her eyes. Weird. I assumed she'd be off with my mom getting everything ready or whatever.

I walk over, totally expecting her to greet me with a cheerful *Hey, let's catch a rideshare together. Are you excited for today?* But when I get closer, I realize her eyes are all red. Has she been crying?

"Carmen?"

She looks up, embarrassment washing over her face, followed swiftly by something else. Shame, maybe?

She gives me a watery smile. "Oh, hi, sweetie."

"Is everything okay?"

"Not really," she says, but when she sees my face, she rushes to add, "With the truck, yes, everything is fine. Your mom is taking care of all of that right now."

Panic stabs through my heart. "The deal?"

"Also fine. You worry too much about that stuff, Fal."

I ignore the slight, the constant old-beyond-my-years refrain I've been hearing practically since birth. "Then what is it?"

When she doesn't say anything, I slide into the booth across from her and set my two boxes of cinnamon rolls on the table. I slide one toward her when she looks up, along with a little plastic fork. Maybe the server will give me another one for Chloe, or maybe the universe knew Carmen was the one who really needed it.

"Mmmm." She dives in, swirling a little chunk around in some of the frosting that dripped inside the box. "I love these, thank you." She reaches out and puts her hand on mine, patting it gently a few times before pulling back, and I shift in my seat, not sure what's going on. "I'm so sorry, Fallon. What your mother and I did was wrong, and Chloe really let me have it last night."

"Yeah, I was asleep when Mom came in last night, but we'll *definitely* be talking later."

"I warned her it was coming." She wipes at her eyes. Is that why she's crying? "And that we deserve it."

"I don't understand why you two thought it was okay. I mean, I almost get where you were coming from, but it's so messed up."

"I know. Chloe said the same thing."

"Where is she, anyway? I was gonna get us a ride, but do you still have the rental car? No sense in all of us paying to get there separately."

Carmen looks up at me, confused. "She didn't tell you?"

"Tell me what?"

"Chloe left."

And I swear to god the whole world stops. She's gone again. She left without saying goodbye again. I can't.

I try to pull it together, my fingers curling into nervous fists against the table. "What? When?"

"She asked me to change her ticket so she could fly back today instead of tomorrow."

"She did?"

*Breathe,* I remind myself, *breathe. This changes nothing. You're still friends. You'll still see her in a few days when you get back. Everything will be fine. A couple days in the grand scheme of things means nothing. We're good.*

"Chloe needed some space," her mom adds slowly. And god, I hate, hate, HATE that word.

"Oh, okay. I'll just see her when I get back," I say, more to myself than anyone else.

"She really hasn't called you?" Carmen asks, and it looks like she might cry some more.

"No, but her phone's always dead." I'm trying desperately to convince myself that's all this is. She's not avoiding me, is she? No, she wouldn't, not after everything we've been through. "I'm sure she'll charge up at the airport or something and call me."

"Fallon, sweetie, she's decided to spend the rest of the summer with her father. She said she needed some time away from me after all this. I can't believe she didn't tell you. She's flying home to get her car, and then driving straight up to her dad's."

"Oh," I say. Which barely begins to cover it. Her dad lives hours and hours away, in a northern Maine town that she absolutely hates. She couldn't get farther away this summer if she tried.

And I can't do this again. I can't.

I pick up my phone and call her, but it goes straight to voice mail. Carmen looks at me sadly, and no. No. I am not getting left behind. Not again. Not without a goodbye. Not without an explanation, even if I have to drag it out of Chloe myself.

I stand up. "When's her flight? Is she already at the airport?"

"No, she took the rental car to the truck. She said she forgot something there. And then she's leaving the rental and taking an Uber. Her flight isn't for hours, but I guess she didn't want to be around me today. You just missed her, though. She left right before I came down here."

Just missed her?

Then maybe—maybe—that means I can still catch up.

# THIRTY-ONE

The wait for a car takes forever—is there always surge pricing in Dallas?—and the ride itself lasts no less than three eternities. It's fine. I need time to figure out my next move. I don't know what I'm going to say when I catch her. *If* I catch her.

I have to catch her.

I hope I come up with something incredible—something that makes her, I don't know, fall in love the second she sees me? Screw being friends. My stomach wouldn't hit the floor at the thought of not seeing her if we were just friends. She wouldn't run if . . .

Look, I know there's a significantly greater than zero chance that I'm reading this all wrong. She could be running away because she wants to, not because she feels like she has to. Not because she's upset that I didn't lean forward and kiss her. Not because I tried to make her pinkie swear to just be friends.

Ugh, who does that? Who pinkie swears "just friends" with a girl who spent the whole previous night with her tongue in their mouth? I was so scared of being hurt again, of being rejected and embarrassed and lonely. But what if I missed something really important—something really special—because of that?

Haserot's Angel, the dinosaur chickens, the creepy stuffed animals—even if she was forced on the trip same as me, she wasn't forced to do any of *that*. That was Chloe. That was *all* Chloe.

And I think maybe I hurt her. It wasn't intentional. I was trying my best and doing what I thought was the right thing when she came to talk to me last night. But sometimes you can be hurt even if the other person doesn't do anything to hurt you, right?

Because there are really only two reasons I can think of for her to ship herself off to a town she hates in Maine: She's just as ridiculously in love with me as I am with her and can't handle the idea of me not reciprocating, or she absolutely can't stand me anymore.

So what do I have to lose by finding out? She'll be gone either way; at least this way, I'll know.

I try her phone again and again until I've memorized every pause and breath in her voice mail message. I send her a bunch of texts just in case, even though I'm almost positive her phone is off or dead. I say, **Wait, we need to talk.** I say **I'm on my way**. Anything to not feel useless. Anything to feel like

I'm doing something. I even start leaving her voice mails. My knee bounces a mile a minute, and all the skin on my body is buzzing, because I need to get to her.

I just need to see her face when she sees my face, and then I'll know.

I have to know.

I pop open the car door even before the driver has completely stopped and yell a quick thank-you. I'll be sure to give him five stars and adjust up to an even bigger tip later, when everything is settled. When the story of me panicking in the back of a rideshare on the way to greatness is something Chloe and I both laugh about together.

Please let us laugh about it together. Let me catch her in time. Please. Let her *want* me to catch her in time.

I hold up my vendor pass as I push through the gates, tapping my foot as they scan the little barcode to make sure it's real and practically ripping the map out of the worker's hand. I shout an apology and run. Well, try to.

Because the crowd is already filling in, packed tightly into this fenced former parking lot—this giant square of asphalt filled to the brim with food trucks of all shapes and sizes and smells. I scan the map, searching desperately for the name Love at First Bite, and find it blissfully not too far away.

I make my way through the crowd, doing my absolute best not to elbow people left and right as I go. I finally find my mom, looking harried and overwhelmed, scooping ice cream alone.

Alone.

I don't see Chloe anywhere.

Shit. Maybe I beat her here, or maybe she changed her mind and went straight to the airport. But I can't think too hard about that right now. I have to find my way to her. She has to be here or on her way here. It has to be true. I need it to be.

"Oh, thank god, you're here!" Mom says, looking relieved. "Carmen was supposed to be here an hour ago, but she didn't show and isn't answering her phone!"

I shake my head. "I have to find Chloe first. Has she been here?"

"You just missed her. I guess she's leaving today. I didn't realize her ticket was for—"

"What?" I say, and I'm going to cry. I'm going to absolutely lose it. "How long ago did she leave?"

"I don't know. Five minutes? Maybe ten? She just grabbed some rocks out of the cupholder and left. Can you put on your apron? I'm dying here."

"Which way did she go?"

"What?"

"I—I'll be right back. I have to find her," I say, and then push back through the crowd in the other direction, praying I'm not too late. My mom shouts my name, but I'm gone, fast, before she can stop me. I have to find Chloe. I have to.

Because if she really came back just for the rocks she picked up, and if it means what I think it does, that she's holding on to good memories same as me, then I can fix this. I really can. I just have to find her.

And yeah, I know, at some point she's going to turn on her phone and get my messages. And maybe we could figure it out then, from whatever state she's in. But I don't want that. I don't want to wait a week to kiss her again. I don't want to have to find a way to get to Maine just to see her smile.

The crowd packs in even more tightly, people rushing in every direction to get their early bird specials. I'm positive that they oversold the early bird VIP passes like most festivals do. If it's this busy now, I don't want to know what it's going to be like later.

I make my way back to the front gate, hoping I'll find her there, waiting for a car or something. But there are just more people streaming in. I climb up on a picnic table, and a guard screams at me to get down, but I ignore her and search the crowd, the road. I search everywhere, but I can't find her. I can't find her.

I'm too late.

The security guard tugs at my hand, and I climb down, feeling heavy, like gravity just intensified times a million. Because she's gone. Again. I lost her. Again.

The crowd pushes me along as I slowly find my way to my mom's truck, desperately trying to hold back the tears.

*It's not that deep,* I tell myself. *It's fine. She'll see my texts when her phone is charged. She'll call me. The magic won't dissipate just because we're out of our little bubble, will it?*

Will it?

The tears start to well up in my eyes, and I swallow hard, trying to fight it as I walk, my head down, not even caring which direction I'm headed anymore. A little kid drops a bag of something in front of me, and I pick it up to hand it back before noticing it's gourmet animal crackers.

Animal crackers.

Which Chloe doesn't travel without.

It's a long shot. Who even knows if she saw the vendor? She could have just grabbed a bag from a gas station, but—

"Where did you get this?" I ask the kid's mom.

She points toward a cluster of vendors I didn't notice before. "Right over there."

"Thank you!" I shout, running in the direction she pointed.

And then I see it: **MANNY'S MAGICAL ANIMAL CRACKER EMPORIUM** painted in giant, zebra-striped letters with Hollywood lights all around them.

"Yes!" Please let her be there. *Please.*

The crowd surges, and I break through. Finally! I can see the line and everyone in it. I start from the end and scan forward. *Not her, not her, definitely not her.* And then, four people from the front . . .

Her.

She's there.

"Chloe!" I yell, rushing forward.

She looks at me, shock and confusion written all over her face. "Fallon?"

"No deal," I say when we're finally face-to-face. I can't believe this is happening. I found her. I did. And she could knock me down with the slightest whisper. She could, depending on what she says.

"No deal?" Chloe asks, looking utterly bewildered.

"Uh-uh." I pant, trying to catch my breath. Suddenly, I feel like crying for an entirely different reason. "No pinkie swears. No promises. Deal's off. I don't want to stay friends."

"Oh, well, fuck you too, then," she snaps.

"No, no." I take her hand as she tries to pull back. "That came out wrong. I don't *not* want to be friends. I want us to be other things too." And her tiny, confused smile encourages me just enough. I surge forward, taking her head in my hands and searching her face. "I don't care about timing. I don't care if we make sense. I don't care about any of that, do you? Do you?!"

"No." She shakes her head, a smile breaking out across her face.

"And maybe you didn't have a preference before; maybe it didn't matter to you if we fixed everything or blew it all up. But do you have a preference now? Because I do."

"Of course I do, Fallon," she says softly. "I have for a while."

I search her eyes. "Is it . . . ?"

"What do you think?" She quirks her head to the side.

"Historically, I'm really bad at guessing what you want, so if you could just fill me in?" I wince, bouncing nervously on my tippy-toes.

"How about this? I want *you*. Is that clear enough?"

"You do?" I smile so wide my cheeks hurt.

She nods. "Are you gonna kiss me now or what?"

And those words. Those eight words are the most perfect words in the history of all words ever spoken.

And so, I do. I kiss her like it's the last minute I'll ever have with her, because it almost was. She kisses me back just as hard, and it's so goddamn perfect.

Until the guy behind us taps me on the shoulder.

I press my forehead against Chloe's, smiling at her for a second before I turn to look at him.

"No butting in line," he snarls.

"Sorry." I laugh—I can't help it—and grab Chloe's hand as she goes to flip him off. "I'm good. I'm not in line. I already have what I need."

And I do.

I do.

# EPILOGUE

*W*henever I imagined this moment, it was always me and Jami, taking in the sights. We would have fun, sure, but there was always an undercurrent to it for me. Even in my mind movies, this trip to Montreal wasn't just about running toward something—our independence, our futures as college freshmen. It was about running away from all the plans I had built in my head around Chloe.

It's not that I thought it would give me some great clarity about life to stare at a giant marble sculpture—you know, the one that the bloody heroine sits in front of at the end of *Too Dead to Die?*—or that it would solve the world's problems or anything like that. But in my head, it was always meant to be a turning point, a reset, a fresh start after a particularly rough year.

Jami's outside buying pretzels across the street, and Prisha, back home, abandoned our Facetime an hour ago in favor of hanging out with Kai. And now, standing here inside this cathedral, I don't want to say it's a little underwhelming, but, yeah, it's a little underwhelming.

I take a step to the right, pacing around the sculpture, trying to find the magic it's supposed to hold. But it's just a statue. A thing. An object. It was Adya Mulroney who brought it to life with her camera and her characters.

That's something else I realized this summer. It's not where you are that matters; it's who you're with. It's the people around you who make things feel big or small. A tent in the woods, a pen full of dinosaur chickens, and even a big marble statue in Canada can feel monumental or like nothing at all, depending on context and company.

Behind me, someone steps on my shoe, and my heel pops out. I spin around, ready to angrily confront another tourist in hushed whispers about the value of personal space, only to be met with a featherlight kiss on the tip of my nose. And suddenly, the magic is right there in front of me.

"You gonna film something here?" Chloe asks, squinting like she's trying to imagine it.

"I would," I say, "if Adya hadn't already done it a thousand times better than I could ever even dream of."

"Nope, none of that," she says. "One semester of college and you'll be the next Scorsese. Trust me."

I laugh, and she squeezes my hand. And oh, yeah, I guess now's a good time to tell you. While I didn't change my planned major—I'm not *that* into going with the flow—I'm looking into the film-related minors UT has to offer. Even my dad says it'll be "a nice balance," which is high praise coming from him.

And Chloe? She's planning to get a degree in hospitality and tourism after our little trip. I've never seen her get as fired up as she does when discussing "ethical tourism" and her future career plans. She's even been doing her schoolwork by choice lately—no nagging needed. She says the sooner she finishes her boring gen ed stuff, the sooner she can get to the good stuff. It's kind of awesome.

"Ten-minute warning," Chloe whispers in my ear, and at least this time she's polite enough not to roll her eyes. To say I meticulously planned out this trip with Jami and Chloe is an understatement. I may have laminated some color-coded itineraries for all of us, although I suspect that Chloe's is buried at the bottom of her carry-on, where it sort of rightly deserves to be, I guess.

And I know what you're thinking: *That's not really living in the moment and going with the flow, Fallon.* But sometimes, going with the flow is a give-and-take, something Chloe and I have been working really hard to balance since our road trip.

Oh, and if you're worried that bringing Chloe along on my trip with Jami was some kind of dick move, just know it was actually Jami's idea. And it wasn't a purely selfless one either. Jami's not outside pretzel shopping alone; she's got Hideki on her heels like the smitten kitten he so obviously is. As luck would have it, he just so happens to live not that far away from here. Sometimes the universe is funny like that, with cinnamon buns and animal crackers and cute French Canadian boys with Broadway dreams popping up just where you need them to be.

"I know, I know," I say, studying the sculpture in front of me. "I'm almost ready."

And suddenly, now that time is running out, I feel weirdly attached to this place. I guess it's a habit of mine. I planned out this trip so much in my head, it's almost hard to appreciate it while I'm standing here in the flesh.

I guess that's kind of what I did to Chloe too. The first time, I mean. The false-start-slash-warm-up, as we've come to call it. I had built it up in my head so much—what it would be like my first time, what it would mean if I kissed Chloe, and all that other stuff too—that I couldn't even appreciate it. I couldn't even enjoy what was right in front of me.

Chloe gestures toward the phone in my hand, and I smirk, hitting record as I slowly scan the statue, the stained glass, the splendor of it all. Because maybe I'm not Adya Mulroney, or Scorsese either, for that matter, but I am me. And I'm here. And yeah, I don't want to miss a second of this.

That's kind of been the theme lately. Chloe never left for Maine, and somehow, I've made watching her study for a test or hanging out in her room while she reads a book for class fun. She comes with me when I meet Kai and Prisha at the batting cages after work, and she even started picking up shifts with me again at the ice cream truck, more because she wants to see me than because she actually wants to help out.

It's still a little bit strained between her and her mom.

My mom and Carmen, for their parts, have gotten the distribution off the ground. They've even hired two new employees to help us keep up with our daily customers on top of shipping stuff out. It's a big step up from where we were at the start of the summer.

They're now looking at a permanent space to lease for equipment of their own. They're thrilled that they'll be able to rent out some of it to other ice cream people who come into town. Say what you want about them meddling in our relationship, but they are always the first to send the elevator back down. They're the ones who taught us how to love and care about people other than ourselves. Even if it took more than a dozen arguments for us to see that.

To say our moms were shocked when we told them we were dating is the understatement of the millennium. Longer than that, probably. Like, I think the big bang was less startling to the universe than Chloe and me dating was to our moms.

In retrospect, my mom was rightfully horrified at the thought of us sharing a hotel room bed. She even tried to make us sleep in separate rooms during our sleepovers this summer. Funny, but that ship had way, way, way already sailed. On her credit card, no less.

Chloe nudges me again, pulling me from my thoughts as she points to her watch.

I pause the recording to pull up the app on my phone—the tracker one I used to create our full itinerary, lest anyone, including myself, lose the laminated one. I asked everyone to download it, but only Jami did. That's why she's a better best friend than Chloe, which has become a bit of a running joke between us all.

Chloe says it's fine, because she wasn't supposed to be my best friend; we just didn't know it yet. She loves to pull out that Einstein quote—you know, the one about judging a fish by how it climbs a tree or whatever? And Jami's always quick to remind Chloe that many of the basic tenets of being a good best friend overlap with being a good girlfriend, which inevitably makes Chloe pout, even though she agrees.

And yeah.

Girlfriend.

I said it.

She is.

We are.

I tried to stay in the moment when we first got back from Texas. I really, truly, honestly did. I thought we could have a super low-key summer thing and see where it went. But, like, have you met me? I lose my mind around this girl.

Chloe was the one to ask me, by the way. I bet you didn't see that one coming. She said the L word first too. Back when we were still in Dallas, even!

After we reassured the guy in line several more times that I wasn't budging, Chloe finally got her animal crackers. But then I kind of ruined the moment, because honestly, I really *was* worried about my mom being alone with that line, so I asked Chloe if we could go back to the truck, which turned into a whole thing.

I don't want to bore you with the details, but let's just say it got icy when Carmen got there. Chloe and I volunteered to go outside and take orders down the line so our parents could scoop and Chloe could "have some space" from her mom. And while we did that, she plugged in her phone to charge it.

The next thing I knew, it was nighttime, the line was finally gone, and we were exhausted. Chloe grabbed her phone from the truck so we'd have it while we walked around together. And then . . .

"You called me thirty-seven times," she said. "And texted me almost twice that." She kept scrolling and laughing as she counted. "Do I even want to listen to these voice mails?"

I grabbed her phone and tried to delete them. I actually did get through deleting half of them, running clear around the parking lot twice in a game of keep-away before she tackled me and tickled me and wrestled it from my hand, which, by the way, was cheating.

"You're in love with me," she said, staring down at her phone. A simple statement of fact, not even a question.

I was scared.

I was so scared.

I opened my mouth to say something like *Maybe a little, but don't worry about it* or *It's not that deep* or god knows what else besides the truth, which was *Yes, I am. I have been for a long time.*

But before I could say anything, she planted a kiss on my forehead and said, "Good, because I think I'm in love with you too."

Fast-forward to today, and we're in Montreal, alone together. Well, alone together with Jami and Hideki. But, you know, close enough. And her rock collection continues to grow with every place we visit.

I hit record again, aiming the camera at her this time. She crosses her eyes and sticks out her tongue when she catches me.

I just shake my head. I'm so gone on this girl, it's not even funny.

"You find what you were looking for?" Chloe asks as she stares up at the sculpture one last time.

"Yeah," I say, watching her take it all in. "I really did."

# · ACKNOWLEDGMENTS ·

**THERE WERE SO** many people who helped put this book in your hands, and I cannot thank them enough. A huge round of applause for: Stephanie Pitts, my editor extraordinaire, who never fails to take my ideas and push them to the next level. My agent, Sara Crowe, who has taken care of this book like her own and is a constant source of inspiration and enthusiasm. Matt Phipps, who keeps everything moving and deserves all of the raises. Catherine Karp, Ana Deboo, Ariela Rudy Zaltzman, and Cindy Howle, my incredibly patient and talented copyeditors. Jeff Östberg, Kelley Brady, and Suki Boynton, for making my book beautiful. My publisher Jen Klonsky, publicist Lizzie Goodell, Felicity Vallence, James Akinaka, Shannon Spann, Bezi Yohannes, Penguin Teen—I am so lucky to have such an amazing team behind my books.

I'd also like to thank Joe, Liv, Brody, Dennis, Rory, Kelsey, Isabel, Karen, Dahlia, Shannon, Jeff, Gina, Kiera, Vinnie, Becky, and my mom. None of this would have been possible without your support.

And last but not least, thank you to my readers and to all the booksellers, bloggers, and other book influencers. I would not be here without you.

*Amber Hooper*

**JENNIFER DUGAN** is a writer, a geek, and a romantic who writes the kinds of stories she wishes she'd had growing up. She's the author of the young adult novels *Some Girls Do, Verona Comics,* and *Hot Dog Girl,* which was called "a great, fizzy rom-com" by *Entertainment Weekly* and "one of the best reads of the year, hands down" by *Paste* magazine. She lives in upstate New York with her family, their dog, a strange kitten who enjoys wearing sweaters, and an evil cat who is no doubt planning to take over the world.

*You can visit Jennifer at*
**JLDugan.com**

*Or follow her on Twitter and Instagram*
**@JL_Dugan**